HILLS HIDE MOUNTAINS

TRAVIS KLEMPAN

MILSPEAK BOOKS

An Imprint Of Milspeak Foundation, Inc.

Manufactured in the United States of America
Library of Congress Cataloging-in-Publication Data
Klempan, Travis, Library of Congress Number: 2023937230

ISBN (paperback): 979-8-9881203-6-0
ISBN (epub): 979-8-9881203-7-7

Design: Michelle Bradford Art
Editing: Samantha Otto Brown

MilSpeak Foundation, Inc.
5097 York Martin Road
Liberty, NC 27298
www.MilSpeakFoundation.org

<h1 style="text-align:center">Additional praise for HILLS HIDE MOUNTAINS</h1>

Klempan's sophomore novel is a cause for celebration while also being a confirmation that his first great novel *Have Snakes, Need Birds* was not a fluke. It's 2012 and a group of people are engaged in operating a rafting company in Montana. But this book, centered around wartime trauma, includes guardian angels, spirit animals, ghost stories, gift magic, touch-insight, and conflicts between the natural and supernatural. Klempan brings all that together in a furious finale. One of those books that will prove to be unforgettable.

—Bill McCloud, author of *The Smell of the Light, Vietnam, 1968-1969*

Bring 'em Back Alive! . . . is the unofficial motto of the Big Steep River Expeditions that cuts through Bonaventure, Montana, and through the heart of Klempan's masterful *Hills Hide Mountains,* a beautiful follow-up to his 2020 debut *Have Snakes, Need Birds*. Like the Big Steep River itself, Klempan's prose is charged and poetic, guiding the reader at their own perfect pace through rock-riddled rapids, placid waters, and emotional eddies. Beneath the surface, *Hills Hide Mountains* is an exploration of the objects, the people, and the memories that keep us afloat on our quest to regain power and purpose after unimaginable loss, all with Klempan's characteristic slow drip of the sinister supernatural, culminating in a heart-pounding showdown that's not just good versus evil, but love versus everything else.

—Brett Allen, author of *Kilroy Was Here* and *Sly Fox Hollow*

"I'd never considered the possibility that the war could come home, that all wars come home . . . " Klempan has discovered a new way to depict the long, strange shadows of America's twenty-first century conflicts. Those readers who first met Mo and John in his powerful debut *Have Snakes, Need Birds* will be thrilled to witness the next episode in their saga, played out along a slow-moving river in "middle-of-nowhere-adjacent" Montana. And for those readers who first cross paths with them in these pages, know that the close of this story need not be the end of the raft-ride.

—Jacquelyn Bengfort, author of *Navy News Service* and *Suitable For All Methods of Communication*

Written in sharp, understated sentences, *Hills Hide Mountains* is full of insight into a human condition inflected by heartache, marked by war and moved by moments of truth and grace. Come for the deeply felt descriptions of life and landscape Klempan offers, stay for [the] beautifully handled supernatural turn.

—Laird Hunt, author of *Zorrie*

Mohini "Mo" Chopra reunites with John Mackenzie in the gorgeous wilderness of Montana four years after she last heard from him. Mo becomes supernaturally empathic and joins a newfound family— [a] good-hearted, well-natured river rafting crew. *Hills Hide Mountains* encompasses anti-prejudice ideas cleverly and subtly, explores the beauty of preserving and nurturing nature, and entertains with paranormal events. A great must-read for anyone who loves nature and adventure with otherworldly powers at play!

—Sairung Wright, co-author of *Separate*

For Charlie, and all the adventures he'll embark upon.

*"The rivers flow not past, but through us,
thrilling, tingling, vibrating every fiber and cell
of the substance of our bodies, making them glide and sing."*

—John Muir

"Life shrinks or expands in proportion to one's courage."

—Anaïs Nin

CHAPTER **ONE**

I almost missed Kirk's declaration. The timing of his arrival, almost too late to help in any significant way other than to stow the box of miniature Bundt cakes in the refrigerator and rearrange the flowers in the vase on the kitchen island, was unsurprising. I wasn't going to tell him about the negative test—not now and maybe not ever—but we could talk about what we both wanted after the party.

The views east over Lake Michigan and the sun setting behind us would set the water to shimmering in time for the anniversary party he'd insisted be held in his condo.

"Mo," he shouted above the playlist I was still busy curating based on his latest tastes, "I said we should take a break."

My fingers worked on their own to pause the playlist, allowing the voices from the living room television to fill the air.

"...*marking one year since the president announced the targeted killing of Osama bin Laden. Jim, how might that play into the president's chances for reelection this fall?*"

Jim didn't get a chance to answer before a dull buzz filled the back of my skull, seeping into my ears and pushing behind my eyes. The sound intensified. For a moment, I thought my head would explode. Laying my hands atop the cool marble counter on the kitchen island reminded me of the ocean, and the pressure disappeared, replaced by...

Nothing, really.

Blaming a terrorist, even a dead one, for the past year of my life felt cheap and unreasonable, but the cheap and unreasonable part of me wanted something to blame other than my own unexpected and embarrassing need to find strength in a man, especially one I'd just met at a party I hadn't wanted to attend after my dream job was taken from me. Throwing the flower vase or the empty cake stand would have felt cliché, but at least the act would leave a mark on Kirk's impossibly clean kitchen.

Impossibly clean because we never cooked in it. He said his salary could buy better food than I could make, and now all the red flags from that May to this May snapped in the breeze unleashed by his revelation.

"That's fine." I unstuck myself from the countertop and went to our bedroom, now *his* bedroom, to pack my things. I couldn't go to Allison's, the only soul in Chicago who might have taken me in. A year ago, she'd welcomed me to her home without question and thrown a party in my honor, though I got the sense the event was a weekly occurrence. Her backyard had been filled with LaSalle Street financiers. She'd tried introducing me to Lawrence, Michael, two guys named Brett, and David before leaving me alone to stew over the loss of my teaching job in Louisiana two days earlier. After avoiding conversation with any of the finance bros or their trophy girlfriends, I'd bumped into Kirk, who seemed different from the rest. His beautiful grin and a bottle of red helped me forget for an evening the seismic shift in my life. He'd escorted me to Allison's roof, what he called *Stephen's* roof, and pointed out the Willis Tower behind and beyond and above the stately suburban trees. We play-argued about it still being the *Sears* Tower in the photo albums of a thousand kids like me, and how could they rename someone's *memories*, and he leaned in to kiss me when word came out that the terrorist was dead. After the heady rush of an impromptu and misplaced celebration, we did kiss. Later that week he took me to Wrigley Field to watch the Cubs lose, but we still marked our anniversary from the announcement of a death a world away. That fatal start set a more appropriate tone for the intervening year than anything else.

This wasn't liberation. It felt more like unmooring, the cutting off of a line and letting the boat drift into the current.

An appropriate image, since I would likely never set foot on his daddy's sailboat again.

"Mohini, can we talk?"

He followed me into the bedroom because that's what movies had told him to do, and I didn't stop him because that's not what evicted tenants do to their former landlords. I ignored the rare utterance of my full name and unearthed the small duffel bag that had, last May, ferried my personal belongings from the classroom I shared with Anita (before she returned to Oakland) and Sera (when she was still alive) into the backseat of the Toyota Camry now occupying Kirk's extra parking spot fifteen stories below. Zeebrugge had been shut down on orders of the state. Our principal, Doc Bellamy, delivered the news, which the residents took without anger, without surprise, focusing on the immediate at the expense of the aspirational.

As a guest teacher, invited to help rebuild after Katrina, I had no place to go within reasonable distance. Though Doc offered help, I declined, guessing at the burdens she had ahead. Boston was too far and I had to go somewhere quickly, so an urgent and half-thought message sent to Allison based on my misunderstanding of geography resulted in a quick offer and eager acceptance of crash landing. We could catch up after years apart and she could tell me about her wedding (*Stephen's family was just so large, and the resort on Saint Lucia so small, so sorry, Mo*) and she granted me use of the second bedroom. Buckley the golden retriever was shuffled aside long enough for me to stay before the room's planned conversion to a nursery, and then Kirk changed my life.

I sorted the clothes on my side of the closet into two piles: one of the things he bought me, and the other of things I brought with me from

Zeebrugge, and St. Louis before that, and Boston before that. T-shirts celebrated bands long sundered; ratty pajama pants had defied Kirk's insistence that I replace them with the fine silken things he gifted me; and a few professional outfits that once served me in the classroom might again in an as-yet undiscovered future. So much of my life had been lived out of a duffel bag and a few cardboard boxes. I had fewer roots here than in Louisiana, and neither was a long-term option.

My teacher clothes were essentially unused because Kirk did not believe I had to work. Even as I sought and secured a Chicago Public Schools substitute teaching license, he steered me from the job I wanted into a part-time gig as a party planner—excuse me, *executive events coordinator*—for the financial firm that showered him with money for moving piles of electrons around the world.

There was the dress, a stunning emerald midi sheath, loaned by Allison for the fateful party and permanently bestowed with the declaration she'd never fit in it again, baby bump or no. My hand paused, almost touching the fabric, wondering if I deserved to keep such a beautiful piece.

"Talk about what?"

I pulled the dress off the hanger and rolled it up, gently inserting it atop the rest of the clothes in the still-roomy duffel. Something small and hard pushed against the green chiffon and I unfurled the dress, remembering that it had pockets. I found a small redwood chip, a piece of mulch plucked from Allison's backyard while I avoided conversation with partygoers who wanted to avoid me even more, but who wanted to avoid *looking* like they wanted to avoid me. Pressing that small chunk of wood into my palm as I sat on my knees on the edge of the closet reminded me why I'd lifted it from the manicured flower bed.

"You can't just leave," Kirk attempted. Gods bless him. Maybe he wanted to *take a break* but still sleep with me; maybe he was trying for another big argument followed by makeup sex. This all felt like another version of the game we'd played for a year, him grinding me down, burning bridges on my behalf and building walls around me. At least this meant no more holidays at his parents' home in Kenilworth—always fucking Kenilworth, never Boston or anywhere *my* family lived. He'd played his last hand.

"Where are you even going to go?"

I lifted the redwood chip to my lips, kissed it, and shoved it back in the bag.

"What do you care?"

HE HAD A POINT. Once again I was being launched without warning from a position I thought stable, my list of landing pads exhausted, both through Kirk's efforts to cut me off from friends and because embarrassment prevented me from returning home to my parents who wouldn't judge, at least not outwardly. Hiding in a town as small as Boston, or anywhere else the Chopra family resided, was nigh on impossible, which crossed another dozen cities off the list.

I found a coffee shop, the caffeine necessary for what promised to be a long night of plotting an egress from Chicago. Destination still undecided, I got the biggest and strongest drink available and chose a spot far from the door from which I could scour my options.

Hope he was able to call his guests and cancel the party, I thought, before realizing Kirk would have had a plan to do so before ever opening his mouth to me.

The fact he still brought home the Bundt cakes baffled me for the time it took to settle in, take the first sip of triple-espresso, and crack open the road atlas that Baba insisted I keep in my car. I turned first to my phone.

Diving into email archives and social media posts provided an uncomfortable descent down a memory hole littered with enough remains of my own destructive tendencies that I extended an unspoken bit of grace to Kirk…until I saw the email from my cousin Priya, saying how sad she was that I couldn't make her wedding in Charlotte. She didn't know that Kirk had said we couldn't afford it, meaning *I* couldn't afford it, but *he* could afford a last-minute trip for the same weekend to see his fraternity brother's nephew's lacrosse game in San Diego.

What could I afford now? Months of organizing fantasy football leagues and video game nights—excuse me, *team-building exercises*—for Kirk and his finance partners had fattened my bank account, but stubborn student loan payments and unexpected expenses starved it almost as quickly. I could buy a last-minute one-way plane ticket in pretty much any direction or a few nights in a local hotel, but not much else, so whatever I came up with tonight had to be realistic and quick.

Friends and acquaintances, distant cousins and sorority sisters. I looked at the giant map splayed across my table, struck by the recollection of the overnight drive from Zeebrugge to Chicago, sunk by my realization that, while Chicago sat near the center of our big awkward nation, it was far from anywhere safe.

Scrolling deeper into my electronic past, thankful that for some reason I saved every single email, a possibility flared. Anita, one of my roommates in Zeebrugge, a similarly bright-eyed young teacher intent on making a difference, was still in Oakland.

Never mind. The next email said she was visiting Guatemala to care for her sick abuela, crossing another option off the list.

I slid my hand into the duffel next to me. There was no reason I needed my clothes with me in the coffee shop, but still the bag came with me. The only other things evacuated from Kirk's apartment stayed in the car. The box of books lifted from their designated half of the hallway bookshelf he'd granted me sat on the backseat next to an ancient typewriter bought from an estate sale in Allison's neighborhood, the first and last time I'd met little Emma. The typewriter was the only item purchased with the only paycheck earned from substitute teaching, those two weeks Kirk granted me to pursue my dream before maneuvering me into his office, because gods forbid I have a life outside of his.

But now I did.

My fingers wrapped around the chunk of wood. Anita wasn't an option, and neither was Sera, but the piece of redwood mulch seemed like my last connection to her, and the breath I took next was purposefully deep. I closed my eyes and counted to ten. Anita and I had escorted Sera's remains to the red-wooded hills of the Lost Coast, and then stayed for her funeral and wake set among ancient trees hardened by a storm-tossed ocean. Her parents were sorrier for us than for Sera or themselves, far more attentive than their only child's roommates deserved, and though they would have taken me in without hesitation, getting to California would be trek enough without having to navigate the twisting seaside highways to try to find their home again.

More than four years had passed since we all parted, the guilt over my part in her death no lighter in the meantime. I'd never told Anita about my fight with Sera, the morning before she left forever, an argument about a man who fell into our lives.

I started typing without wiping away the tears gathering in the edges of my eyes.

John. Total shot in the dark, but you once said if I ever needed anything to ask. Well, I need a place to crash, ASAP, and you're literally the last person I can ask.
-Mo

How the hell had *he* survived a war zone and our friend, the woman we both loved, hadn't survived in America? I didn't hate John Mackenzie. Couldn't hate him, never had, but for his role in altering Sera's course, sending her sideways into disaster, for being the last man to touch her before she died...

I dropped the wood chip and the phone, leaned my head forward to rest against my arms atop the atlas, atop the awkwardly small table in the back of a coffee shop in Aurora, and cried. Surely I wasn't the first woman to cry as the sun set and the sky darkened over the cafe with a pun-based name, for the barista left me alone, but damn it I deserved to cry even if I was now cut loose from the unmovable man. I could have stayed a thousand years and Kirk's condo would be as unadorned, as cold, and as sterile as he liked it. Returning, if it were even an option, would be surrendering, waiting for him to grant me some smaller place in his life, a spot on his shelf where he could grind me even further into nothing. He deprived me of even the chance to mourn a relationship that, unfortunately, was my longest one since high school by removing my ability to pine for any of it, and how fucking stupid was that?

John's role in Sera's death was tangential, momentum transferred from the collision into her life afforded by the fortnight he'd spent under our roof in Louisiana. He may have blamed himself, if he remembered her or me, but as soon as the thought appeared I knew he could never forget either. Sitting around our dinner table to a meal he'd cooked for Sera and Anita and me, I had accused John of everything short of war crimes. He had taken it, questioned his own role in an unjust war, even came close to thanking me for challenging him so bravely and so boldly, as he'd put it in his email to me from Iraq a few weeks later. I'd felt neither brave nor bold, then or now, but Sera loved us back in different ways.

Am I a fool for thinking he'll answer my SOS?

John's sincere simplicity never came off like an affectation. Sera claimed he could talk to birds. Not just talk. Plenty of people talked to birds; my baba's sister held ongoing one-sided conversations with the doves that swarmed her house in Jaipur. John understood what they said. Sera saw him share a message from a heron that hung around Zeebrugge, a bird our students had named *Jesus*, and something about the encounter convinced her he wasn't bluffing, that he was privy to a mysterious avian dialogue. As unlikely as it was, such a skill would fit the rest of his personality. His ability to answer the questions he could and admit his ignorance when he couldn't, his steady demeanor in all climates, the innate guts it took to weather multiple deployments to a country riven by a war that we—

Wait. Was John still in the Army?

I lifted my head and searched for him online, an avalanche of results for men with that unremarkable name more than could be sifted through in one night. Adding *united states army* to the search bar returned stories of an award ceremony, cryptic references in a military news article about heroism in a firefight, the lives he saved both Iraqi and American.

Just because it was nighttime in Chicago didn't mean it was night all over the world. As likely as not he was over there again, or this time in Afghanistan.

I shoved away the impulse to add *killed in action* to the search.

My phone buzzed. A new email appeared, bold and unread.

Mo. Of course. Anything I can do to help. Come whenever you need to. John

"Wow."

He provided an address in a place called Bonaventure. My brain flashed back to grade school geography bees to decipher *MT* as *Montana*.

Last I knew he was in Georgia, debating whether to stay in the Army or get out. Were there even military bases in Montana? If he were still near Atlanta, I could empty my checking account for an airplane ticket, but...

Could someone even fly to Montana?

I flipped the atlas pages to find Bonaventure tucked in the far south-west corner of that state, a little jaunt above Yellowstone National Park, and then shuffled back to the country at large. I dragged my fingertip along the blue highway line from the blob of Chicago up the flank of Lake Michigan, across Wisconsin and Minnesota, across the length of a Dakota into Wyoming and ended back in Montana.

The sudden novelty of a road trip, rolling down highways bound for mountains and pine trees and buffalo, shook some of the past few hours off my shoulders. The past year would require more powerful magic to undo, if that were even possible. A few days hiding out in the Rocky Mountains could at least offer me a chance to come up with a real plan.

"Bonaventure." Just breathing the word into existence gave me hope.

Electrified fingers typed out a reply and hit *send* before I could stop myself.

CHAPTER TWO

The FM stations blasting country music disappeared after leaving Sioux Falls. The AM broadcasts about crop price predictions for the coming season in the morning faded into angry denunciations of the *election year enemy* in the afternoon. My little Toyota's speakers squawked, tinny and haunting, like messages transmitted from inside a can at the bottom of a mineshaft. The radio eventually gave out entirely, disintegrating into static as I wondered if there would be a safe place to stop for the night.

Muscle memory allowed me to riffle through my CD binder, another artifact in a shrinking collection of items accompanying my stumbling journey across the nation, and pop discs in and out of the dashboard player without taking my eyes off the unbelievably straight highway. The familiar music set my mind to wandering, which unfortunately let Kirk in. Every time my nostalgic memory landed on an amazing date or fancy excursion or wondered what my haste was in leaving immediately and not staying to, as Kirk asked, *talk things out*, my rational brain blamed me for just leaning back and taking a year's worth of shit, for embracing the high life as payment for the hard times in Zeebrugge and before, as makeup for opportunities missed in putting my job ahead of myself, and maybe I hadn't left quickly enough.

In return for his indulgences, I became the woman who had a cocktail ready for her man when he came home, and then the woman who had a cocktail while waiting for him to come home. For a few months in the darkest part of winter, I'd nearly lost myself inside a series of bottles. The heavy slate sky prevented me from seeing anything more than the next few hours, over and over until bedtime, when sleep came without dreaming, if I drank hard enough. The return of light in the spring gave me energy to cut back on the drinking, but not enough to bring the dreams back or to cut myself free.

Thankfully, Kirk provided the unloosing.

To call the road ahead a "whim" suggested choices, selecting one from among many. It discounted all the other points along my path when the ability and even the weight of doing the reasonable thing made sense. Driving to Montana with so little forethought that it required a last-minute trip to a thrift store to procure a fleece jacket, down vest, and warm gloves was not, truth be told, the craziest thing I'd ever done.

This also wasn't the frontier days, setting out west into the great unknown. I wasn't launching myself on a raft in hopes of a better life. This wasn't getting on a plane to give children born and unborn a better life in an unknown country, this wasn't even *that crazy* simply because it was a reversible decision. In all likelihood, I would crash with John for a few days, maybe a week or two to decompress in the great outdoors and get my head on straight before retreating to Boston, this time for good.

I sent my parents a text, letting them know I had left Chicago and would be staying with a friend for a bit. They wished me well, asking only that I keep them posted, and be safe, and did I know my younger sister was expecting and that I'd be an auntie again and I should call her.

They'd left home as two smart but hapless people and with luck and connection landed in Massachusetts, he to earn a position teaching high school algebra, she English literature, though both had been professors at university in Jaipur. They'd always been dubious about my plans, the third of four daughters, happy when I was happy and waiting when I wasn't. Nieces and nephews scattered across the far reaches of the continent provided plenty of opportunity for them to dote. Mama and Baba never hinted at my own lack of husband and children and stopped asking after long-term partners and holiday visits, content to know I was, in their estimation, doing *all right*.

Do I deserve more than all right? The crows on the power lines flanking the highway couldn't hear my question. They took off in a dark whirl. Even if they could have heard they wouldn't have replied, and even if they had, I would not understand their answer. *Had I done enough to earn more than all right?*

College in St Louis, followed by Teach for America, and then a magazine ad had caught my eye and drew me south to Zeebrugge, a town in a state I knew nothing about, in a parish of the same name. (Who, outside Louisiana, even knew they didn't have counties but parishes?) The small town had been hit hard by Katrina and looked to reinvent itself in the aftermath.

Selfishly, I thought I could help with the reinvention.

Anita had answered the call as well, another college town daughter of immigrants, and when we got to Zeebrugge we found Sera, who already had a home rented and set up for our arrival, as though she knew we were coming. The three of us were the only ones to respond to the advertisement. She took us in without question and we got to work, not as missionaries or heroes, but as teachers. We helped the children so *they* would go off and study and return and outsiders like us could move on. Hard work, and good, and we convinced each other we made enough headway each day to feel less like bumbling aliens and more like well-intentioned weirdos.

Two years after we parachuted in, Sera had taken a weekend off and chose the most random but appropriately *Sera* way to fill the time: a Christian music festival in the dry September belly of Oklahoma. She wasn't Christian, of course. At most she could be considered a pagan, or more accurately a heathen, and being from the Lost Coast she was less religious than that, but she showed a great curiosity about a great many things. That curiosity led her to find John, a soldier on leave from the war in Iraq in the middle of a storm or the middle of a song, or both, and it wasn't the music or the spirit or anything other than her own bravery that lowered her guard enough to let her say *yes* to the whim she felt in her chest, always *yes* with her.

I shook my head at a water tower speeding past me in the opposite direction.

"Fucking whims," I said, wasting a curse on an undeserving target.

She'd brought John back to Zeebrugge to test her courage, Sera said. I'd called her ridiculous. She was the bravest person I knew. Finding a lost young soldier in our kitchen was odd but not *that* odd, since she'd never brought a man home before, and for two weeks he fit into our little family.

They lived under a deadline. John had to return to Iraq to protect his men, to survive the rest of his time in a combat zone, and Sera had promised him, though I never knew exactly what or how much. She cut off enough of her heart and he his to guarantee not just a reunion but a commitment. Sera had asked us to write to him as well and shared some of the messages they exchanged and the plans they made.

A month later she'd died. Another random weekend trip, this time to the Mississippi Delta, led her straight into the path of a truck with failed brakes. John couldn't attend the funeral, though not for lack of trying. *The Army*, he'd told me in one of his last emails from Iraq, *doesn't grant emergency leave for soulmates*. We'd traded a few more messages, his tour neared its conclusion, and then…silence.

I could still turn south for Denver, or plow ahead and bypass Bonaventure for Seattle, impose on the good graces of cousins and aunties and subject myself to a (perhaps deserved) review of my life choices.

You could go back.

The steering wheel didn't deserve the sudden pressure from my fingers.

You should go back.

The lack of traffic meant my abrupt lane change didn't endanger anyone else.

Go back.

The car shuddered as it pulled onto the shoulder.

Go back go back go back.

The voice wasn't mine, wasn't Kirk's, but rang as clear in my head as if someone were sitting next to me shouting. Angry, insistent, threatening… *familiar?*

Going back meant going back to *him.* I could temper my words, constrict myself even smaller, and Kirk would reward me with lacy pajamas and box seats and trips to Cabo if only I could be the girl he wanted me to be. Plenty of people carved themselves into something else, someone they didn't want to be, but there was safety and predictability and comfort in conforming.

There was also the negative test, the one I never told him about because we hadn't been trying, hadn't even *talked* about trying. My brief but overwhelming scare couldn't be shared with anyone, not Allison or Mama or Sera, and I threw the little white stick in the lobby trash bin so Kirk wouldn't find it and I still got ready for the party.

The pain in my chest made me want to decide something, anything, if only to stop the throbbing inside my head drowning out the last song as the disc ended and slid out of the player. I rolled my window down, desperate to get some air, and reached for the passenger seat. The binder of music had fallen to the floor after my cut across two lanes of interstate. Reaching beneath the seat, the feel of an unexpected object pierced the foggy trance brought on by my thoughts at war with the intrusive voice.

The sudden stop had dislodged something smooth and cool. The survivability of a loose compact disc exiled under the seat was questionable, though the penmanship and message on the label convinced me that I had to try.

A burned CD—the successor to the custom mixtapes of my awkward teen years—the date written in precise black marker chronicling its creation two days before my best friend's trip to the Delta, the names caught the breath in my lungs.

Made for: Mohini Chopra
Made by: Sera Quarron

The drone in my head faded. I wiped away tears with the back of my hand. Even years after she was gone Sera knew when I needed her. The anger, fear, excitement, sorrow, and hope of the last few days swelled and threatened to consume me, made heavier by contemplating the imposing emptiness of the landscape in every direction, but as I slid the disc into the player, I knew her gift was made as an act of love.

In place of songs ripped from the internet or burned from other CDs, Sera accompanied herself with a guitar, presumably the beat-up sticker-covered hand-me-down she'd bought for more than it was worth from a Zeebrugge yard sale. I hugged the steering wheel, pressed the hot and grimy leather into my forehead, and broke. My chest heaved in time with the songs, sobbing but not wanting to stop the music. I had so little to remember her by. I wanted to commit her voice to memory, to etch the lyrics on my heart as surely as they were carved onto the disc.

She sang me ten songs of love and courage, songs she and Anita and I had belted out on road trips, and others I'd never heard. *How did she do it?* Our house was tiny, the walls thin, and we could hear everything from any other room, but somehow she recorded herself playing that rickety guitar and singing messages into a bottle, a time traveling note of cover songs beautifully rendered to appear for me when I needed them most, when I was more lost than ever.

Each song brought strength, brought joy. The car shuddered each time a semi-truck flew past. I barely felt the disturbances. The disc repeated as the sun touched the horizon. By the time it started the playlist for a third time I was ready to sing along.

The disc skipped, the player whined.

"No," I whispered. "No, no. Come on."

The sounds coming from the guts of the dashboard horrified me.

Smashing the eject button made the player jump from song to song, taunting me with the first three seconds of each, and then it shrieked, a cacophony of grinding accompanied by the faint smell of smoke. *Please, gods.*

The disc emerged halfway, squealing as it appeared. Before I could grab the edge, the player sucked it back in. I wanted to scream at the car, the player, Kirk, the world, and would have, had I any energy left to do so. Scratching at the dashboard might have felt good, but it wouldn't rescue the disc, currently being torn apart, sight unseen. My forehead sunk to the steering wheel.

"What the hell am I doing?"

Hey Mo, you beautiful human being. As fast as the world is being destroyed, we have to learn to love even faster.

I lifted my head at the sound of Sera's voice, four seconds of the silly mantra we shared each morning in Zeebrugge. The message hadn't played any of the previous times through the playlist, but there it was, a hidden eleventh track.

THE BAYOU THUNDERSTORM had hammered the porch with such force it had felt like the whole world was caught in the downpour. I'd found John leaning against the least rotted of the timbers holding up the tar paper roof, the one we'd put off fixing time and again. Any money left at the end of the month went back into our classrooms, and we deferred all offers from parents to patch up the holes in our home. They had enough to focus on in theirs.

John had spent part of the past ten days repairing things around the house while we were at school, cooked us dinner more often than not, and would leave the following morning. The roof could wait for his return or collapse in the meantime.

Hope the roof holds one more day, at least.

The screen door slammed shut behind me. John hadn't moved except to sip from a mug, maybe filled with coffee, maybe something stronger.

Doc Bellamy had called Sera to the school, interrupting their last afternoon together. Tomorrow, we would pack him and his few belongings into my car for the trip to the airport in Dallas, from where he'd return to Iraq and war.

I frowned at this latest injustice in the midst of so many more, a few hours stolen from two kind people in a cruel world. They'd promised to write actual letters to each other, emails to fill in the time between mail calls, and they planned to reunite when his tour was over. For knowing each other less than a fortnight, it wasn't the worst idea, though I'd had my reservations.

John's face had changed over the course of those two weeks. Some of that came from not shaving every morning, some from getting three regular meals a day and some from actually sleeping, as much as he and Sera managed. I'd caught him the day before, by accident, stepping out of the bathroom, a towel around his waist, and he looked filled in. Healthy. The look of haunted panic he wore on that first morning in our kitchen had long since faded, replaced by a deeper calm. Any lingering tension from our argument at the dinner table was long gone, replaced by a detente based on our mutual feelings for Sera. His imminent departure weighed on him, as it did Sera, but he'd looked as ready as he could be.

For what, we had no idea.

"Did Sera make you watch the spaghetti Western?" I asked.

"How'd you know?"

"It comes on, like, every Wednesday. She's made me and Anita watch it at least twice." I looked at him. "It's not bad."

The storm burled in on itself, intensifying as it sucked up the heat and moisture from the Gulf of Mexico and Keep's Creek and Bayou Araignée, setting the water loose among the clouds to come down as a deluge. The ground was already so drunk that the rain spilled into the streets. The residents had survived worse, but surely this downpour sent chills through a town still catching its breath after Katrina tore through.

"The moment the storm breaks, that first fall of water…" Thunder nearly swallowed up my words. "That's the fever letting go, but you know it'll come back. Always does."

John looked into his mug. "The rain falls on the just and wicked alike."

"No one gets to walk between the rain."

"Into each life comes some rain."

I waited a moment. "Are you this philosophical when you and Sera fuck?"

"Wow." He'd flinched, like a lightning bolt caught him on the arm. "How did you—"

My laughter competed with the storm and, for a moment, won. "Holy *shit*, soldier, you guys aren't that loud, but this house ain't that big." I caught his eye. "She seems to like you, though. Maybe more."

"Do you…" He hesitated. "Do you love her?"

I had leaned against the other timber, felt it bend beneath my weight, and wondered if the whole roof would come tumbling down on us. "Do you?" I asked him.

I SAT ON THE SIDE OF THE INTERSTATE with the shards of the compact disc in my hands, the prairie wind whipping my hair across my face to stick to my cheeks where the tears fell. Brushing away the dark tangles I could see my palms were unmarked, but deep inside they felt sliced and bloodied, the fire and power in my grasp threatening to consume me and the entire world.

The pain subsided, leaving me with aching numbness and three chunks of a disc. Fitting together the fragments revealed the letters inked on the surface years before.

A passing truck rocked me backward and fixed my attention to the west, where the highway melted into the sunset and, hopefully, Montana. I had all the time in the world and only a few minutes to make the decision to keep going or turn back, which meant going back to *him*.

And I might have made a U-turn at the nearest available exit, an hour before, if my hand hadn't found the disc from Sera, lost beneath my seat for who knows how many years.

I knew. She had inked the date she made it. In the days before our last argument, she recorded herself playing ten songs, songs I'd never heard before and songs I loved, sung just to me as explanation and acceptance, and then tucked the disc in my car as a surprise, discovered only now and lost just as quickly.

Sera drove by herself up state and county roads to the Delta. She'd asked me that morning, in the midst of our argument, if I wanted to keep talking, to come with her, and I refused, committed to winning this fight or putting it off until her return.

I got up, dumped the pieces of the disc into the cup holder, and wiped my hands on my shorts. Nothing cut, nothing bleeding, at least not to the naked eye. The tears stopped. Sera had given me one last gift, and her gift gave me direction and momentum.

John wasn't Kirk. He wasn't anything, really, other than a man from years before who now offered help without condition. Maybe he really could talk to birds, but most importantly he'd been good to Sera, to Anita, and to our students, even to me, though I hadn't deserved it. Sera loved him fiercely and that could be a sign on its own.

CHAPTER THREE

Despite the thousand miles traveled over the past three days, the hours of solitude, and the acres of contemplation, I'd given no thought to how I should greet John. A hug felt out of place and a handshake less than necessary to mark the oddity of this encounter. He and I faced each other, shivering in the encroaching darkness brought about by the early twilight of the mountains surrounding this little cabin where the engine of my little Toyota ticked in relief, idle after a marathon day that started almost twelve hours before. Snow crunched under my feet.

John extended a hand holding a mug. "It's tea," he said. "Green tea. Figured coffee might not be the best idea this time of day."

"How'd you know?" I held my face low over the steam and breathed it in, the warmth invigorating even through thin cotton gloves.

"In your email, you sounded…" He searched for a word.

"Desperate?"

"Anxious. Maybe anxious. I didn't want to assume too much, just thought you'd be arriving as quickly as you could."

The cabin looked bigger than it did a few minutes before when my lone remaining headlight had illuminated the outside walls, landing on a flannel-clad man rising from a rocking chair on a covered porch. Pine trees flanked the gravel driveway. The slope behind the cabin rose quickly from the valley floor, the darkness probably amplifying my vertigo. The diet of gas station food and the fitful, dreamless sleep that accompanied me from Chicago didn't help my nerves.

The tea was serendipity in a mug, comfort in liquid form, but not enough to keep me on my feet for much longer.

"Is it still winter here?"

The smile beneath his beard was enough to convince me, if I had any doubt, that it was really him. He'd given that smile freely to the school children of Zeebrugge, to Anita and me at dinner each night when we told him about our days, and to Sera whenever they were together.

"It's been a snowy spring. Do you have a coat to go with that beanie? Real gloves?"

I pulled the knit cap lower over my head before ducking inside the car. I emerged holding the puffy vest purchased in panic based on the Montana weather forecast. "Can we go inside? My blood is still operating on Chicago temperatures."

"This is chilly even for me," he admitted. "Supposed to be true spring any day now. Need a hand bringing stuff in?" He took the duffel bag from me, and then the box of books.

"You were just sitting out here in the dark waiting for me? I sent that email…what, days ago?"

"You didn't say when you were coming, or even that you were coming from Chicago. I've been spending a little time out here around sunset each day since. There's plenty of chores to keep me busy." He pointed to a small tool shed and the driveway, mostly free of snow and ice. A conifer, smaller than any other, just to the side of a gravel path, caught my attention. "Figured the most likely thing was you'd arrive at night, or close to it."

I blinked and shook my head, unsure what about the little Charlie Brown tree was so insistent.

"Mind if I bring something…impractical inside?" Without waiting for his answer, I hauled the typewriter out. "Don't ask. Not yet."

He led me up the porch steps and held the door open.

"This is…unexpected," I said.

He set my luggage down on a bench next to the entryway and departed down a short hallway, leaving me to examine the room: mismatched sofa and armchair with blankets draped over their backs…tall bookshelves properly filled…a fire crackling in a stone hearth.

John reappeared carrying a tray, which he placed on a wooden steamer trunk that served as a coffee table. I set the typewriter down next to my luggage, kicked off my boots, sank into the cushions of the armchair, and pulled the wool blanket over my shoulders.

"You have an actual lived-in living room."

"Did you see the sunset on your way in?"

Grilled cheese sandwiches, tomato soup, and apple slices demanded my immediate attention. The simple food reminded me of rainy weekends in Boston, Baba and his ships in bottles, Mama deep in another book. I filled him in on the details of my road trip between bites, avoiding anything like substantive updates from the intervening…*gods*, four years since we talked last, saving the topic of Sera's CD for another day.

"Do we have to worry about bears?"

"Bears?" He paused before taking my empty bowl to the kitchen. "Like, coming inside?"

"When I told my parents I was coming to Montana, they wanted to know about bears."

"There are definitely bear in the woods around here." He returned with more apple slices and a small plate of shortbread, taking some of both for himself. He refilled my mug with hot water and a fresh tea bag before he sat. "Mostly black bear. We're on the edge of wilderness, but the grizzlies stay closer to the national parks."

"I'd like to see Yellowstone, if that's OK."

My body felt submerged, not just in the armchair or under the blanket, but like every heaviness of the world descended on my shoulders and held me underwater. Each bite of fruit snapped like a firecracker between my teeth, granting my muscles energy to stay afloat for a minute longer.

"Of course," he said.

Had he not also spent the last few days reliving our encounters? John seemed open and welcoming, neutral edging toward warm, but there was something else at work beneath the surface of his otherwise quiet demeanor.

"If the bears stay outside, do I have to worry about them if I have to, y'know, use the outhouse in the middle of the night?" An attempt at a smile crossed my face.

"This *is* Montana," he replied, wearing a grin of his own, "but we have indoor plumbing. Hot and cold running water, even. Bathroom on this floor is right over there, just across the hall from your room."

My room.

"I'm glad you made it," he said. "Glad you felt comfortable enough asking, if you needed someplace to crash for a few days, but can I ask—"

"Why didn't I go home? Stay with my parents?" He nodded. "Part of it was practical. Right now they're getting ready to take their students to Europe."

"Europe?"

"They teach honors courses, and each summer they take the kids to Europe. Kind of a reward for all the hard work they do, being huge nerds all year and missing out on a social life."

"Did you get to go when you were in high school?"

"Thanks for assuming I was an honors student. I didn't want to go back to Boston and hang around an empty house for a month. Can I ask you the same thing?"

"Why I ended up in Louisiana," he said, "instead of being with family? Middle of a combat tour, you'd be right in thinking most guys head home.

My dad was long gone by the time I joined the Army, and I lost my mom in a car accident."

"Oh, gods, John."

"I have a sister, but we haven't talked much since then."

We listened to the hum and crackle of the fire.

"Do you miss Sera?" I regretted my question as soon as I asked it, but wanted to know how much her loss weighed on him, all these years later.

He countered with one of his own. "Have you been thinking of her? That's a long way, Chicago to Montana."

"Hard not to." My chest tightened. "Every day since we lost her. I'm sorry the Army didn't let you come to the service."

The fire shrunk lower, the room now too dim for me to see his face. He stood, walked to the nearest bookcase, and pulled a small leather-bound parcel from the highest shelf. He handed it to me before returning to his seat.

"After I came back from Iraq," he said, "that was my last time over there. After I came back, I visited her parents. They gave me that." He pointed at what I could now see was a journal, embossed with Sera's initials, the ones she'd chosen for herself as an adult. "They said she wanted me to have it. I've never opened it," he admitted. "Didn't know when she stopped writing in it, what she said, and I didn't know if I wanted to know. Funny thing, though, it helped me rejoin the world after I left the Army."

I hated that my voice shook. "How?"

"She told you about…" He paused. "You know about me and birds, right?" I nodded, not wanting to hear my voice shake again. "Ever since her parents gave that to me, it's helped me hear more of what the birds say."

"Sera called your power *birdspeak*."

"She's the one who came up with it. I never had a name for it, it was always just kind of…there. I thought I lost the ability in Iraq. It went silent for a long time, but having that journal." He leaned forward, elbows on his knees, and clasped his hands beneath his chin. "It helped. I could hear them again." He set his feet on the steamer trunk. "You seem pretty willing to believe in something as weird as birdspeak."

"I'm trying to be open to more possibilities. The universe is pretty strange." I ran my fingertips across the smooth leather, traced the letters *SEQ*, and found I couldn't open the cover either, let alone read a single page. I looked up at John. "This was in the box of things Anita and I took from her room in Zeebrugge and gave to her folks," I said. "They were so kind, at the funeral. Almost too kind, considering why we were there."

"Funny to think of someone being *too kind*." He let out a breath.

"That's not what I…" The food was gone and the buzzing sound returned to the back of my head for the first time in days. "Not what I meant. I can go."

Standing too quickly sapped every bit of energy left to me. I tried to pass him the mug, but dropped it. I fell to my knees next to the puddle, desperately trying to sweep the hot liquid off the smooth timbers of the floor back into the mug. My hair fell across my face and eyes so I didn't see when he knelt next to me. I felt his hands on mine, stopping me from scalding them further.

His hands were warm, but I flinched from the jolt of electricity, the same sensation the broken shards of Sera's disc had sent up my arms and down my body.

"Hey." His voice was soft. The buzzing disappeared. "It's just tea, Mo." He picked up the mug. "See? Didn't even break."

John offered to stay up until the fire went out. The last log in the hearth popped and the flames consumed everything, not one chunk after another, but every tree in the world, and I felt sorry not for the wood so much as for the fire and its need to burn.

John asked how long I was staying. *How long*, not *if*.

We patched in some of the missing pieces from our last many years, coloring in the intervening time as a way to prolong the evening. At first, we stuck to geographic and journalistic facts, avoiding editorial embellishment. I shared what happened the night bin Laden died and the year that followed without diving into too many gritty details, not wanting to open that particular wound just yet, if ever again. My eyelids drooped and my head bobbed, but I fought to stay awake when he reciprocated with the story of his final combat tour, what happened after he'd left Louisiana and returned to Iraq. The line between his tale and my own dreams, newly returned and strengthened by their prolonged absence, blurred as he spoke about firefights and roadside bombs, demons from America let loose upon an innocent city, a tornado that threatened to destroy the world, and a small black dog.

My eyes snapped open and my leg shook hard enough to knock the blanket off my lap. My muscles ached and I did not want John to have to carry me anywhere. A nagging, lingering thought from the dreamscape, a demand that I examine the connection between a CD made for me and a journal given to John persisted until I stood and stretched.

I had questions that needed answers before I left Montana, but I needed sleep before I fell down.

Now, on the first night in a new place, no forest noises outside the window of the guest room—*my room*—hearing only my breathing kept me awake, despite everything hanging over me. Kirk blasted the air conditioning in our—*his*—condo every night, summer or winter, and I had grown accustomed to falling asleep to the sound of the aggressive hum. Here in a room with an actual bed on an actual frame, covered in soft sheets with a heavy quilt folded neatly at my feet, flanked by mismatched furniture, a modest lamp and of course another bookshelf in the corner, the glassy night hidden behind deep blue window sashes, I wrapped my arms around myself and cried, though only for a minute.

Finished with my tears, I held my hand, still tingling from the disc shards, where my fingers had brushed against John's and the tea.

TALL KHAKI BUILDINGS blot out the sun. The warm glow from hot bricks illuminates John kneeling next to me, clad in camouflage and bulky with gear, cradling a rifle like a baby. Dream knowledge tells me the wooden gate and the red door on the far side of the courtyard are the only exits to the rest of the world. One leads to sanctuary, the other doom. Danger surrounds us, infuses our muscles. John worries because he can't see the rooftops and the windows have no glass in them, staring down at us like empty eye sockets. The sound of a basketball bouncing on pavement fills the air. Laundry on a line snaps like flags in a hot breeze that stirs the sand, the wind gathering its strength.

Death stalks the small squad of soldiers waiting on his order, each man with John's face, some younger and some older, all scared.

A small bird named *hoopoe* flits in and out of shadows, circles a canine body splayed in the middle of the courtyard. John's ability to understand birdspeak means I can understand what the hoopoe says, knowledge transmitted secondhand.

Get up, urges the bird. *Save them.*

John whispers to a version of himself, points to the far side. I want to warn him which route is safe, but no one can know that because there's no such thing as *safe*. We can't even save the dog, so how can we save ourselves?

A younger John darts out to check the gate. Locked. The bird bows before him, then resumes its hopeless mission to rouse the dog. A second, even younger John, impossibly young, runs to check the door.

Watch out. My mouth fails to form the words and they resonate inside my head.

A snake lunges from shadows and the hoopoe takes flight, not quickly enough. The viper snaps its jaws shut around the bird's chest. Each John clutches his chest, agony on their faces, and the youngest John stumbles, crashing through the door. The entire world shudders and the snake with triangle eyes laughs around the bird in its mouth. I slap my hands over my ears but my hands and ears are gone and the wind howls to the center of my head and knocks us all to the ground. The John next to me shouts and bullets fly in slow and deadly paths across the world.

The snake with triangle eyes wrestles the bird to the ground and John can't bring his weapon to bear. None of the men can move. Even if they could, they couldn't. Reality tears apart at the seams. This is the end of time.

Wake up.

New motion at the edge of chaos catches my attention, moving with dream-heavy muscles to watch. Sera in a dress the color of oceans at night, of far-off mountains, of cabin window sashes walks from the edge of existence into the courtyard, purposeful and filled with life. The wind shrieks but cannot touch her. John tries to warn her but she does not stop. She marches forward, clasps her hands together, and dives into the body of the dog. The creature comes alive, turns on the serpent, and catches the monster in its jaws. The snake releases the bird, and every John in the squad can move.

Sera and the dog pin the snake to the ground as heaven and earth shatter. The tornado around us bellows and expands, sucking down the towers and smashing them to atoms, but the storm knows it has lost, same as the snake. John aims his gun and dream knowledge tells me that his bullet will kill the snake and stop the storm, but Sera will disappear, this time forever, again.

His gun makes no sound as a bullet leaves the barrel and the dream ends before the shot lands.

CHAPTER FOUR

When I emerged from under the quilt, my eyelids held fast against the warm light pouring through frosted glass. I remembered my drive into the hills and wilds of Montana, recalled the snow still packed hard upon the ground, and longed for another grilled cheese sandwich.

The soft edges of illumination suggested morning, though I had no idea which direction my room faced.

My room. Did people care about cardinal directions out here, *out west,* and would I remember which was north and all the others? The lake insisted on reminding everyone in Chicago which way was east, though there and in Zeebrugge I'd navigated not by compass points, but by landmark and memory, and still got lost.

I kicked off the quilt and sat up, forcing my eyes to open fully in hopes of shocking my brain into usable shape. The lingering chill convinced me to retrieve a portion of the blanket. I slid my foot out to test the floor.

"Damn." I rescued my frozen toes and looked over the edge of the bed. My entire slumbering life was an unwinnable battle between overheated and freezing, collateral casualties stretching back to my childhood cat Benji. The pile of clothes I'd shed during the night had landed on the hardwood floor next to a pair of leather slippers. Not mine, but left for me.

I rested my head on the pillow and stared at the ceiling.

"Bonaventure."

A house, clean and comfortable, owned—*did John own the place?*—occupied by a man whose path had crossed mine half a decade prior, and what did he *do* here on the edge of the wilderness? How long would he let me stay?

How long could I stay right here?

My empty stomach compelled me out of bed. Feet inserted into wool socks and then the slippers, a flannel button-up extracted from the duffel resting on the chair by the bookshelf and thrown over my tank top and leggings, and damn if I didn't pull that knit beanie down over my ears as well. My fingertips grazed the spines of the books, each touch providing fleeting ethereal images of the people and dragons within.

Despite my hunger and lingering weariness, even after the mini-panic attack over spilled tea, emerging from the first dream in…months…one that felt far too real, I felt…*refreshed?*

"Restored," I told the room.

My room, according to John.

Windows in the hallway admitted light sufficient to animate the intricate networks of melting ice, rivulets on glass casting shifting patterns on the rug. In the kitchen, someone who wasn't John worked over a gas stove, blue flames leaping to touch a pair of cast iron pans. The smell of melting butter warmed the cabin.

The man moved without speaking, confidently laying strips of bacon into one pan while cracking egg after egg into the other. John had not mentioned a roommate. A dog curled at the man's feet woke when my foot fell on a kitchen floorboard. The audible creak caused the dog to lift and tilt her large shaggy head. A cross between a shepherd and some breed lost to prehistory, her eyes narrowed with a guarded toughness. After a moment she was satisfied with her inspection of me, relaxing and turning her attention to the man at the stove, perhaps hoping to partake of the coming feast.

"You like turkey bacon and fried eggs?" He only half-turned to me, still tending to the pans.

"Yes, thank you. Over easy, if you're taking orders."

He wiped his hands on a dish towel and faced me, a smile fixed naturally on his face. "That way you can sop up the yolk with toast, right?" His gaze lingered on the wall behind me. I took his hand and his eyes flickered to meet mine. "You met Badger. She don't make much of a guard dog, but she knows where the bacon's kept. I'm Carter."

Badger stood, did a better downward-facing *her* than I could ever hope to accomplish, and then walked from the stove toward a door that looked to lead outside. She threw herself into a pile of towels next to a small bench covered in boots and shoes.

"Carter. Is it all right if I pet Badger?"

He nodded, returning to his duty on the stove, flipping eggs one after the other with a deft touch. "She's off-duty right now. I know my way around the cabin well enough, it's just getting around outside she helps with."

Badger pressed against my leg, encouraging me to give her scratches behind both ears.

"She's a good girl, looks like. Who's a good girl?" My fingernails dug into the thick ruff of fur around her chest and set her tail to wagging. She radiated security, the way a big dog should, a bastion of certainty in a turbulent world, but she'd not always been safe…the thought was hard to hold. The more I massaged her shoulders and neck the more she told me what it was like not to know what tomorrow would bring, and to be afraid. That was in her past, and she lived in the now, unburdened by memories or worries.

"She's a rescue."

"Kinda," he said. "Careful you don't spoil her, now."

I shook my head and intensified my affections. "Are you kidding? I haven't spoiled a dog like this in *months*. Who's a big girl? Who's a sweet big girl?"

"She's good at her job, but she might be deaf."

"Deaf? Isn't that ironic, if you're—"

I cut myself off. "Guess it is." Carter laughed. "Though I'm not all-the-way blind, just most-of-the-way." He turned his head over his shoulder. "If you want toast to sop up those yolks…"

The way he trailed off and left me a gracious opening made me feel silly. I stood as Badger nestled back into her pile of towels. "Sorry. I'm Mo. Mohini, but my friends call me Mo."

"Sounds good, Mo. John said he was expecting company, though not much more. I was saying, if you want toast for your eggs." He pointed the spatula at a toaster and bread bag.

A glass dish of butter on the table and a clean table knife retrieved from an actual cutlery drawer provided more clues that this wasn't the stereotypical bachelor pad, and I decided to accept the signs for now and see where they led.

By the time I dressed a stack of warm toast and Carter finished crisping the bacon, John stepped through the door from what might have been the backyard, though the whole state felt like a backyard to me. Badger leapt to her feet to greet him, his breath set to steaming, coat speckled with moisture. The air he ushered inside was cold enough for a few large flakes to put up a good fight against the radiance of the stove.

"Got some fresh snow last night. Not much. Might be the last snow-storm this season." He stomped his feet before stepping out of his boots. "Sure you've seen some frost on the windows."

"Montana isn't in the same time zone as Chicago," I said, ferrying plates to the table, careful to step around Badger, "but it has to be the same *month* here, right?" My fingers wrapped around a mug of coffee, fortified with a spoonful of cocoa powder from the pantry, guarding its heat. "The kitchen warmed up plenty, what with Chef Carter cooking up a storm—"

"She made the toast," he cut in, halfway between a warning and a joke.

"—and my room was more than comfortable, but the rest of the state seems not to know it's May."

"We have extra blankets." John shoveled eggs to join the bacon on his toast. "And I can chop some more wood for tonight if you're uncomfortable."

My fork came down harder than I'd intended. Badger's head popped up to rest on my thigh and both men fixed their stares on me. I grabbed the edge of the table to steady my breathing and found the dog's ears to scratch.

"You guys just, without any sort of, you know, warning or questions, you said *OK, let her come, let her stay*? Damn it, John, the last time we saw each other I was yelling at you in the rain the day before you flew back to a war, daring you not to, sure you were going there to die."

John rubbed his coffee mug. "You didn't yell that much."

Badger relented and returned to her bed.

"Fine. *Lecturing*, whatever you want to call it." I released my hold on the table. "That's the last time the three of us were all…"

John set his mug down much more quietly than I had my fork, but something worked at him just the same. "I miss Sera, too," he said. "And I had no idea what kind of situation you could find yourself in where you thought reaching out to me was your last option, or your only."

I laughed, once, a sort of coughing exhalation that fled my chest, taking most of the tension with it. "On the drive out here, you know how on long road trips there's only so much to think about, so many hours you can listen to the radio, so you think about all sorts of things. In this social psych class, the professor had us read a study that suggested the more options you have, the less satisfied you are." I wiped my nose with the back of my hand. "You're in the store and you've twenty types of peanut butter, maybe you'd be happier if you only have crunchy or creamy to choose from." I picked up my fork, not wanting to let the food go cold, because damn if Carter couldn't cook the hell out of some eggs.

"Is John crunchy or creamy?" the cook asked.

My laughter was sincere this time. "He's like…something out of a different aisle."

Carter nodded. "He is, ain't he?"

I used my toast as planned, finishing up the yolks set to runny perfection by a caring hand, the heat from John's fire creeping in from the hearth to replace the lost warmth of the stove. "So, what the heck *do* you boys do around here? You have jobs?"

They looked at each other and Carter shrugged his response.

John leaned forward. "Ever heard of the Big Steep River?"

THE ICY RIVER broke up under the midmorning sun. The dark current tumbled over rocks still slicked by frost, rushing before three humans and a canine perched on the sandy bank above. We'd crunched across the near-frozen highway, steam rising from the asphalt, and came upon the swift water not a stone's throw from John's cabin. After watching the river run past, bound with purpose for the bottom of the canyon east of us, I turned to John.

"I still don't get it."

"The Big Steep River," John said.

Carter sat comfortably upon a rock despite the permeating chill, hands deep in Badger's mane. "A river neither big nor steep," he said. The dog's short puffs matched his in icy clouds. Outside the cabin, on duty, she was focused and mindful of her charge.

The river flowed west to east, left to right, bending around a giant curve below the bank. Steep pine-covered hillsides behind us, behind the cabin, looked across the canyon at bare slopes. The river sounded not so much a roar as a disgruntled murmur.

"Looks plenty big and steep to a city kid like me. You guys go whitewater rafting?"

"Not whitewater." John held a stick in his hands, tapped it against his leg. "Not enough true rapids for that. We run the river during the summer. We put in just past town, ride it a couple miles to where it dumps into Lake Pando."

"You guys own a boating company?" My voice lifted. "Like, boats with people in them?"

"Tourists." John fidgeted with the stick. "And rafts, not boats. Big Steep and Bonaventure aren't really on the way to or from anywhere."

"Not exactly middle of nowhere," Carter chimed in, "but middle-of-no-where-adjacent."

"We don't get a lot of traffic like they do closer to Yellowstone. The rivers down there, especially around Gardiner, they see lots more folks, the road-tripping family types. We get enough through the summer to stay in business, though truth be told, the last few summers it's been *barely* in business."

"We'll probably start running around Memorial Day," Carter said, "hope to run until Labor Day, maybe a little later, considering all the snow we got."

"What does snow have to do with—" I stared at the hillsides around us, tracked the course of the river back up the valley and beyond to its imagined source, high in the mountains west of us, picturing snow-capped peaks likely to remain so for a few more weeks, if not well into June. Clouds newly freed of their precipitation prompted me to take a deep breath, take in the topography and weather, all of it inevitable and unstoppable. "Oh." I blew air into my gloves. "You guys own a rafting company."

John smiled at Carter, a grin already shaping his face.

"She's gotta meet Ollie," John said.

CHAPTER **FIVE**

John narrated points of interest as we passed through Bonaventure. An old movie palace-turned-bar called Diamond Rough was just stirring after a long winter nap. The cluster of buildings called Little Woodstock for the influx of hippies and painters and poets that arrived years ago to protest a local uranium mine was formerly a feedlot. The old artists mixed with a newer, wealthier strain of craftsperson attracted by the dramatic landscapes. A train yard hearkened back to the heyday of agriculture, some families in the valley having farmed three or more generations.

He showed me where the rafts put in, just past the edges of town, a few of the highlights of the course visible from the road. John promised the ride was *a little* more exciting from the water, but Carter said from the backseat that it mostly attracted a *more sedate* clientele than faster rivers.

We pulled into a gravel parking lot between two ramshackle buildings, perhaps the first and only things in my life I'd ever described with that flashcard word. The walls may have been painted red in a previous lifetime, but they had faded to a shade like old leather. A tarpaper roof peeled under the sunshine gathering strength as the sun crested over the eastern border of Lake Pando.

A crisp breeze blew off the water to counter the approaching warmth, and I was glad for the beanie. The tops of only the tallest trees on the far shore were visible through the shimmering haze.

Carter let Badger guide him to a bench near the shoreline as John led me up a short flight of rickety steps to a squeaky screen door swinging in time with the wind, bumping against the cock-eyed jamb. John nudged a stone with his foot, propping the door open. Sounds from a bird's nest tucked into the eaves above the doorway hinted at new life.

The room was cramped and dark, the light trickling in through heavy glass in a small window enough to illuminate piles of boxes, life vests stacked haphazardly, and a small counter, behind and over which stood a man bent over a yellow-papered ledger.

Another word from my school days, only ever used on a test before—*wizened.*

The man frowned without looking up.

"Jen, ewer laid."

Excuse me?

"Check your clock, Ollie," John replied. "Me and Carter were scheduled for noon, but we came in early. Gotta test the rigging on the trailer and catalog the life preservers. Roof needs fixing, same as the door." He pointed out the window smudged with age against the sunlight. "Can't run the river yet, still too much ice."

"Beckon mayday weed half." His words snapped like twigs as his mouth twisted into a grin. My mind spun trying to decipher the strange dialect.

John, you're late. Back in my day we'd have.

John leaned on the counter and tapped on the book. "Ollie, I'd like to introduce you to someone. This is my friend Mo."

The old man lifted his head. Tufts of white hair splayed from under a ball cap as faded as the walls outside, flaps covering his ears against the persistent chill in this unheated room. The hat was maybe dark green before the Montana sun bleached it to the color of parched mint. He wore a flannel shirt, neat and clean, under bib overalls. His knuckles, cracked by wind and rain and ice, rested on the ledger as he turned his gaze to me. He squinted at me from behind Coke bottle lenses and rubbed his nose between thumb and forefinger before clapping his hands together.

"Hue on a jab?"

"Excuse me?"

"Dome one a hair you a few dome one a work."

"She's not looking for a job, Ollie, I just wanted to—"John cut himself off. "We never actually settled on how long you were staying, what your plans for summer are. Do you?"

My mind swam, floundering like a sailor lost at sea. "Do I what?"

"We *are* down a person, Ollie," he said. "Glenn called day before yesterday, said he isn't coming this summer. Got that job in Seattle. Gabby's ready to take his spot in the raft, which means we'll need a new office manager." He smiled. "You never liked Glenn anyway."

"Nittany good," he replied.

"She's super-smart, and guaranteed she has a better work ethic than Glenn. You don't want to run the office by yourself or ride the river with us. How about it?" He faced me. "Unless you have other plans, you have a job here."

How did he know?

Had John, in some way, knowing this man Ollie would be down a person, that he would offer the position to the first person who blew in past the flimsy screen door? Gods, maybe I *wasn't* heading back to Chicago anytime soon, if ever, and Boston and the rest of the world felt like they'd never take me back, and I had bills to pay, and wasn't a mooch, but I knew nothing about running boats on a river, let alone *rafts* down a river bigger and steeper than anything I'd ever been on. John and Carter could joke because they were river guides and I was, what, a former elementary school teacher and part-time social events manager for a Midwestern financial firm? Even if this job didn't take me on the river there would be tourists, real people, and did I want one more favor dispensed, a piece of pity thrown my way?

John wouldn't ask for rent or gas money and would let me stay without obligation or a plan, expecting nothing in return. He wasn't offering a job the way an angler offered a hook.

Sera would never have trusted Kirk. She trusted John.

"How much does it pay?" Even stumbling into a job offer didn't mean I'd accept without at least *pretending* to weigh my options. John had called me *anxious*, after all, not desperate.

Ollie cocked his head to the side to weigh *his* options, reminding me of Baba's uncle, the engineer, a man I'd met only a few times on whirlwind trips to Jaipur to see as many family members as we could in the time we had, and holy hell if Ollie didn't strike some kind of chord all the sudden. He nodded at John, who straightened up off the counter.

"We try to run three trips a day to start," he said, "maybe fit a fourth later in the summer when the days get longer. We'll run six days a week, season's about twelve weeks long, give or take, and we pool our tips…" John tapped thumb to fingertip a few times before quoting me a figure for the entire summer that was less than the amount doled out for planning one finance bro party. Mindless labor with little in the way of creativity or challenge, that kind of stupidly easy remuneration induced a certain amount of guilt in someone used to working for a living. Kirk made a small fortune off speculation and leveraging and things that could lead to the next market crash, yet *he* never felt guilty. Now, faced with relative peanuts for a job guaranteed to end before the baseball season did, with a level of responsibility for families and children and old folks on a river through one of the last little wild parts of the American West, and how much would I have to learn just to keep up?

"When do we start?"

"Win lass cushion, Mizz Mo. Hue gone beer holler summer?"

I grinned at John and offered my hand to Ollie. "Yes sir—I'll be here all summer."

JOHN MADE FISH AND RICE, steamed vegetables on the side, a cobbler full of last season's berries for dessert, and the three of us stayed up late, trading stories out of order, free from context, anecdotes from our lives chosen solely for their power to amuse. Badger snored from her spot on the rug next to her human in the armchair and I split the couch with John as we emptied the freezer of ice cream to put atop the huckleberries.

Carter Momsen spent much of the year in Florida, running tourists from the north down lazy crystal rivers. *Not so much running*, he clarified, *as lollygagging*. He preferred the muscular waterways of Montana, Badger at his side in the bow of his raft, and the tales of Sunshine State antics had us in stitches. He slept in the third bedroom, upstairs next to John's. Once spring deepened into summer he would move to a pop-up camper parked in the pines behind the cabin.

When Carter and Badger excused themselves for the evening, John moved to clear the coffee table. I reached out and lay a hand on his forearm. He sat back down and I took our dishes to the kitchen. He knelt next to the hearth and broke up the fire. He said he would be a few minutes more, but that I should go to sleep if I needed to.

"Thank you."

"You're welcome." He looked up. "For what?"

The longer I'd stayed with Kirk, the less I dreamed, either asleep or awake, until I couldn't remember the last time my mind had been free to wander. His was an enervating presence, his power blocking out thoughts of anything other than his plans and priorities, and I was flotsam pulled in his wake through momentum and sheer willpower. Now, in the nights since slicing my hands apart with the shards of Sera's CD, since coming to Bonaventure, I was learning to dream again. John was a part of that magic, same as he'd been part of Sera's magic all those years ago.

LIFE POURS IN through every open window, waters warm and rushing as the ocean fills a citadel. I do not panic but walk through each doorway into vast halls of worlds built by dreaming.

John, asleep in his bed, beset by his own dreams of snakes and tornadoes swirling around him, resting when he dreams of Sera, calls out for her and the noise sounds like wings flapping to break free.

Here, a giant ship foundering in arctic waters, a man thin as whispers carries heavy iron bullets to shoot at the horizon, the sea shooting back at us. The aurora borealis burns across the sky, a living tapestry of neon greens and copper reds raking claws across the firmament.

There, a dog runs through the forest, cars in place of trees, other dogs run with us and Badger is the leader, urgency and need propels the group. Each creature here has proven her worth to the others and the pack, not through deeds but by the fact of life, their very lives enough debt paid for protection and strength and love, if not love then safety, and aren't those the same? We come upon another pack snapping and snarling and *please leave us from a fight*, for even in winning each of us is weakened, and dogs aren't foes to other dogs.

THE PILLOWCASE BENEATH MY EYES was wet, and this time the tears flowed, no holding back. This wouldn't be the last time I cried, but it was the last time I would cry alone.

chapter SIX

We fixed the screen door before lunch. After sandwiches and potato chips, we rigged a panel below the bird nests to keep the droppings at bay. Ollie invited me to the roof to assist with shingle repair before the sun grew too strong. We cleared sheds of antiquated gear and swept them clean of mouse turds and other, less identifiable debris. We hauled out the rugged relics from the Reagan Era, the fourth generation of watercraft since Big Steep River Expeditions first ventured out, and patched them back to serviceable shape. Carter brought me up to speed on terminology, though my knowledge acquired by dint of living on the banks of the Charles River and the Mississippi and the edge of Keep's Creek and the shores of Lake Michigan gave me a little bit of a starting point.

John caught me in the afternoon staring at the pride and joy of BSR Expeditions.

"You ever go on the river in *that*?" The giant wooden boat resting under a grove of pine trees looked ancient and powerful.

"Ollie used to," he replied. "Fifty years ago. Takes a real even temper to handle the Durham, so he says. Built it himself when he moved here from Minnesota." He held up an armful of life preservers. "C'mon, we're going to drive the river."

We piled into his truck and retraced the water's path upriver to the Slip, the preferred launching point for each run. We walked the banks each day until the last chunks of river ice tumbled clear, the water now nominally warm enough to survive if anyone fell in. Badger stuck close to her man's thigh while John detailed the procedures for putting in, getting organized, how many rafts could fit at once; even though I'd be stuck in the office, he insisted I gain as much knowledge about the river as could be absorbed.

Ollie dumped piles of maps and sketches from previous seasons on the counter, cracked open journals filled with notes from rafters retired or otherwise departed, and I studied these until I could draw the Big Steep with my eyes closed.

My dreams returned full force each night. Physical contact made with other living beings animated my sleep, offering what felt like insights I had no right to know. As inexplicable as John's alleged birdspeak, this weird piece of magic seemed to come from that burning disc, the pieces imparting something from Sera. Not ready to call it a gift, not with the bombardment of images and emotions bleeding into my waking hours, I avoided touching others as much as possible until I could talk to John.

In the meantime, rafters from across the country trickled in.

"The rivers in Florida," Carter said, "the rivers there're just slobs. A real zoo. All over the place. This river." He saluted the Big Steep across the highway from the cabin, holding his half-empty bottle aloft, stifling an enchilada burp. "This river might not live up to its name, but it's got places to go."

Carter was a sharp rafter. He would sit in the bow with Badger pressed to his side, sounding and monitoring the course and progress of the river, relaying circumstances and changes to the man at the tiller. When I asked who that would be, Carter and John begged off answering.

The next morning two floppy-haired kids showed up claiming to be river guides. Mickey and Lucky, friends of the inseparable variety, with energy to shame a Tasmanian devil. They made quick work of the grunt labor John saved for their arrival. They came to Montana from New Jersey, before that from two countries almost as far apart as possible, united by their love of rock music. John said they had two full seasons under their belts, which made them better than rookies. They rode the river together, swapping bow and stern, and injected some much-needed energy to the boathouse. After a dinner of aromatic sausages and crispy potatoes, Lucky related the story about how he and Mickey had settled on their Americanized nicknames in kindergarten, and then performed for us a backyard boom box concert, complete with air guitar solos inspired by Springsteen.

Gabrielle Richmond appeared the next morning. Not much older than Mickey or Lucky, she came up only to their chins, but damn if she was not the perfect lens to focus their excitement into concerted effort. She was a force of nature, freed for a fifth summer from the confines of a prim Savannah upbringing and college chemistry exams. The minute John promoted her from office manager to full-time river guide she quickly and gleefully dispelled any notion we were making any progress toward a Memorial Day opening, and did so in the most cordially foul-mouthed manner possible. Everything she surveyed was *awful shit, loves,* the place *in such a sad state of ever-loving disrepair, darlings,* and she accused John of *dorking around all winter,* declaring if not for my *heaven-sent happenstance arrival* then *there'd've been no blessed hope* for anything being ready this year, let alone in one week, *thank the Maker.*

Deacon Redtail was the only one among us who grew up in Montana and had family in town. He drove the bus and the trailer of rafts from the boathouse to the Slip, but didn't go on the water, which meant he had plenty of time each day to spend around the office. Older than John, nowhere near as old as Ollie, he radiated a calm that balanced the Jersey boys' collective exuberance and Gabby's crisp declarations. He rocked denim outfits—vests over pants, even adding a denim shirt one day, much to Mickey and Lucky's enjoyment—and swapped stories with me while the rafters were on the river.

Ollie blessed us with an early release on the day before the last guide was due to arrive, before our first run of an ice-free, but still ice-cold, Big

Steep. We celebrated with another raucous cookout, taking turns on the grill. Gabby came close to permanently banning John from cooking duty after she cataloged his crimes against hot dogs, *holy hell, honey, how hard is cooking a frank.* The beer stayed cold in the last of the snow sheltered in the shade of the cabin. Our conversations touched on everything in existence except the impending practice run, not out of any sense of foreboding or superstition, but because, for this night, we were just a family catching up on months apart. Even as the newest member, dropped unexpectedly into their midst, I felt only love.

THE MONTANA SUN CAME UP fully warm and chased away the last of the moping winter and false spring, revealing true May. The clothes from Chicago and before stayed in my room in favor of a wardrobe from the lost and found bin, detritus accumulated over years of shuttling cargo down and sometimes plucking them from the Big Steep. All of the clothes were freshly laundered by Lucky, bless him.

I shielded my eyes from the glare off the lake with a clipboard, and then turned to answer Gabby's question.

"Sure, I've plenty of experience on boats. Mostly as a passenger."

Carter and John worked inside the raft strapped aboard a trailer hitched to an old school bus emblazoned with our outfit's name. Deacon sat on a stool next to the bus, finished with replacing one of the tires.

I'd seen crew shells aplenty up and down the Charles, from single-seater sculls to the giant eights that muscled everything else off the water. My little sister sat coxswain for the boys' team at our high school, granting me additional secondhand rowing knowledge. Our family took summer vacations, the length of the drive into the wilds of New England a bargain between how adventurous Baba felt and how far from the highway Mama allowed. We paddled down more than a few placid Maine rivers in rented canoes.

John slid out of the raft and passed a tool to Carter. We waited in the parking lot for the arrival of our final rafter, after which we would review the river's course together, and then ride as one crew in one raft, taking turns sitting bow and stern. I would play the part of paying passenger.

Home from university one summer, I'd hooked up with a cute duck boat operator who'd liberated one of his charges after his shift ended and crashed it into a channel marker while trying to make out with me and steer.

"We didn't sink. But almost."

Gabby laughed. "That's just plum damn ridiculous, love."

Boston whalers. Little aluminum jon boats. Trawlers and day-sailers, crab scratchers and dinghies. Ferries, barges, pleasure craft with second- and third-wives' names on the transoms…a person couldn't grow up along the Atlantic and *not* be beaten about the ears with oars by the people who loved the water. The harbor had been school enough for observing and absorbing nautical information, but none of it was anything close to what we were about to do, or what we intended this summer to be.

I lowered the clipboard and gestured to the wooden behemoth beneath the pines. "We should take the Durham out. You know, just for fun."

John considered my question carefully, though it was at least the tenth time I'd asked. Whether it was still seaworthy after fifty years in the snow and shade was a separate issue.

"Not really a Durham," he replied, though not to my question. "I looked it up once; it's not quite the same as the original design. Ollie said he made some improvements—*modern Durham*, he called it."

Carter clambered out of the raft. "Considering he built it when Eisenhower was president, no way it's a modern *anything*."

The Durham took up residence in my heart at first sight, authentic to its ancestors or not. Wide at the middle, prominent prow and rounded stern, the enormous craft could carry more than twelve paying passengers and two crew with room to spare. Wood planks ran the length of its side, heavy and smooth, worn but cared for, and the vessel gave off vibrations like it could go more than just a few miles on the Big Steep, like maybe it could mount the Diamond Dam at the eastern lip of Lake Pando and travel the length of the Jefferson River to the Missouri, paddle all the way to the Gulf of Mexico.

The screen door swung open without a sound, closing gently behind Ollie as he stepped onto the porch. He clattered down the steps, gnarled hands holding a cleaning rag. I made a note on the clipboard to inspect and repair the staircase.

"Ollie," I said, "you sure you don't wanna take the Durham out? John says you're the only one talented enough to do it."

His hands twisted the rag before sliding it into the back pocket of his coveralls. "Don't want a chance of breaking her. Had too many close calls on the water. She's safer on land."

"But aren't boats like that made for danger?" His distinctive accent took surprisingly little effort to decipher, having spent more than a few hours in his company over the past week.

"The river'll trick you, Miss Mo. Keep that in mind." He held his breath long enough that Badger lifted her head and cocked it from one side to the other before Ollie broke out in full-on belly laughs. He strode back up the steps to the office, whistling a few tone-deaf notes from a children's song, and I nudged John.

"Sure you don't want him in the raft with Carter? He's still got it."

Carter shrugged. "He's only about five hundred years old, give or take."

"Looks good for his age." Lucky took a break from tossing rocks into a bucket with his buddy.

"I heard he was in the war," Mickey said.

"Which bloody war?" Gabby asked. "Been lots of damn wars, honey, so many they gotta number 'em." She was eager to run the river, if only to direct some of her energy into something big and wild, and if this mysterious final guide didn't show in the next few minutes she'd probably do it with or without him, or us, with or without a raft beneath her.

"Ollie was a merchant mariner in World War II," John said.

"A Marine?" Lucky sat up. Mickey used the distraction to land a pebble in the bucket, his expression and Lucky's reaction suggesting he won their game.

"Mariner," John repeated. "Not a, you know, cargo ships. He sailed convoys of war materiel on the Murmansk Run, north of the Arctic Circle, Halifax to Iceland to the Soviet Union. Did that, what, ten times? Fifteen?"

"More, to hear him tell it," Carter said. "He crossed the border into Canada before Pearl Harbor. Got his ship sunk out from under him by a German submarine on his last trip. Spent a few nights in a much smaller raft than what we have, in much colder waters. Saved three other guys, too."

A memory of my dream, the night after shaking Ollie's hand, made me shiver. The unexplainable insights came after touching someone, so avoiding handshakes until I understood what was happening seemed a logical step. Funny thing, though, even standing close to others invited intrusions of… feelings, emotions, urges. I stood apart from the group when it got too much to handle, but sometimes I didn't care and let the feelings in.

"If he fought in World War II," Lucky said, "that would make him at least ninety years old, yes?"

"He's never really said," John said, "but my guess is he's even older than that."

I shelved my concerns about Ollie's wartime experiences barging into my dreams and looked again upon the Durham. The boat was constructed half a century ago by a man nearly killed by Nazis while delivering supplies to a country that no longer existed, and the thing looked brand new. Running my hands over the wood connected me to something deep and powerful, to ancient secrets, glimpses into the memories of the trees that gave their lives for the planks.

Our own rafts were good at what they did, though they contained nothing like the charisma of the Durham. They could carry a fair bit of *cargo* (as John half-jokingly called the tourists) and keep them safe on our sedate river, but did so without any grace or history. After today's practice run, I would be doing none of it. The office would be my place of duty, taking payments and making sure that everyone knew to wear their protective gear before leaving the riverbank. John emphasized safety constantly, even with the seasoned rafters, and his references about *wrangling the unexpected shifting or inappropriate behavior of the cargo* felt too specific not to come from firsthand experience.

After days of cram sessions with Carter and Gabby, I still had lots to learn. Even with a week of practice runs ahead for the crew, I knew that, despite the teasing and joking, they would soon have actual responsibility for actual human beings, some quite young, others almost as old as Ollie. John tempered my nerves by reminding me that the guides were all experienced, the Big Steep was relatively tame, and the families who would show up had low or no expectations. Even Mickey and Lucky, he pointed out, could run the river nearly unsupervised.

"*Nearly,*" he repeated.

The bristling purr of an engine demanded our attention. A white Land Rover raced into the lot, kicking up gravel the entire way and sliding to a stop *near* our cars and bikes, but not *that* near, a trick guys like Kirk invented to avoid errant door dings in less-than-reputable areas. A young man hopped out. Neither he nor the vehicle were spotless, as nothing in Montana stayed dust-free for long, but both had been washed more recently than anything else in the lot.

He was the first person I'd seen in days wearing something other than sneakers, sandals, or cowboy boots. In fact, his entire outfit evoked the choices of a very specific and familiar demographic: boat shoes, pleated coral shorts, a light blue polo, and a white cap to match his car, *DUKE* in exclamatory letters across the brow. He carried a cup from the only coffee shop in Bonaventure. He also wore a huge grin as he waltzed up to the group and tossed a set of car keys to Mickey, who caught them in midair.

Whoever was in charge of such things hadn't broken the fancy high-priced mold after the first overly confident, underly self-aware frat bro was minted, all those unfortunate rush weeks before, and the factory just kept churning them out. If this man wasn't Kirk's carbon copy, he was damn close.

John shook the man's free hand and tilted his head toward the car. "Wasn't it green?"

His grin crinkled at one corner of his mouth. "That was a 2011, John. This is a 2012. Who do we have here?"

"Mo, this is JJ Kane."

"Just Jared." He knocked his sunglasses to the end of his nose to squint at me over the reflective lenses. "Monique?"

"Not a terrible guess." The back of my neck tingled. "Mohini, actually, but my friends call me—"

"Mo it is," he declared. "And I'm just Jared."

"Ah. Got it."

The Jersey boys showed the same golden retriever ebullience about his arrival as they did everything in their world and Carter tipped an imaginary cap in JJ's direction. Gabby looked annoyed that he was late, agitated now that he was here, and relieved that we were one step closer to running the river. Deacon waved from his seat next to the bus.

John stepped up to the map tacked to the wall of the boathouse, the one we'd all reviewed a hundred times, the one we would review once more before getting on the water, but JJ held his coffee cup aloft, calling for attention.

"Is Ollie around?" he asked. "I have an announcement and he wants to be here for it."

"Is it a damn surprise?" Gabby muttered.

Ollie appeared at the office door and let out a whooping yell at the sight of the young man. He nearly skipped down the steps before taking JJ's hand in both of his, talking too fast for any of us to understand.

JJ gently ushered Ollie to the side of the map and maneuvered himself to take John's spot in front of the group. "I can't tell you guys how happy I am to be back in Montana," he said. "And to meet our newest team member. C'mon, let's give Mo a proper Big Steep welcome."

The applause made my cheeks flush just the tiniest bit and I hated that they did. We'd all been here at least a week, some of us longer, and had weeks of work still to do before Memorial Day, and here was JJ preparing to give a speech, walking around like he owned the—

Oh, shit.

I couldn't find a way to warn John, though maybe he also saw the other boat shoe about to drop.

"Everyone knows I grew up back east." JJ winked at me. "Well, *now* everyone knows. I may be just a kid from North Carolina, but my family has been coming to Montana and the Big Steep River for generations. We have a summerhouse outside Rabbit Springs, though this place feels like more than just a second home. In fact, my grandfather was one of Ollie's first rafters back in the day." He started to pace in front of the map. "It's no secret that, while I've enjoyed some great success with Kane Financial, the time has come for me to step out on my own, put my mark on the world." He stepped to one side and clasped a hand on the older man's shoulder. "After the end of last season, I approached a handful of investors, presented them with a detailed pitch, and got my father to buy in as well. Over the winter we generated interest from some very exciting players, and I'm proud to say we've secured a sweetheart of a deal with nowhere to go but up." Lights of awareness flickered on the faces of the rafters. Ollie looked as downright giddy as a century-old boatwright could be. "Phase one involved buying out our friend and mentor." JJ gave him a playful jostle. "Phase two starts immediately. An influx of capital will do more than just keep BSR Expeditions on the water for years to come."

Here it comes.

"We're looking at a major and comprehensive investment in, upgrade to, and reinvention of the town of Bonaventure and all of Pando County." JJ raised his voice. "As the new President and CEO of BSR Expeditions, Incorporated, I plan on retaining Mr. Ollie Berdahl as Senior Vice President and *Chief River Officer*. I'd love to keep you all on, if you want jobs for the summer."

CHAPTER seven

Nervous glances passed between Mickey and Lucky, Gabby and Carter. Deacon by the bus looked unsurprised. As we all considered this new reality with its unknown consequences we looked to John, one by one, until all eyes were fixed on him, and his not on JJ, but on Ollie. John weighed the attention. He didn't outwardly acknowledge our unspoken entreaties. He seemed to calm himself, descended into his mental center, and thought about how this would impact the rest of us. The strength of my insight unnerved me, as we were nowhere near touching, but that could be another problem for another time.

John took the span of several breaths to assess this monumental shift and what it meant for Ollie, who appeared relieved, even excited. This investment offered him the chance to retire if he wanted, though none of us, even those who knew him better than I did, had a hint there was anything other than the river and the rafts to occupy his time. He never talked about kids or grandchildren, family of any kind, and slept most nights in a space on the second floor of the boathouse that was less a bedroom and more a closet.

If the sudden infusion of cash meant Ollie could dial his energies back a notch, John quickly came to terms with the idea. As for the rest of it… wheels turned in his head, matching my own realization that this was not just a golden bucket bailout for seasonal rafters. JJ mentioned reinventing the entire county, and when rich kids with MBAs parachuted into impoverished locations with grand notions—

I saw it up close in Louisiana. John lived it in Iraq.

The tentative smiles around the semicircle gave me pause. *Am I being too critical?* Everyone here had far more experience with JJ and they all appeared less outwardly conflicted than I felt or John looked. Uncertainty hung on all of us, but maybe my more recent and intimate experiences with frat boys and finance bros and shuttered towns led me to an overreaction.

JJ seemed unaware of the internal turmoil coming out through our furtive glances, finally breaking the five seconds or so of silence with a clap of his hands.

"And John," he said, clearly leaning into a rehearsed speech, "if you're up for it, I'd like to make you *Head River Guide*, right here and right now. We'll work out the details of your contract later. I can guarantee you'll be handsomely rewarded for your experience and leadership."

His pronouncement may have been meant to ease the tension, backslaps and grinning nods from the others testament to its effect, but it electrified the hairs on the back of my neck. How could he refuse? Not that John would want to, but was JJ deftly weaving some sort of web of obligation? Had I gone from bumming around with a casual river outfit to being thrust into a network of intrigue and—

Now you are *overreacting.*

John answered with his smile. "We still need someone to ride with Carter and Badger. Want to stay on one more season as their tiller-man?"

Everyone laughed at this, even me, and JJ mock-doffed his spotless hat at John's gracious counter-offer. "If you'll have me," he said. "Now, John, before I interrupted the meeting, please. My plan is to keep as much in place for now as possible, steady as she goes and all that. If you want to lead the review for our practice run, I'll step back into my role as humble rafter for the moment." The two men traded places, the strain replaced with anticipation. The sand beneath the gravel under our feet had shifted, though nothing on the surface changed.

I propped the sunglasses atop my head and hugged the clipboard to my chest. John allowed the crew a few breaths more to collectively channel their emotions before focusing us on the task at hand.

"We find ourselves once again, as always, off the beaten path." His voice rang out clear and confident. He hadn't practiced anything like a speech, not at the boathouse or in the cabin, and he consulted no notes. He spoke like he did this every day, not like we stood at the edge of a monumental new adventure.

I could not keep my smile from widening.

"The Big Steep River is not on the path to or from Yellowstone," he continued, "or the Tetons, or Glacier, or much of anywhere. Our cargo will be tourists whose GPS took a dive, or fathers who didn't do their research in the grip of a cold Ohio winter, or mothers minutes from giving up, just trying to get home without leaving the kids on the side of the road." He stepped back, nearly touching the map pinned to the wall. "Random busloads of visitors fooled by counterfeit guidebooks may appear without warning. One year, the bachelor and bachelorette parties from the same engagement ended up here on the same day at the same time." Mickey and Lucky nudged each other. Gabby beamed and Badger leaned forward. "Our people are the lost and the unknowing. Our job is to show them the river, share the adventure for a morning or an afternoon, and bring them back alive."

Bring 'em Back Alive was printed in big yellow letters on the back of Carter's gray shirt, made at the end of a particularly rough season a few years back, and had become BSR's unofficial motto. Whether it would survive JJ's corporate rebranding remained to be seen. It was also how John described his mission in Iraq when I grilled him at that dinner table in Louisiana, confronting him on the militaristic bullshit he represented in my imagination. I finally got the complete picture, the truth. He saw his crew and their charges as his responsibility, our safety his duty.

The tone he used with us now made me wonder how he gave up the yelling and cursing from his time in the Army, this thought overtaken on its heels by the curiosity of what kind of soldier he'd been. Was he just as soft, direct, and unthreatening in uniform? Sera hinted at some of his stories, shared others with me and Anita secondhand after he went back to the war. In none of them did he come across like a caricature, not the grunting macho a-hole from the movies, and even today he didn't fit the stereotype of the traumatized veteran, hiding from the world, or bragging and sticking out his chest demanding to be thanked for his service. He just…*was.*

"This used to be a river valley." John slung me back to the present when he pointed east. "FDR and his boys stopped it up with the Diamond Dam, made themselves a lake where none had been. They put dams all over Montana, and a half dozen of their little reservoirs feed into our river. The Big Steep might not be the Snake or the Columbia, but this stretch of water, from the Slip to Lake Pando, it's ours to care for, ours to share with friends we haven't met yet, and the river is wild enough for our purposes."

No cheers or applause greeted his declaration, this not being a movie, but steely determination now replaced any lingering hesitancy. John stepped aside, letting all eyes shift to the map on the wall. His finger traced the length of the river. Each of us had studied this image for hours, some of us for days, and everyone except me had run the course scores, if not hundreds of times before. We all moved closer.

The crew would put two rafts in at the Slip, several miles upriver from the boathouse, a few miles downriver from town, and run three trips per day, fitting in a fourth as the days lengthened. Safety briefings for every outing, John reminded us, no exceptions, and even JJ nodded. Each tourist would get a life preserver before they ever left the parking lot. Allowances were made for the crew. According to Gabby, the vests made nice cushions late in the day. Anyone who fell over the side would float along with the sedate current until the rafters could work together to fish the dunked soul from the water. We would spend the next week running as often as we could to test these skills over and over, before the first paying passenger ever set foot in a raft.

"After the Slip," John said, "the river sort of leans to the south, then settles down for a spell. This here's the Frying Pan." He pointed to a spot on the map where a hot spring was marked with a red V. "The cargo likes to verify for themselves that it's hot. After they soak their paws, Blue Creek joins from the north and douses us with cold water. That's the Icebox. This little section wraps up with the Microwave, a gentle eddy that can spin a raft easily enough if you're not paying attention."

Gabby picked up the thread. "Once we leave the damn Kitchen behind, we pass under the Natty Gann Bridge. Freight trains run over twice a week, and the silly little sightseeing locomotive from town goes across four times a day. We try to run it so the cargo can get their sweet, stupid pictures."

Carter took his time describing the Mill Pond. After sliding between the trestles of the Natty Gann, eerily calm water could bewitch a crew, losing themselves in the thick vegetation along the shore. Douglas fir, larch, birch, and quaking aspen came down right to the water's edge, offering another prime photo opportunity.

"Mickey, Lucky." John broke in. "What happened there last year?"

"We won't get stuck in the reeds." Lucky suppressed a chuckle.

"Not again," Mickey added.

"And it's in the reeds that the ducks and geese live," Carter said, reclaiming his time. "Other waterfowl, if you listen for them. That's a good chance for the cargo to see wildlife."

"*Wildlife* means deer and elk, Mister Momsen," Gabby said. "Buffalo and bears. At least according to the damn brochures the cargo always bring along. High expectations, thinking we're fucking Yellowstone or something."

"Birds are still wildlife, Gabrielle," Carter replied.

"What's after the Mill Pond?" John said, steering the conversation out of the weeds.

"Northern Exposure." My classroom voice masked my sudden nerves. "We clear the little forest and the hills to the north bend down some. They're not very big, but up close they're enough to hide mountains. Good photo opp for the last run of the day." I tapped the clipboard against my leg. "The Mill Pond narrows here. While the cargo take their pictures, we get caught up."

Lucky nodded. "Deception Point, right? Where the Pond tightens there is a hydrodynamic trick, the water gets *super* deep, right, and the current starts to rocking." He used his hands to punctuate the narration. "It scours the river bottom clean, and catches the rafts up before we shoot the Twins." A pair of rocks so prominent even Carter couldn't miss, according to Gabby.

Mickey parceled out his words to continue the spiel. "The Speedway. Whoever gets there first goes first, then runs down to Teflon Flats."

Ollie's smile, broad and powerful since JJ's announcement, faded as he excused himself without a word, stepping aside and shuffling up the stairs into the office. John waited for the door to swing shut before he continued. "The north bank makes a kind of point after the Speedway," he said, voice quieter than before. "Navigating past Liza's Hope can be tricky. There's an old stone foundation where a cabin used to stand. Late in the summer when the snowmelt starts to ebb, the sandbar here is harder to navigate than the reeds in the Mill Pond. You get stuck, the cargo have to help get the raft off the rocks, and you don't want to hang out near the Hope any longer than you have to."

JJ cleared his throat. "A short stretch of river after the Hope spits us back onto Lake Pando." He tried to inject some enthusiasm back into the brief. "Bear hard right and you'll make it home. The river flows hard enough that if you miss the docks you'll have to convince the passengers to row you back to the boathouse." John took the hint and stepped aside as JJ clapped his hands together. "Great job, everyone, real nice. Couple of things, though.

New boss, new rules, right? First, I'd like it if we could please stop referring to the paying customers or passengers as *cargo*."

"Why the hell why?" Gabby asked. "We never call 'em that to their faces, but won't your investor money keep us afloat this summer, not just our charm and good looks?" She was clever enough to temper her words and still express her disdain without entirely naming the odd situation we all found ourselves in, needling but not puncturing JJ's benevolent rich guy persona.

"Well, part of the idea is we'd like to see a return on our investment," he said. "Along with our investors, I've put a lot of my own money toward this project. Also, we're in the adventure business, certainly, but now we're also in the customer service business, where the customer is king. Or queen. We want them to come back next summer, and the summers after. We want them to see Bonaventure as a destination."

"And the other couple things?" Carter asked.

JJ avoided looking directly at Gabby when he announced there'd be no more swearing, in or around the rafts or the boathouse, not while on the clock. "It's a professionalism thing, guys."

Gabrielle, suddenly deprived of a not-insignificant portion of her vocabulary, dug her toe in the gravel.

"And John, I know we've always joked about us being on the path to nowhere. Heck, Granddad made that joke when *he* worked for Ollie."

Final shoe, I thought, *prepare to drop*.

"But as part of our investment strategy we've leveraged a large amount of energy toward building an online presence. We can finally take reservations over the internet! We're essentially booked up through June. I'm surprised none of you saw the social media campaign that started last fall. We were all over the web anytime someone searched for *Montana*."

For some reason, everyone looked at me.

"Oh, shi—shoot. I Googled the weather before I came, but had no idea what John was up to out here. I'd never even heard of Bonaventure."

"People will hear the name now. We're gonna make Bonaventure the adventure capital of the West. And John must've known something was up," he said, glancing between the two of us, "arranging for someone to come and run the office, picking someone so clearly perfect for the role."

What did that *mean?*

JJ plowed on. "Starting on Memorial Day, we're going to have more tourists than we've ever had before. We'll run as often as we can until we hire some additional hands, maybe hire some guides away from the rafting companies down in Gardiner. More trips mean more money for our investors, but also more money for all of you. I hope everyone's ready for a summer that'll change your lives."

I looked over my shoulder to the school bus. Deacon's expression hadn't changed.

CHAPTER EIGHT

"Where're all these people even gonna stay?" Carter unstrapped the tie-downs and stepped back as Lucky and I dragged the raft to the edge of the Slip. "Not like Bonaventure has a surplus of hotel rooms."

John waded into flowing water up to his knees and held the nose of the raft. Deacon tied the stern line to a stump.

"I'll wait until you're loaded and pointed in the right direction before I leave," he said.

"The river does most of the navigating," John replied.

"Aren't there a lot of campsites in Pando County?" Lucky asked.

"Not like these fancy flipping dips JJ is advertising to are the ding-dang roughing-it types." Gabby tested the feel and force behind her new vocabulary, frowning at the results.

Deacon tilted his head town-ward. "There've been rumors all winter about a big development up in Rabbit Springs. A hotel, some new restaurants, a health spa. At the time, no one had any clue why they would build so much so quickly."

"Well, now we know." John tossed life preservers to each of us. "Remember, when you're a passenger," he said, managing to use the proper word without snark, "even a pretend one, you gotta wear one of these. When you're sitting in the bow or stern you can take it off."

"Is that still allowed?" Lucky asked.

"Until we're told otherwise," John replied. "I'll sit tiller first today, and then—"

JJ's car interrupted us again as it pulled off the highway onto the shoulder. Mickey hopped out and opened the back. He hauled a giant sandbag in his arms, clearly as heavy as…well, I could say *shit* in my own head. Lucky scrambled to help. A quartet of other bags sat in the back of the car, and *yes*, they were indeed heavy.

"These should be enough to simulate a full load of twelve passengers," JJ explained, "and two crew. We want to make sure the rafts can take the weight."

John set his bag down on the edge of the raft and frowned. "The rafts Ollie's been running down the river for, what, thirty years?" His tone sounded calm, but hid a glimpse of something harder.

"Our investors weren't happy with the lack of business records. I had to reconstruct most of it on my own, filling in gaps where I could, making best-guesses for the rest, and if it weren't for the Kane family name," he said, a self-congratulatory smile enough to make me roll my eyes, "they might not have trusted any of it. One of the conditions of ongoing investment is that we start producing some documentation. First priority has to be safety."

"You also said *twelve* passengers." John let the statement hang without a question mark.

"That's right. Second priority, right behind safety, is profit. We crunched the numbers, and we have to increase the loads. We've run with eight people, one or two rafters depending on conditions, but I want to maximize our capacity each trip. BSR has reservations for twelve-person trips starting next week."

Mickey produced a marker from somewhere and drew faces on the sandbags. Lucky named them, and within minutes we had a cartoonish family to accompany us down the river.

"Let's load up the living." John's voice rang out louder than I'd ever heard before. "I'll sit tiller first. JJ, why don't you start in the bow before we rotate you to the stern?"

He pulled up short. "Oh. I drove the Land Rover here." JJ looked over his shoulder at the car. "Plus I've got a mountain of paperwork back at the office." He winked at me. "Don't worry, Mo, it's corporate stuff, not day-to-day. Besides, John, we do this every year."

A hard edge emerged in John's eyes. "If we do it every year, then we do it every year. That means everyone who goes on the water goes on the practice run. CEO, head guide, heck, even the office manager."

"Look, John, I've dropped a bunch of changes without a lot of notice, and you might not be used to taking orders, but this is a real business now. We've got to have a chain of command."

The way JJ said it, like he didn't know that John had taken and given orders under fire, and something in the frat boy's coral shorts and early season tanned skin and spotless Duke hat grated on me, and *gods* even John was acting obstinate when the sunlight was almost midway gone, and this could not be the first day of promised magical river-running and—

"You boys done, or should we put the raft back on the trailer?"

Everyone looked at me. Hell, *I* would have looked at me if I could. Gabby tensed at my side, Mickey and Lucky averted their eyes, and even Badger found a beetle on the ground to occupy her canine attention.

JJ's face flashed, a range of emotions in an instant, none of them pleasant. His expression finally settled on forced conciliation, a mean kind of smile pretending to be otherwise, and I'd seen that look often enough in the past year on a different handsome face. If JJ were keeping score, then I was suddenly the first and only one here with a strike against her.

John's face, though…a flare of misdirected angst, turning from JJ to me, and then shock when he recognized it, shame and embarrassment for acting like an ass, and he knew he had a responsibility, not just as *head guide*, but as a person and a man. I remembered our first and biggest argument years ago, around the dinner table in Zeebrugge, me accusing him of things I couldn't know, fitting him to a caricature and hurling the blame for a world on fire at his feet. We'd hurt each other that night, Sera playing peacemaker, and even now, I felt on uneven ground around him, unsure how much those thoughts echoed in his memory. I no longer had the excuse of being exhausted from life or ejected from Chicago and Louisiana and every other place I failed to set down roots. There was a reason I'd emailed John, a reason he'd accepted. This was my place for however long I wanted it, as much as anywhere else in the world, and these were my people, for better or worse.

John was not the kind to keep score against anyone but himself.

JJ broke first, fidgeting with the sunglasses dangling from his neck. "I'll need a ride back from the boathouse," he said. "To get the Land Rover."

John grinned without forcing the gesture. "Sure thing."

The new CEO glanced once more at his car. "Think it'll be…safe?"

John nodded. "That's what we're selling the tourists, right?"

WE DROVE THE COURSE EVERY DAY coming to the boathouse, and several times after to study it. I memorized the map and pored over the notes left by rafters long retired. One day we walked the entire length, plunging our hands in at the banks of the Kitchen and the Mill Pond and where the waters of the Big Steep mixed with Lake Pando. Every night since, the river came alive in my dreams.

And here I was, a pretend tourist preparing to take the reins as office manager. When we pushed off, I knew none of the days leading to this or those to come could touch the excitement once the current took hold.

We barely had time to turn and wave farewell to Deacon before vegetation blocked our view. Everyone turned forward, eager for the journey, and my eyes lingered on John for a second. He returned my gaze and nodded his thanks. He pointed to the river, encouraging me to ride and forget the past five minutes, maybe even the past year, if only for the time it took us to return to dry land. Despite being this close to so many people, their thoughts didn't overwhelm so much as comfort with collective sympathetic vibrations.

Over the Rocky Mountains to the west, storms Pacific only in their origins spent most of the year depositing snow, heaping up piles to suffer under the relentless eye of the springtime sun. Gravity pulled the meltwater down fierce and quick past alpine tundra and through evergreen forests, tumbling over cascades and rapids. Reinforced by the Little Flat Creek and Goat River and a dozen unnamed waterways, many of them blocked up by their own Depression-era dams, the Big Steep River was born.

We were seven humans, a dog, and a bunch of sandbags. Life was perfect in that moment.

JJ welcomed those of us playing along from his perch in the bow, his frat boy exterior drawing back to reveal a kid giddy to ride the river once more.

I slung an arm around the sack to my right, sunglasses and beard hastily scrawled on its surface, and hugged it. My free hand trailed in the water and yes, it was even warmer than expected. I shivered when we reached the Icebox. John used the simple tiller to steer the raft, letting us bob in the Microwave for an extra moment, giving us a chance to feel the river at work. We had no means of propulsion save for two short canoe paddles in each raft. These were only for emergency use or, as Carter gleefully hinted, to help occupy those passengers with an inappropriate sense of their utility. Asking a loud-mouthed father to *paddle us down the river* or *keep us off those rocks*, Carter said, was a great way for them to burn off some energy while feeling like they could contribute.

Alongside knot-tying and first aid, between cleaning and repairing and more cleaning, the guides prided themselves on developing their humor. No scripted performances, no prepared jokes, but each raft developed its own personality, honed over the course of a season and refined year after year. They teased the self-important braggarts, indulged the imaginations of the youngest riders, and delighted in never giving the same tour twice.

John and JJ swapped places with Gabby and Lucky as we exited the Kitchen. John mixed up the crews on purpose, making sure each of the guides knew how to be comfortable with anyone else in any position. He wanted them to be confident not just in themselves but with each other.

"There it is." Gabby sang out from the stern, not so much muscling the tiller as leaning her whole body into it. She barely sat, her energy more than could be contained. "There it is, folks, the ding-dang Natty Gann Bridge, bigger than stinkin' life. Take your dad-blasted pictures, folks."

I pointed a pretend camera at the landmark. We saw the bridge often enough from the road, but now, slipping beneath its monumental trestles for the first time, even without an antique steam engine passing over this cold reminder of age and strength, a relic and messenger from a different era, I felt compelled to bring a real camera next time, if only in a futile attempt to capture the immensity above us.

We slid between four giant pillars of iron and wood sunk into stone and I made a silent apology to the Big Steep on behalf of whoever had stabbed a bridge into its river belly. Neither the bridge nor the river replied.

I teased Gabby when the moment was over. "I can see why the flipping-dip passengers want to take their gad-dang pictures."

The Mill Pond, reeds not yet fully grown in, trees in early leaf, birds darting and swinging through the air and—

"Holy shit!" I leaned out of my seat, pointing for the benefit of my sandbag boyfriend. "A deer."

Even had we not been acting the part of tourists we would have gawked. Maybe not the others, and it wasn't as if I'd never seen a *deer* before, but this one, from the big floppy ears to the dark tuft of a tail, was the first big animal, the first *real* wildlife I'd seen since setting foot in the wilderness. This place suddenly felt more like a home, however long I might end up staying.

"Carter." John sat alongside a sandbag with a mustache and monocle. "Take the tiller. Mo, you're up front."

I was too shocked to question so moved to the bow, unzipping my vest along the way, setting it on the nose of the raft, taking up the post like it was something I knew how to do.

"Wait a second." I turned to the man settling in at the stern. "How—"

"Call it out, Mohini," Carter replied.

I lifted a hand to continue my protest and noticed Badger sitting tight between her human's legs, eyes locked on me. The dog leaned into Carter, pressing against him in the direction my hand pointed. I tried the other direction and my trust in the mutt grew a hundredfold.

Small movements and slow decisions mattered most on the river. The water moved us on a path already set down. We just had to follow. Carter spun us in the Mill Pond, smells of green growth filling our nostrils, birdsong filling our ears. We practiced turning, he and Badger and I, until the deer departed, and danced downriver with just my hands and a dog.

The weight of the raft shifted as John approached the bow, sitting close behind me, radiating calm. "Want to take us past Northern Exposure?" he asked. "Try to shoot the Twins?"

"What about Mickey? He hasn't had a turn yet."

"You run the Speedway with Gabby in the bow, Mickey can steer us past Liza's Hope and home to the boathouse."

I wanted to say *yes*, and *no*, and to jump in and float all the way past the lake and over the dam into the next river, and the next, until the ocean took me. Where had this water been, not all my life, but in those terrible times…after Sera's accident…in the days leading to her funeral…any time I saw a news report from Iraq or Afghanistan, uncertain if John was there or somewhere else or nowhere at all…the entire year of, *gods*, not even soul-crushing under Kirk's eye. He wasn't the type to crush anything, let alone something as strong as a soul, just slowly leached the energy out of it, muting all sound and color in my life until I felt relief in him breaking it off.

Here, among the ducks and wrens and a mule deer maybe still watching us from a thicket, I sat up and ran the back of a hand across my nose. Balancing myself on John's shoulder on my way to the stern let me feel the river through him, seeing past the calm to the unsettled power in him and the water, and he thought of Sera in that moment, too.

I squeezed the tiller and felt the weight of the duty before me: six humans and a dog and yes even those sandbags were my responsibility. Badger and her human lolled in the middle of the raft, as relaxed as they'd been on the porch last night. Mickey and Lucky pretended to be (or maybe really were) actual goofy teenagers, not fearless refugees carrying hopes of a new world on their backs, just a couple of buddies flirting with a sandbag between them. Gabby sat in the bow, grip tight on a safety line, not for support, but for something tangible into which she could infuse her energy, urging us onward.

JJ watched John watching me.

John nodded.

Bring 'em back alive.

CHAPTER nine

Jukebox guitar riffs and cowbells welcomed us into the Diamond Rough. Carter described the bar as *the only decent place in town to get a drink*. It had been off limits until after our first run. I steeled myself for the flood of emotions a palatial old movie house filled with people might unleash. I needn't have bothered. A few artists rubbed elbows with ranchers, but the place was otherwise empty. A four-sided bar sat like an island in the middle of what was once the lobby, and beyond that the rows of theater chairs were replaced with tables arranged around a dance floor. A previous owner had knocked down the wall separating the lobby from the auditorium and left the balconies on either side, creating a single cavernous space.

Sawdust covered the wood floor, hiding notches made by boots and high heels. Antlers, farm equipment, and paintings of Egypt decorated the walls alongside old cinema posters hanging between faux sandstone pillars. John told me the Diamond Rough used to be lit with nothing but neon signs, now retired without replacement when they expired. Two advertisements for beers no longer brewed served as the last garish holdouts from the previous proprietor, occupying wall space alongside the new owner's attempts to restore the original art deco interior.

This place would be our gathering place for many upcoming summer nights. Right now I felt unmoored, still wobbly from running the Speedway.

Carter and Badger found a table while Mickey and Lucky made a beeline for the giant jukebox, a friendly argument over the upcoming playlist muffled by the current lyrics croaked out by Fogerty and his buddies. The Jersey boys pumped quarters into the ancient machine while Gabby headed to the bar. John pulled a few extra chairs up to the table.

"Expecting company?" I asked. "Are JJ and Ollie going to join us? I know Deacon has his wife and kids in town."

"Might be nice for the new boss to hang out with the working stiffs," John said. "Considering the number of changes he's thrown at us in one day, this season's likely not going to have any previous comparison." We sat down facing each other. "Then again, maybe the CEO doesn't want to get too familiar."

"*Too* familiar?" Carter echoed. "Was it last summer or the one before when he got midday drunk, stripped naked, and took a bath in the Kitchen?"

Gabby approached, a bar tray balanced on her shoulder, subbing in as server for our little party. "Sometimes you gotta be OK not seeing everything, honey." She passed out bottles covered in icy sweat that dripped onto the tabletop. She caught Mickey's attention and pointed at two cups and a pitcher waiting for him and Lucky at the bar.

"He wasn't *totally* naked," John said.

"And Ollie?" I repeated my question. "Does he come out with us?"

"He remains an enigma."

The four of us held a silent debate, glancing between the door and the unclaimed bottles. By the time the kids joined us with their root beer, we made the collective, unspoken decision to proceed. Glasses clinked and my face relaxed after a long pull. This local brand I'd never heard of brought me the biggest smile since arriving in Montana.

"You shot the Twins like you'd done it before," John said.

"When you put it like that…" Two hulking rocks, clear as day, marked the first part of Big Steep where we couldn't see the course ahead, the entrance to the closest portion that could be called *rapids*. For a few minutes from the Twins to Teflon Flats I felt…free.

"Mo?"

I shook my head and leaned toward Gabby. "What was that?"

"I said *congratulations*, babe. We never let a first-timer, let alone someone not even going on the river, do what you did, and you kicked ass. Maybe that's a new tradition."

"To go along with the other new tradition?" Our raft had passed Liza's Hope, the crew full of energy and excitement that overshadowed the weird vibes from what Carter half-jokingly called *a haunted point of land*. My own joy transmitted back at my friends, and we all whooped and hollered. When we drifted by the Hope, Mickey and Lucky heaved their sandbag ashore. After that, we all threw the sacks as hard as we could. The inked faces betrayed neither shock after being abandoned nor horror at the rotting timbers and crumbled stone foundation surrounding them. JJ protested only to point out that someone had to come back and retrieve the bags. The Hope could only be accessed via the river, so getting them off would require a special trip. We ignored him perhaps more pointedly than we should have, given his new position, but that was a tomorrow problem.

A discussion of food arose, the Diamond Rough evidently expanding its menu beyond grilling everything and deep-frying the rest in preparation for high-class tourists. Fogerty gave way to Springsteen.

"The Boss!" Mickey and Lucky shouted, air guitars blazing.

I closed my eyes and tried something, slowing my breath and extending imaginary arms outward. Farmers and ranchers and truckers confirmed by their hats and clothing ate next to aging painters and sculptors with roots in the stones and soil of the land dating back decades, all of them weary for their own reasons. Younger creative types moved to town, drawn by the magic of the light and mountains in hopes of making names for themselves. They knew our table, didn't know our faces, but recognized our exuberance and our youth.

I opened my eyes and approached the chicken sandwich before me with the same excited anticipation I used to shoot the Twins. For long moments none of us talked, Bruce did that for us, and I wondered at this newfound wrinkle in the way I could feel others, even without touching them, exerting a sliver of control over something I still did not comprehend.

I knew JJ would step through the door before it swung open. Suppressing my access to knowledge without explanation, I waved at him with French fries in my hand. "JJ! Come on over, boss."

"The boss!" the kids shouted again, toasting JJ and their idol together. He wore a new polo shirt, dark blue instead of light, and looked freshly showered, no hat to hide his long blond curls.

"Wish you guys had waited." He took the proffered chair and grinned. "The first round was supposed to be on me." He held a credit card aloft as proof.

"Second round tastes as good as the first," Carter said. "Even better when it's free."

"Let me catch you up." I downed my beer, stood, and snatched the card from JJ's hand in one motion, our fingertips touching long enough to send a disorienting blaze of electricity down my arm. I looked at the label on the bottles and waved for Gabby to join me at the bar.

"It pays to be careful." Her voice was soft and close.

I watched the room as the barkeeper filled our order. Gabby didn't give off the impression that she felt anything other than completely at home, so far from her Georgia roots, letting the casual and not-so-casual looks run right over her.

"Does it get any easier, Gabby?"

The boys at the table laughed and teased each other, bonds between men pretending to be brothers sometimes easier to forge than those between summer sisters, but Gabby's confidence played a part in my own inching back, and maybe we could share in more than being outsiders in a place that—

No. We were *not* out of place. No one would be, ever again, not if I could help it, not here or anywhere.

She nodded. "You did great on the water, Mo," she said. "Truly. The guys will respect you for that, but they already respected you. The way you stopped that little tiff at the Slip?" She shook her head. "I never seen John act like that."

"And JJ?"

She snorted. "Let's talk about something else."

"Are you more excited for school to start, or sad that this is your last year on the river?"

"Crazy to have to plan for school already, summer hasn't really started, and I never even thought I'd be here this many seasons. My dad *insisted* we see Yellowstone, then *we* got lost…shit, if John knew we were the wayward souls he likes to tease. Anyway, first summer here, I never would've picked myself to get caught up by the river. Now?" She sighed. "Probably time to move on. Four more years of school, couple more as an intern and a resident is a hell of a lot to look forward to, but you know how much we need doctors who'll take women's health seriously, especially in Atlanta, especially in the South. Maybe we'll come back when we're older, when I can afford what JJ's gonna do to the place."

I couldn't control my insight enough to know what she meant, and decided I wouldn't pry.

Her plan reminded me that every summer ended, as this one would. A profound and dumb statement, simple as a sunrise and just as real. I gave little thought to anything beyond a few weeks, if pressed, trying to focus on the tasks at hand, but any conception of a future terminated around Labor Day, fuzzy images of John pushing into my dreams each day, growing firmer, pictures filling in. None of it made complete sense yet.

"Drinks are here," Gabby said, interrupting my thoughts.

We returned to the table, waited for JJ to down his first beer to catch up, and then took the second round slower, together.

"*More* Springsteen?" Gabby narrowed her eyes at the Jersey boys. "Exactly how many ding-dang quarters did you kids shove in that gad-blasted thing?"

"I appreciate a jukebox as much as the next man," Carter announced, "or woman. And this particular box is good, great even, perhaps the only one of its kind still in existence. I for one can't wait until Sophie gets here."

"Sophie?" I asked.

"Oh, damn," Gabby said. "John, how've you not told Mo about Sophie yet?"

The rafters exchanged silent looks around the table, unspoken communication obviously a byproduct of months on the water together, but even by the end of this season, with access to insight from a touch, would I be able to—

Not yet, I told myself.

John leaned forward. "Philosophy Maria Cage," he said, "Sophie, the local…what would you all call her?"

"Musician," JJ replied.

"Part-time tattoo artist." Carter showed off the inked designs wrapping his forearm.

"Fucking witch," Gabby said.

"She is a character, certainly," Lucky said. "She's like a, what is the word? A cover artist."

John frowned. "I wouldn't say that to her face."

Lucky pointed at the jukebox. "Not just cover artist like a tribute band. Sophie does the tattoos, right?" He pointed at John's arm, letters and numbers sketched from wrist to shoulder. "She covers up the old ones, makes them new, makes them better. She sings the songs, she does them better. When Sophie sings, it's like, it's like—"

"A whole new song," Mickey finished for his friend.

I'd seen my fair share and more of covers and tributes, in Beantown and Saint Lou and the Big Easy, Windy City was full of them, and they always felt, if not *wrong*, then just *off*. Covers could be sung out of love, certainly, both for the artist being heralded and for the audience who wanted something familiar to hang their ears on, gambling on seeing a new act and wanting a reassurance, a reminder they weren't completely lost, a promise that they wouldn't be left behind.

Damn, I thought. *This is good beer.*

"When does she show up?" The collective shrugs suggested a spirit as free as Sophie's was not bound by concepts like calendars. With nothing further offered, the conversation moved on. "So, JJ, boss, what's on the agenda for the rest of the week?"

"Head guide, you wanna field that one?"

"We run the river some more," John said. "Forecast is for rain tomorrow morning, which will give us a chance to do our CPR recertification in the boathouse. If it clears by lunchtime, then we'll take two rafts out, keep mixing up the crews. We can practice our rescues, first in the lake, and then on the river. We'll do some role playing. You know, difficult customer interactions." He smiled at me and finished his beer. "All based on true events. If the office isn't keeping you too busy, we could use an unruly passenger."

"Don't forget," JJ said, "we have to get the sandbags off Liza's Hope."

CHAPTER TEN

The office kept me busy. While the rafters ran the river as many times a day as they could, I tried to shape a semblance of order out of what had been, until my last-minute arrival, the disaster that was Ollie's domain. Gabby told me she'd left it in a respectable state at the end of the previous season. John stayed in Bonaventure the whole year, the only rafter who did, but hunkered down in his cabin, never visiting the boathouse, leaving the boatwright to his own devices, free to shuffle and reorder things in a way that he found pleasing, if unintelligible to others. Like his speech, though, a little attention and patience helped decipher his organizational code.

In getting my feet under me and boxes out from every conceivable corner and crawlspace, I spent a fair bit of time with the sage. He was a font of river knowledge and, despite the lack of formal schooling past fifth grade, could recite detailed lore from almost any previous season as we wrestled old bits of equipment out of the office and boathouse and into the parking lot. Ollie acquiesced to my gently couched suggestion to part ways with anything that didn't work and couldn't be fixed, though he and Deacon could tackle any project short of actually manufacturing replacement parts. Information stored in Ollie's still-sharp memory appeared without warning, all of which helped me and JJ build a clearer picture of the enterprise dating back to the Nixon years. Any specific business information from a pre-Watergate era was declared *lost to history*.

Ollie had still lived in Minnesota when the Bighorn Dam and Blue Creek Dam and all the others went in, fought for his life in the Arctic Ocean while the first rafters went down the Big Steep, but moved to Montana after the war and started his own company, outlasting all others. He was here when updated earthen embankments replaced the simple dams, threatening the flow down to Lake Pando. He negotiated a sweetheart of a deal with the Forest Service to keep the reservoirs west of us filled with enough water leftover from farming to shovel some cargo—*passengers*, I reminded Ollie gently—down the river for a few months each year.

The prospect of keeping BSR Expeditions afloat for the foreseeable future thrilled him, since he had no intention of pulling up roots and rotting away in some retirement home in Arizona or worse, Florida, *thank you very much*. As far as JJ's grandiose plans to change the town and the rest of the county, he had less to say, hinting only that *the only constant's change* and we left it there. Ollie wasn't frustrated by the frat boy's internet plans because he refused even to acknowledge the existence of a digital world. Rigging an old transistor radio to catch the college station out of Bozeman and play it in the office was a minor technological victory. The student DJs loved to play songs from what counted as Ollie's middle age.

It fell to me to catch up on translating the backlog of online reservations into real-life boat assignments and, when JJ asked me to build out a simple website and increase our social media presence, I agreed, if only to move the conversation along.

At the beginning of each day, I pretended to be cargo—*a passenger*, I reminded myself gently—and I didn't want to miss the bus listening to one of JJ's business school speeches.

Moving from party planning to office management wasn't a huge shift in professional skills and would have felt virtually identical in many respects were it not for the first faint glimmerings of my own nascent river knowledge. The crew ran the Big Steep more in the five days after the first practice run than they would for any other week of the summer. The task was easier without having to shepherd, ferry, or otherwise babysit passengers. John coached me on acting the part to test the guides, all of his farfetched suggestions based on encounters with actual human beings. Each trip down the river taught me something new about the rafts, the water, the rafters, and myself.

Carter knew the river cold and, in some ways, better than anyone, but was prone to daydreaming, especially near the Natty Gann Bridge whenever a train crossed. He blamed it on the whistle and a nostalgic disposition. Badger did her best to keep his focus on the water.

Word-hoarder Mickey and gabfest Lucky weren't particularly strong on their own. Put them in the same raft and they shared more than a brain, springing into life as an unstoppable duo. John ran them separately during the practice week in hopes of boosting their solo confidence, and I had to remind myself that they were still just teenagers. Even kids could surprise the grownups.

Gabby's role as floating guide meant she had to know bow and tiller positions and work with every rafter in order to swap out and let them take breaks. She tested her ability to narrate given the new vocabulary restrictions and her energy filled the raft, spilling into the river.

After the number of years he'd spent on the Big Steep, JJ was more than skilled, but where Gabby was poised and confident, he was cocky and loud. He rode mostly with Carter by default, as that man cared least about JJ's posturing masquerading as good cheer.

Then there was John.

He reminded me of the Mill Pond: quiet on the surface, deep and potentially challenging, but the steady beating heart of the river. Sometimes, though, I just wanted him to say *something*. Towards the middle of the week, as the riders settled into their roles, I rode with John more than with anyone else. He let me steer, but never told me what to do or how to do it. We spent long stretches with no words exchanged and I lost count of how many times I bumped another raft or grazed the struts under the Natty Gann or beached on the sand bar by Liza's Hope. I once nearly flipped the raft, a feat which Gabby claimed was *frackin' impossible*, and each time he let me figure things out on my own. As the days drew on, *yes*, I erred less often, but *damn it*, just tell me what to do.

"You know what the problem is, John." Both of us struggled in frigid water up to our waists, feet digging into muddy riverbed at the entrance to the Mill Pond. His grunt came from either exertion or assent. "These dang rafts," I continued. "They're not—" The bottom lifted free and I jumped in, swinging my bare feet over the side as John climbed aboard, shoving us away from land with the emergency paddle. "They're not real boats, but we just call them by number. Raft one, raft two." I picked up the other paddle, knowing it was useless, and slapped the water, startling a clutch of geese congregating near the reeds.

He looked past me, squinting at the rafts waiting to run the Twins, and I could feel him give the geese an apology on my behalf. "What do you mean?"

I don't know if it was the heat of the afternoon, the chill of the water on my legs and shorts, if it was John's habit of asking questions in response to questions or how he could talk to birds yet never made a big deal about it, but I used the paddle to splash water on him. To his goofy credit, he smiled.

"They're *rafts*, John, watercraft with a mission and a purpose. Don't they need *names*?" His apparent seriousness in considering my flippant inquiry amused me. I held the paddle against my chest like a guitar, though I couldn't play, and closed my eyes. "C'mon." I dragged out the second syllable. "This shouldn't require scientific analysis or philosophical introspection. Rafts: names or no names?"

John sat up in the stern.

"How about it, JJ?" he shouted. "You think our passengers would rather ride in rafts with proper names?"

"But I *like* raft four," Carter drawled.

JJ stayed uncharacteristically quiet while he thought it over. My shorts dried in the sunshine and a giant dragonfly took that moment to alight on the tiller near John. It folded its wings, stretched them, and the moment lingered, almost too long.

"Mo," JJ said. "You're the office manager now. If you can convince Ollie, then sure, let's name the darn things."

OLLIE TOOK MY SUGGESTION *under advisement,* and we thought nothing of it until the next morning when he announced we had the day to come up with names before holding a ceremony at sunset. The way the rafters reacted to the word *sunset* seemed odd, their feelings hidden by their buzzing excitement over our last day of practice runs. We had a free day tomorrow before the first passengers would arrive on Monday. We finished our eighth and last scheduled run of the day just as the sun touched the tops of the mountains west of us. We hauled the rafts onto the boat ramp and cleaned them as thoroughly as we could, inside and out. Deacon presented three bottles of champagne and one of sparkling cider, for the Jersey boys, and revealed polished wooden planks upon which we would paint the names in bright red letters.

JJ corralled Ollie for another in a long line of business conversations. John found me and Gabby. "The old man's changed," he said. "Ever since JJ dropped a fortune on his head, he's been different."

"Money does that to people." Gabby laughed. "Especially a wazoo-full of money."

John held a cloth in his hands, wringing it over and over.

"Looks like you squeezed all the water out of that thing," I said. "Is that why you hesitated to bring up the naming thing? Ollie's the kind of guy averse to change, and one more might be too much?"

He shook his head and tossed the rag in a bucket. "The man's seen nothing *but* decades of change, a lot more forced on him than of his own choosing. Gabby's right, money will change a man, but JJ gave him more than that. He gave Ollie a kind of freedom. Even if he never leaves Bonaventure, even if he does this for *another* sixty years, now he has the freedom to *choose* that course." He looked at us. "Ollie opened up to the idea of naming rafts that never had names. I don't know what other kinds of changes come with that."

WE TOOK TURNS carefully painting the handmade wooden plates, little plaques to hang in the boathouse, one more thing to eventually weather and fade away, worn down by wind and rain and maybe even tourists putting their silly paws on them, but we found comfort in the impermanence. The years could wear away our own names, and at different times we were different people to different people. For now we were us, we were for each other, and that was strong enough.

No explanations offered or asked for. The names came from each crew and needed no justification.

Little Durham. Born to Run. Magnolia.

And John's raft was reborn as *Blondie.* It took me a moment to tease out, wondered if I was right, knew I could touch his shoulder and confirm, but didn't begrudge him the memorial, appreciated the subtle reminder of Sera's favorite movie.

Instead of cracking bottles over bows, we poured a small amount of bubbly into each raft, split the rest among a clutch of paper cups, and toasted each other as the sun set behind the mountains. Memories and emotions surged each time I hugged someone, an immense outpouring that would result in dreams as confusing as the clouds piling up over the peaks.

"Diamond Rough?" I asked. "Doesn't the mysterious Sophie Cage arrive tonight?"

The others grinned as Ollie excused himself. The sound of the bus roaring to life and headlights piercing the darkness caught me by surprise. Blondie sat on the trailer.

"One thing first," John said. "Another tradition."

RUNNING THE BIG STEEP gave me a thrill at any time of day. Shooting the Twins and zipping down the Speedway that first time still made my heart leap a week later. On Tuesday, I'd lost a bet to the Jersey boys and had to travel the whole river standing on the bow, not making it to the Natty Gann before falling out, John fishing me from the water with a smile. Elk and bighorn sheep joined the mule deer, rare sights for even the more seasoned rafters, and yesterday's morning trip ended with a flock of pelicans swooping low overhead on their way to Lake Pando.

None of those experiences held a candle to my first nighttime run.

We settled into Blondie, each of us armed with a short paddle, and pushed off from the Slip. The river shook us when Deacon released the rope, the current somehow faster, more confident in the dark, as if it knew we had places to go before we slept, if we ever could again. Carter reminded us this was how he did it every day, but then fell silent, all remaining jokes left ashore, my ears growing three sizes until I heard birds and frogs and insects unseen calling to one another, the grunts and chirps of some creatures bedding down for the night, others just stirring for nocturnal adventures. Even if I couldn't understand the words their messages permeated my body, sundering my connection to the land and my past. The same power Sera gifted me through the shards of a disc that allowed insight into the humans around me worked with *wildlife*, big or small. They didn't speak in sentences or nouns or verbs, but *gods* they told stories, recounted the happenings of the day, wondered at the urgency of the night ahead and days beyond, and yes, there was love.

Oh, was there love.

Nature and humanity shared the color red in tooth and claw, though wilderness was not gratuitous with violence. In the pursuit and escape there was a love that transfixed us all, insights or no. A mother deer taught her fawn how best to hide, confident in lore passed down through generations… bees hummed in the hollow of a rotten tree, eager for tomorrow's flowers, thankful for peace in numbers…a bobcat stalked a rabbit to the water's edge and we sat witness to it all.

A dragonfly flashed in the last glitter of sunlight as it landed on my knee, the same one I had seen the day before. Its wings moved gently, glistening for only a second before springing into action, speeding away and leaving me to follow its flight as long as possible, privy to new knowledge granted by a hunting insect. Where its six feet landed a tingle lingered. I lost track of the dragonfly as it leapt toward the heavens.

The stars.

I was no stranger to the ocean, far from land the last best place from which to see the night sky without our own mocking artificial lights interfering. An undergraduate astronomy elective included midnight field trips to the Ozarks with the goal of identifying constellations, but here, with ridgelines blocking the dim glow from town and no human settlement bigger than Bonaventure within miles, I couldn't recognize a single pattern from that class.

I saw *all* of them, watching the heavens and knowing why our ancestors lived in awe and fear of the sky, and considered doing so again.

The sound of collective breath inhaled brought me back to Earth, to the river and our raft, and we'd all been holding ours together.

Mickey and Lucky huddled close and I felt a sudden protective urge in my heart. Carter leaned his back against Gabby's, neither knowing what came next but both eager for the thrill. Her fingers stroked Badger's mane, the dog more alert and alive than I'd ever seen the canine, feeling not just her own blood, but that of every wolf and hound who'd ever hunted coursing through her veins. JJ sat silent, the majesty and mystery of sky and wilderness enough to transcend even his cocksure shell and inspire the child within.

John's leg pressed against mine, contact between his bare knee and mine enough to transmit his answer to why he said *yes* when I asked for help before my rocket ship departure from Chicago, why he provided a place for me to crash in the wilderness. My insights came now from mere proximity while actual physical contact provided knowledge that threatened to overwhelm me. Each time we touched—fingertips over spilled tea, hands pulling me from the water, legs touching as we moved through the Mill Pond—another layer of defense pulled back, in both directions.

Sera told me everything she knew about John after the love of her life left her in Louisiana, going back to war in hopes of bringing his men back alive, promising to return himself as well. She confirmed her love for him so strongly that she made me believe *she* believed, if nothing else, in him. She'd told me that this man who showed her his entire heart in ten days and earned hers in return could talk to birds, and I knew now I was a fool for ever doubting her.

At the time, I'd railed at her, incredulous she gave so much to someone she knew so little of, and so quickly, to someone with such a claim, and she had responded with kindness and sorrow and not a small amount of her own incredulity at my lack of faith. Whenever we fought, she came at me with love, never set on winning the argument but on preserving our friendship. That morning had been brutal. I was dead set on showing her the folly of trusting John, of trusting *anyone*, and she responded with our daily greeting. Hearing it in the moment had just made me mad.

As fast as the world is being destroyed, she'd said, *we have to learn to love even faster.* The day we met she'd asked if I was comfortable with hugs, and every time we spent more than a few hours apart she offered an embrace upon our reunion. That day, she'd tried to leave me with a hug, her version of aloha, and then got in that doomed car.

Was John part of the explanation behind my touch insight? Were we all experiencing a piece of his power, each of us listening to and gaining knowledge from avian dialogue, or was this a collective delusion, agreeable and believable though it was? I didn't want to break the silence, but if I pressed my knee against John's again, harder, what answers would that provide?

We passed the Twins and ran the Speedway, heart-pounding in the dark, unseen rocks and waves more than enough to pounce on our foolhardiness with ice-cold admonishment. We landed in Teflon Flats and crept upon Liza's Hope. JJ cleared his throat and the spell ended, nature hushed and inscrutable again.

"We still have to get the sandbags."

John replied, voice low, as though he didn't want to disturb the remainder of what JJ scattered aside. "We should do that in daylight," he said. "I'll take someone tomorrow."

I thought this might be another point of friction, unsure why John hesitated, if he was picking a pointless fight over something silly. We were already here, there was starlight and plenty to spare, and with all of us lugging sacks, it would take less time than it would for two to return on our first full day off since the first practice run and the last before the tourists arrived. I was already planning to sleep in, and John could, too.

We neared the point of land, outlined audibly in the darkness by the river lapping at its rocky shore. Carter called it *haunted*, and until this moment I'd thought he was joking.

The foundation of a one-time structure was visible thanks to the profusion of stars, but the more I looked at it, listened to and for it, trying to sense the wildlife in the cabin's ruins, taking in the entirety of Liza's Hope, the more I felt…nothing. An absence. A hole in space, a veil hiding something sinister…and the less I felt like obeying JJ's orders and more like following John's lead.

Clouds moved across the sky and turned the lingering warmth of the late May sun into a shroud. Surely the sacks would still be there in the morning. No one had disturbed them in a week, and no one would mess with them in the meantime. It's not like anyone *lived* on—

Oh, shit.

"C'mon, JJ. I vote we get the sacks tomorrow." Something about the stacked stones and charred timbers made me suddenly want never to set foot there, least of all at night, and I wanted to get back on solid ground as quickly as possible. The others chimed in until JJ relented, though he asserted his authority one last time in the pettiest way possible.

"Fine," he announced, "but I want Mickey and Lucky to do it. First thing tomorrow."

CHAPTER eleven

The ride from the boathouse to the Diamond Rough allowed time and space to reflect on what we'd seen, what each of us had felt on the water, and to wonder at what the summer could bring. Part of me wished for an evening of reflection and solitude, to carry that silent contemplation and finally examine what power this touch insight really held.

Walking into the bar shocked me harder than a lightning bolt. The promised hordes of tourists arrived, early and in force.

JJ had informed the local merchants, tried to prepare them for the sudden appearance of Bonaventure on the maps of the world, sold them on his plans for an influx of hundreds of humans and their dollars over the next few months, and suggested they brace for impact. Based on the crowd before us, the blurs that were two servers and the barkeeper laden with trays, desperate shouts from the kitchen, and the press of humanity in the small space, his warnings didn't appear sufficient.

John touched my shoulder as he passed, his grazing fingertips reminding me of the electricity transmitted not even an hour ago, something more than just a touch, an unanswered and unanswerable question as yet unasked.

He led us past the bar and through the crowd to a table marked with a small hand-scribbled sign reading *Reserved*. Still off-balance from eavesdropping on predators and dragonflies, unsure what consequences this magic invited, ill at ease over an argument about a sandbag rescue mission, and queasy from the raw power emanating from dark stones and timbers, I blinked back tears, wondering how he knew the sign meant *for us*.

Of course he knew.

The jukebox worked overtime to keep up with the sudden demand for entertainment. Shania asked after boots under a bed, Martina declared her independence, and Bruce reminded us what we were born to do. As we drank and ate I realized that what had been until today a platform to store extra tables and chairs was, in fact, a stage from days long past when a pianist had accompanied silent films, now rigged with speakers, a microphone angled over an electric keyboard, and a single wooden stool, tiny and defiant in the cavernous auditorium.

"Live music?" The syllables rasped against my unused throat, the first I'd uttered since urging JJ to put off the retrieval of our erstwhile sandbag companions.

John leaned close, his voice just audible over the songs bought a quarter at a time.

"Sophie."

"The one and only." A woman materialized beside our table, conjured by John's whispers and holy gods in rivers and on mountaintops. She was just as I had imagined and still blew me away. The crew cheered her arrival. She shared the edge of Carter's chair and offered smiles around the table. Gabby beamed and the Jersey boys sat starstruck. Sophie took up hardly any space, but commanded the room. Ranchers and sculptors now elbow-to-elbow with guidebook dads and moms negotiating meals with their children picked up on the energy that crackled from her impossibly blood red and midnight black curly hair. She wore gloriously large hoop earrings, a vest made of denim, and a leather skirt.

"Sophie," John said, "this is Mo. She's the newest member of the crew."

Her off-kilter grin and charisma made me giddy. Was this some blockbuster artist in disguise, sneaking off for the summer to a mountain dive bar, or was she an undiscovered star, a true talent hidden from the world and uninterested in paltry things like fame or money? She had yet to sing a note, but we ached for the music just the same.

"Nice to meet you, Mo." Her voice felt as warm and cool as the river.

Carter saved me from mumbling something dumb in return when he rapped on the table with his knuckles. "Sophie," he said, "can you explain to young Lucky here the difference between a *cover artist* and, well, whatever it is you call yourself."

"I don't call myself much of anything," she replied, "but *cover artist* isn't an insult." Her smile eased any reprimand the Jersey boy may have felt, her hands on his and Carter's a peace offering. "Besides, I sing my own songs, too, so maybe it's more about tribute. Cover artists, the good ones, if they're going to play someone else's songs, they won't do it just the same each time so you can't tell the difference, maybe only sanding off the edges and setting it down in cotton. A good artist makes it her own *and* honors the original effort."

JJ set his bottle down loudly enough to cut through the crowd's murmur, but not *quite* loud enough for the gesture to qualify as rude. Very measured. Deliberate.

"A tribute band is still just, like, unoriginal." He stifled a belch. "They might think they're doing it outta respect." He picked up a shot glass full of amber fire and paused before slamming it back. "But if I pay to see a band, I wanna hear something you can't hear on the radio."

"Good thing I play for free." Sophie gazed into his eyes. "Think of all those bands, the ones people demand play the same live exactly as they do on their albums." She looked at JJ while speaking to the rest of us, maybe to the whole bar. "Lots of time they could be damn good lyricists and mu-sicians in their own right." Her voice fluttered between an iron rasp and a wood flute. "And when people demand they play their songs the same as they always have, we all lose. Nostalgia's not what we're after."

"What's wrong with nostalgia?" Lucky asked.

"It's longing for something that don't exist anymore. That's a powerful force, and anything that powerful comes with danger attached."

"Love is powerful," Mickey said.

"And love is dangerous," Sophie replied. "Stronger than a boxer."

JJ leaned forward and cranked his voice up another notch, returning her look but also not speaking directly to her. "Ever see someone do that Simon an' Garfunkel song at karaoke? The person ends up just, y'know, standing there at the end, just…" He lifted the bottle to his mouth. "*La-la-lie,*" he sang in a mocking falsetto. "Over an' over. Stands there like a dumbass for, what, two minutes."

"Oh, JJ," Sophie said. "Where have all the cowboys gone?"

He bristled, replicating a very Kirk-like reaction, and I wondered what road we suddenly traveled. Over the past week his entitlement and surface-level combativeness competed with an eagerness to please—that was just JJ being JJ, everyone told me—but he kept the conflict mostly in check.

"C'mon, Sophie." A measure of his fire lessened. "It's been, what, eight months?"

"Heard you bought the town," she said. "Might explain why we have a midsummer's crowd before Memorial Day and the Diamond Rough is already almost out of beer."

"We did a lot of advertising," he said. "And I gave the chamber of commerce plenty of heads up. *More tourists* mean more money, including more money for struggling local musicians playing in run-down movie theaters."

John cut in. "In two years, you won't recognize the place."

"Oh, but you will." JJ perked up in his seat. "It'll feel even more real than it does now, more like the Old West these people expect to find out here. Leather and wrought iron, weathered wood and sepia tones. We'll give them what they want, authentic without feeling antique. This is a blank slate out here."

"Some of us actually *live* here," John said. "It's not *out* anywhere, it's home."

"And soon it'll be a home you can be proud of. Bonaventure." He swept a hand through the air. "Home of the Big Sky experience and the Big Steep River. Our investors are already thinking of installing ziplines, bringing in ATVs, all the top-of-the-line tourist attractions."

"You gonna turn this place back into a company town?" Sophie asked. "I didn't know rich people could still do that, and I didn't think you were rich enough to pull it off."

"I was just joking about the karaoke," JJ said.

"Just joking, just Jared," she replied. "Except I've never known you to make a real joke."

"There it is." He regained his head of steam. "Good old Sophie, standing up for the downtrodden even as she sings their songs. I'm trying to bring jobs to town, because jobs mean money, money means taxes, and taxes pay for things like schools and clean water. I want to give this town a future."

Zeebrugge was an entire community condemned for want of a future, its citizens tossed to the wind. A few months after I landed in Chicago, a hedge fund bought the town and somehow turned a profit on the loss.

"I just call it like I see it." He pointed his empty bottle at her. "In vino veritas."

"And in whiskey odium," she said. "You ever sing karaoke, JJ? Not in front of underage coeds—in a place like this." She didn't move her arms, but somehow encompassed the entire bar with her words, maybe all of Montana. "Strangers, JJ, people who can't help but recognize you as different and you sing anyway. That's brave, and nobody who does karaoke like that can be a dumbass."

"But you sing in front of strangers," Mickey said, playing peacemaker.

"Oh, Mickey," she drawled, voice and gaze softening, "you blow my mind. They're all just friends whose names I've forgot. Plus, a karaoke rookie is braver than a trained singer the same way a first-time skydiver is braver than a professional. Or maybe they don't know enough to be scared."

"Do y'all remember those white bread kids?" Carter asked, shepherding the conversation back to even ground. "That bunch of boy scouts from Provo. Now *those* kids were a cover band."

"That was their actual name," Gabby said. "The frickin' Wonder Bread Kids."

"Only ones I've ever seen smooth the edges off Journey," Carter finished. "They made everyone stop believing. Elevator music, except the elevator only goes up one floor."

"Gotta listen to something on an elevator." JJ hadn't completely deflated, but wasn't getting any angrier. He pounded the last dregs of his beer and stood, managing to hide most of the wobble. "Hope everyone enjoys their day off tomorrow. Mikhail'n'Luc," he slurred, "don't forget the sandbags are still on Liza's Hope. They've been there a week now. You two might be the only sober ones come morning, so I want you guys to stop procrastinating and get the bags off. Just be careful doing it." He turned to the rest of us. "Sophie Maria, always a pleasure." He snapped off a mock salute as he departed.

I leaned forward to catch her attention. "So, what *do* you do, Sophie?"

"Whatever we want, Mo."

"The crowd feels…restless. You think maybe it wants some music? You know, not the kind you hear from an album."

When she laughed her hair shook, red streaks parting to reveal deep purple and bright green among the richer black curls. "The crowd doesn't always know what it wants, but sometimes they recognize it when they hear it."

I was torn between believing her and not wanting to surrender the last of my wits.

Sophie stood, gave Mickey a loving squeeze on his shoulder, and I wondered what could be learned from her touch. Alcohol seemed to blunt my insight, despite how close we sat, and Sophie emitted her own magic, though I couldn't parse it. She wove through the crowd, occasionally stopping to say hello or hug a familiar local. Everyone she passed, even those she didn't greet or touch, fell quiet. The silence spread to the rest of the bar like a boat's wake until the whole place watched the spark approach the stage, ready to ignite. She sat upon her stool, cracked her knuckles, and looked to our table.

When her fingers touched the keyboard, the crowd leaned in like swimmers on the blocks. She drew forth music, growing our hearts when she became that poor boy whose story was seldom told, and sang us silent until we all, in the company of strangers, stood in that clearing with her, and we sang along for minutes at the end, none of us dumb for trying to be brave. I almost wept for him, the poor boy, and for Sophie, and for all of us who'd been bled and would bleed again by winter, even for JJ and Kirk and the man whose car killed Sera, and she cut me until I cried out.

chapter TWELVE

John hadn't slept in either. I found him on his back with his feet propped on one arm of the couch, a book open and face down on his chest.

"Do you still jog?"

He looked up like it was his first time seeing me.

"Not a hard question, John." I moved around the couch and sat on the armchair. An oversized lost-and-found hoodie nearly swallowed me up. "You were in the Army, so I imagine they made you run everywhere. You went out for a jog when you stayed with us in Zeebrugge."

He sat up and closed the book. "Maybe you forgot," he said, "but that didn't end well."

"A few parents phoned the school, said they saw a *crazy white boy* trying to run in the bayou heat, swore you passed out on their sidewalk."

"I did."

Part of me wanted to go back to sleep, or at least bed, but the rest of me knew the energy infused by Sophie's performance had to go somewhere, the lingering dizziness from that last beer needed steadying, and the nerves from the nighttime trip down the Big Steep needed settling.

I stood up.

"Do you or do you not, John Mackenzie, still flail your arms and legs from time to time in the vain hope of burning calories and making yourself feel less permanently awful?"

He pointed at a plate of crumbs on the trunk that served as a coffee table. "I just had breakfast."

"Leftover pizza is not breakfast."

"Anything is breakfast if you eat it early enough."

I hopped from one foot to the other. "It's our last day off for who knows how long. Carter said he'd be *indisposed* and not to wait around for him, Gabby's not answering her phone, and the Jersey boys are taking care of the sandbags."

"I told them to let me handle it."

"In any case, they don't have a hangover to take care of. Running always helped me feel better the morning after a party."

He stood and stretched. "Yeah, Mo, I still jog. Not every day, but I can flail my arms and legs."

"Then get ready." I unzipped the hoodie and tossed it on the chair. "I'm going to run one way or another, but I don't want to get lost…or get eaten by a bear."

WHAT MONTANA LACKED in humidity it made up for with altitude. The effort expended getting John off the couch would have been better saved for shepherding oxygen from the thin atmosphere into my overtaxed lungs. I'd been in Montana a few weeks already and had mostly acclimated, though the combination of late nights and early mornings had so far prevented me from establishing a regular workout routine. Even in Chicago, that much closer to sea level, I'd never jogged much. Kirk had granted me access to his condo's fitness center, accompanied by his unsubtle suggestions to lose weight and keep it off, but I preferred getting my heart pumping in a pool. His office had an onsite workout program that rivaled most pay-to-play gyms. He and his buddies were in a chest-and-arms phase when we met. During the summer they'd shifted focus to something called *combat fitness*, and fixated on the latest exercise fad when their political idol gave an interview about it.

"This used to be a logging road." John's words slid out easily between footfalls. For a guy who claimed not to run every day he set a fine pace. I didn't begrudge him the difficulties he faced in that swampy air all those years ago.

"A logging road," I said, "now a jogging road." Maybe all the squirrels darting up the pine trees and scolding us from the branches stole the oxygen molecules, but John laughed at my out-of-breath joke.

Upon first hightailing it out of Illinois, I'd tried and failed to shove every memory of the previous year aside. The night before, as Sophie sang to us of love and adventure, I decided to forget the attempt to forget. She shared song after song about independence and the strength we found in ourselves, and I realized that the twelve months idling or waiting or getting sanded down by Kirk's inertia would no longer make me sad. He transformed over time from a fun nighttime and weekend partner to an adequate boyfriend to a psychologically manipulative jerk, and he could be a jerk for the next woman and the next. Even as I jogged alongside this taciturn river guide down a crunchy gravel road a million miles from anywhere I'd ever been, thinking of Kirk gave him no power…not over me, over what used to be *us*, and definitely not over our story.

My story. Sophie's performance had also reminded me who the heroine in my story was. Forgetting that truth may have been my biggest sin.

Kirk was the kind of guy who adopted trendy habits because others did it, not to impress them, but to do it better than they did. Whether that was P90X workouts, frat-pack movies, or something called *cryptocurrency*, all his interests wrapped around a very specific aesthetic. He moved on when things bored him, or when he found out that he wasn't as good at them as he thought he would be. If the man wanted to embrace the superficial and the flashy, more power to him.

"Not my problem," I puffed out.

"What's that?"

"Nothing." John couldn't see my smile. "Not my problem. Never was."

I made a mental note to text Kirk the address for the boathouse and ask for the balance of what he called *my portion of the mortgage* but was really just *rent*. Hopefully it would cover groceries and my cell phone bill until the first BSR paycheck cleared. Even with JJ's promised raise over what John had offered, every penny would count this summer, and the pennies had yet to pour in.

The old logging road took on a rougher character, rising to challenge us, pines thinning as we gained elevation. John chugged along, silent even in his breathing, and I spat a loogie to the side of the road to see if he'd react. He crept ahead, just enough to outpace me, and my grin grew wider.

Not today.

I swam competitively from elementary to high school. After trying to start a field hockey team in college with no takers, I'd switched to yoga and kickboxing, habits that fell away and resurrected themselves over the moves from Missouri to Louisiana to Illinois. Maybe I would try again in Montana. Right now, I was not going to let John win, at least not easily.

We made it to the top of the hill and I stumbled to a halt. The views took what little breath I had away. Enormous white clouds with hard gray edges tempered the sunlight, allowing me to turn in place and see to the horizon in every direction.

"Wow."

"Yeah."

The wind whistled past my ears and whipped my ponytail against my neck. "How have we not come up here yet?" I could see Lake Pando, the little inlet where the boathouse sat hard against the shore, almost obscured by a stand of aspens and evergreens. I traced the path of the Big Steep backward, traveling up its length, naming the points of interest all the way to the Slip. There was Bonaventure, the Diamond Rough smack dab in the center of town, other buildings spread along the riverbanks.

"Do you still write?" A gust nearly stole my words.

"Not as much as I used to," he said, "or want to."

Mountains piled up west of us, like a pair of giant hands had crumpled a map and covered it with pine and snow. The dark bottoms of the clouds connected heaven and Earth for a moment.

"Could be rain later," he said.

"If I told you something weird was happening," I said, "would you believe me?" I faced him. He wore a loose t-shirt, sleeves long since cut away, and shorts. It was just about the simplest workout gear someone could get away with, none of it crafted for the purpose, but put to use just the same. I'd seen him often enough in the past few weeks in various stages of dress and almost-undress. As housemates, it was nearly impossible not to, and on the river clothes were worn and shed quick and easy, and *yes*, he was in good shape. We all were, considering the functional fitness that wrestling rafts demanded. A diet of food grabbed on the run, if at all, meant we'd collectively lost more than a few pounds in just a few days of working on the water.

How to tell John what bubbled under the surface of my consciousness since holding that shredded CD in my hands? Our fingertips brushed over spilled tea and that first night I dreamed of him at war. Shaking Ollie's hand resulted in a vision of him as a young man on a merchant ship in a frozen ocean. Tousling Badger's mane let me live the life of a stray dog for a night, and in the days since the power seemed to grow. Now, even being near someone let their feelings push into my vision. My knee pressed against John's last night in the raft gave me more than an impression of what roiled beneath his stoic exterior. Being on a mountaintop with him was like eavesdropping on his inner dialogue. Every contact with another living creature offered insight, and I didn't know how to control any of it… but I had an idea.

Last night, between rounds of drinks and sets of music at the Diamond

Rough, I'd tested my idea with gentle touches and casual contact with the rafters. Each time offered me knowledge of their emotions, or their past, but most often cryptic and garbled messages I couldn't fully interpret. I even tried seeking out information, though I didn't get far in my attempts. When I brushed past Sophie I was nearly consumed by the touch, like grabbing a live wire. The way she'd looked at me after suggested she knew something was up, but left her thoughts unsaid. My dreams had been fitful, energetic, and expansive.

If I focused hard enough, the writing on John's arms could be the real confirmation that I'd stumbled into an ability without rational explanation. He was the only other person in my life with any exposure to the supernatural, and his birdspeak meant he might be at least open to the notion of another phenomenon at work.

I didn't object to tattoos, though my own-ill advised bow-tied rabbit was, thankfully, hidden in polite company, and the Gamma-Phi-Beta on my ankle could be explained as a reminder of my sorority years. Soldiers and veterans got their bodies inked almost religiously, but John's artwork had been outdone by Sera's long-gone body tapestry. I never asked if part of their attraction was the mutual proliferation of ink across flesh. Gods, was she gorgeous. Any idiot who saw her understood that immediately. She was clever and witty and loyal to a goddamned fault, possessed a billion other virtues, but something had to first catch John's attention in that Oklahoma desert amid the religious rock music. Had it been the gallery on her skin? Something in the trees and wings and poetry hinted at her humor, her mind, her heart—

"Of course." His reply caught me in the middle of a hiccup. "Are you all right?"

I stepped closer. "These are names, right?" He looked down at his arm, and then lifted it for my inspection. *Here goes nothing.* I took his wrist, turned it to fully expose the letters, and read, starting high, near his shoulder.

Spillman. Grieg. Gutierrez. Aspen. Washington. Kid Rocket. I traced my fingers across darker ink, not as faded. *Cisneros. Ledbetter. Bergstrom. Stavanger. Smith.* A gap at the crook of his elbow, and then, in bold script, *Atwood.*

Thunder heralded the approaching storm.

Rosenthal. Tompkins. Manzanillo. Yarrow. Another *Smith.* I pressed my thumb over those last names and closed my eyes.

"Are they…" I tried to concentrate. "These were—"

"Yes."

Tears came and my jaw popped. "You don't even know what I was going to ask." I released his arm and spun away, not wanting to look at anything in that moment.

"I'm sorry," he said. "What do you want to know?"

Even without looking at or holding him, their stories bombarded me, caught the breath in my throat. Not all of them, but so, *so* much, like static electricity trapped in my skull, faces and stories of men I'd never met, would never meet, glimpses of the parts of their lives when their paths crossed John's.

"Kid Rocket." I choked the words out. "He was young. Too young. He lied about his age, even his name, just to join up." My chest tightened, not needing to see his nod of affirmation. "Five of your men died at once. Cisneros, Ledbetter, the Swedes, and a Smith. And Manzanillo was your… he was a captain. Hector. He died in that courtyard, with the bird and the snake." I turned back to face him, my eyes fixing on that gap at his elbow. "When was that?" My fingertip nearly smashed into the blank space between the first Smith and Atwood. I held back, not sure if I could suffer another rush of insight.

He traced a finger down his arm, starting at Spillman. "This was 2004. This ends in 2007." He came to rest on the second Smith, just above his wrist. "We didn't lose anyone the first time over there, even though that was what everyone called *the war.* The second time." His voice faded. "And the third…"

"That gap," I said, "that gap is for Sera." The realization shook me. "You think she's another casualty of war? You marked the loss of…" I counted the names on his arm. "Gods, *seventeen* other people, but you can't bring yourself to put her name to flesh?"

"Should I?"

"She's dead, John," I snapped. "Commemorating her loss wouldn't make her any more dead. And you're not responsible for her death. She wasn't one of your soldiers."

A thought radiated off of him and slammed into me, the insight pushing its way into my subconscious, his unspoken voice ringing inside my head. *She might as well have been.*

"You weren't there that last day," I said. "You didn't get the call from a small town sheriff looking for her next of kin. You don't know that I was the one who—"

Was I angry on her behalf or my own?

A bird called out, snapping the tension as we both watched it wheel away on an updraft. John might have known what it said, but he didn't share the insight with me.

"Before she left," I said, preparing to cut myself open and spill a secret not even Anita knew, one I tried keeping from myself. "Before she went on that weekend trip to Mississippi, we fought. About you, about what I can't remember exactly, but it was dumb. Of course it was. Any argument that's the last thing you say to a person has to be dumb, if you can't leave on good terms."

"You couldn't know."

"She always gave me a hug, whenever she saw me, whenever we departed. It was a lot, sometimes, but I liked it. No matter what was going on, she offered a hug and I accepted. Except…that last morning, I got so…*angry*, I refused. She tried calling a couple of times from the road." John took a small step in my direction. "That's the thing, isn't it?" My eyes burned against the wind and memories. "That's all that's left. I miss her." I folded my arms across my chest, hugged my arms. "It's been years, but every day I miss her."

He turned his eyes to the mountains blocked by hills, there just the same even if we couldn't see them, and I knew he missed her just as fiercely. *What would it be like to get only two weeks with your soulmate?*

"You know how they say when you're in love," he said, "every song reminds you of the one you love?" He faced me. "They don't tell you that's true even after they're gone."

John didn't challenge me on my unexplained insights into the names on his arm. A decade of war would invade my dreams tonight, and seventeen dead men would die again, but he seemed to accept my trick, his own magic perhaps enough to trust mine.

"Does anyone else here know you were in the Army?" I asked. "Do they know what you did, what you saw, what you lost?"

"Why do you ask?"

"The way JJ throws words like *chain of command* around." I wiped my cheeks with the back of my hand. "The way he treats you, like he doesn't know what you've been through."

"Should he?" John slipped back into his question-for-a-question habit. "Would that make the way he treats me better or worse?"

"He shouldn't get to be a jerk about it," I said, "even if that's just his nature. Maybe he should get a chance to be a jerk in other ways."

"Carter knows I was in, but doesn't know everything," John said. "If he's told Gabby, she hasn't said anything. Deacon and Ollie know a little more than they do. I've told Sophie all of it." His gaze drifted down to his arm, and then up to me. "I left a space for Sera, but wasn't sure at the time why. Still not sure. She wasn't over there with us, not really, but neither was Gus."

My chest relaxed, letting me breathe again. "Gus...Julius Atwood."

He tapped the name gently, with love. "He was on leave in Florida, died in a car accident. His wife and kids survived, thankfully."

I shivered at the memory of the phone call from the small-town sheriff who'd spent a whole day tracking down someone to call after Sera was taken in her own car accident. What did it take to receive that kind of news in a war zone—twice?

"Gus was my best friend over there."

I unfolded my arms and decided against kicking a rock over the edge of the hilltop. "Jesus, John, I didn't mean to…I don't know why I brought any of this up, here and now."

"This place brings it out of people," he said. "Being this high above everything else, you feel kind of…able, I guess, like you can do things. When we go back down, when we get home, it's different, except maybe out on the water. I don't know what else to say." He pointed at my hands. "Whatever you've discovered, it's powerful, which means there's danger, too. We can talk about what it means, or about Sera, all of it or none of it, up here or on the road, at the boathouse or the cabin."

"We do have a long way back to the cabin," I said. "And a long summer ahead."

"Not that far back." He stepped closer to the edge. "Take a look. Just down there."

Trees blocked most of the view, but there it was, a pair of pines taller than the rest standing right outside *my* room.

"C'mon," I said. "It's my turn to cook breakfast."

"I already had breakfast."

"You had pizza."

CHAPTER THIRTEEN

John entered the kitchen as I slid the last pancake onto a plate. His freshly trimmed beard held droplets of water from the shower. My own wet hair hung loose over an actual shirt of my own, not a refugee from the lost and found bin. He leaned against the fridge, maybe thinking about our conversation on the hilltop, or about the day ahead. I didn't try my insight on him to find out.

I handed him butter and syrup before he had a chance to snatch a pancake. "Probably too late to get started," I said, "and not sure when our next day off comes, but we should go to Yellowstone this summer. See the geysers and the animals."

"That's a thing people do." He followed me onto the porch.

"What's *that* supposed to mean? Do I have to wait for August until Yellowstone is snow-free? I wanna see a *buffalo*, some *wildlife*, damn it."

"Most of the snow should be gone by now, probably the rest of it in a few weeks. Right now is when the park starts filling up with people, though."

"And you don't like crowds?" I stabbed a piece of flapjack.

"Bonaventure had a crowd last night, Mo, but Yellowstone is *crowded*."

"Listen, mountain man, I just came from a year in Chicago. I grew up in Boston. You frontier kids think one's company, two's a mob, but I can handle myself around a bunch of tourists."

"I'm certain you can."

I glanced at him sideways before gazing into the pine forest that surrounded the back of the cabin. "Thanks for listening to me up there. I don't have a clue what's happening, but it's nice to have someone else with a…with experience to talk to." I turned back to him. "So, John, what *are* we gonna do today?"

"What do you want to—"

"No!" I ratcheted my voice into mock indignation and almost hurled a pancake at him. "You're the local boy. You know the people, places, things. You pick."

He sipped from a mug before answering. "I'm not actually a local. Northern Colorado," he revealed. "Did a year of college in Wyoming before joining the Army. After I got out, I bounced around a bit, then came up here." He nodded over his shoulder at the cabin. "This is the only thing I ever got from my dad's side of the family, other than the last name."

"Why'd you leave?" Maybe we could just talk until lunch, then talk until dinner, and end with drinks at the Diamond Rough. The answers could come from a simple touch, but I wanted to hear him tell me.

"The Army?" he replied. "Or college?"

"How long are those stories?"

He held his response. He hadn't just *been* over there, he'd *fought* over there. The names on his arm were evidence enough of what he experienced, what he lost, a scar on his other arm hinting at something he'd yet to divulge, something I'd yet to uncover. The glimpses revealed so far were surely just the tip of a ferocious iceberg.

Good thing I could swim.

"It's a long summer," he said.

"Fine." I returned to my breakfast. "But I'm not leaving Montana without some answers."

Before we could examine what *leaving Montana* meant the Jersey boys raced up on their bikes. They hopped off, flush with excitement and laden with canvas shopping bags. JJ was tied up in meetings all over town, the local merchants raking him over the coals for not giving them a complete picture of the mobs this season promised. The infusion of tourist dollars was nice, but stores already ran low on supplies, trash appeared on roadsides overnight, and the out-of-towners camped wherever they pleased. Part of me wished to be a fly on the wall for those discussions, another part knew I would get the feel of them the next time we saw JJ, and the rest of me felt a little bit sorry for a man in over his head.

The boys set up a badminton net after they started their food in the slow cooker. John ducked inside and returned with the book interrupted by our morning jog, and the day slipped away between rotating matches. I woke when my chair gently rocked, looking up to a can of ginger ale and a plate of savory vegetable stew over rice.

"There's a few things at the boathouse I need to do," John said. "Might not rain for a bit yet, but I have to get those sandbags off Liza's Hope."

"Do you want help?" Lucky asked. "JJ wanted me and Mickey to do it."

"I know what he said."

I sat up in the chair and accepted John's offerings. "You sure you don't want company? Or—" I looked around the yard. "Where're Carter and Gabby?" The studious neutrality on John's face wasn't enough to cover a fleeting smile, which was answer enough. I propped my foot on a short stool and set the plate on my lap.

"Sophie said she might swing by before dinner," John said. "She's playing again tonight, but we don't want to stay out too late before our first official day."

I settled my sunglasses on the end of my nose and stared up at him over the lenses. "You might not notice, John Mackenzie, but hardly anyone around here talks in terms of *numbers* when it comes to, y'know, *time*. Just mentioning it, given that you and the crew are set to run rafts full of human beings down the Big Steep River on a precise corporate schedule in about…"

I looked at the freckles on my wrist. "Some number of hours from now."

"Not knowing the time has never stopped us before."

THE INTRUSION OF A CHILL BREEZE broke me from my dreams.

Sleeping in a rocking chair might not have been the best idea, but the combination of warm sun and full belly had been more than enough to send me off to revisit the men from John's arm. The past week and year had sapped me of more energy than I realized, and I wondered if it would ever return in full.

John was gone on his errand. Mickey and Lucky had left during my nap. Carter and Gabby were—I smiled to myself. Even with the touch insight, I'd missed what was right in front of my nose. I was happy for them.

I stood, carefully and slowly, flexing my limbs back into working order. I wore no watch, my phone was inside, and I was not yet Montanan enough to tell time by the position of the sun, though its proximity to the tops of the ridges beyond the cabin suggested the day was nearly done, but not all the way gone. I shielded my eyes from the light of the departing sun before blinking back tears at the recollection of a dream still dissolving in my mind and on my tongue. Five men gone in a flash, but the details slipped away like minnows in the Mill Pond. Grabbing the porch railing steadied my breathing, touching something that couldn't touch back. Maybe a late afternoon walk would clear the fog.

I stepped inside long enough to throw on socks and real shoes and slip a flannel shirt over my tank top. I skipped the steps coming back down the porch to the driveway, passed the little Charlie Brown tree, and brushed my fingertips across its branches. I shivered at the unbidden and unexpected thought of cold ocean waves crashing against cliffs, wondering where the images came from.

Pine needles covered the ground near the highway. *Duff*, Carter called it. I followed the road away from town, higher into the hills, away from the logging-slash-jogging road. The morning excursion, a few rounds of badminton—Lucky and Mickey had challenged me and John to a winner-take-all doubles match, handily beating us—and a couple of good meals helped me feel…*good*, a silly realization that still surprised me after almost a month in this restorative hideaway: that simple pleasures were still pleasures.

The smell of evergreens and the sound of wind through their branches filled me with the confidence to follow another gravel road off the highway, one I hadn't noticed before. No sidewalks bordered this part of creation, and I passed fewer and fewer houses as my route took me deeper into the foothills. Keeping to this path would let me navigate my way back. John was right. The rain held off, and despite the bracing chill on the breeze, I felt strong. Insects droned in the bushes, unseen but powerful just the same.

Maybe approaching the connection between touch and insight from a more critical, more scientific perspective would teach me something new. Neurons and synapses misfired all the time. Feelings of déjà vu could be attributed to improperly wired memories, sensations of deeper intuition could come on the back of lucky guesses and educated assumptions. Trauma prevented feelings and thoughts from being stored properly, if at all…and that was the first time I saw my time in Chicago as trauma.

My mind had operated on autopilot for much of the previous year. Coming to Montana challenged me, opening me up in ways I had yet to explore. Maybe this alleged power was my mind just cleaning out accumulated debris after finally having a chance to rest, my long-dormant imagination making it feel like there was something special about me or my situation. I had missed the whole Carter and Gabby situation, after all, so this *touch insight* was still fallible, if it even existed.

The buzz of insects grew louder.

Of course dream-Ollie would appear aboard a ship at sea. Surrounded by rafts and water, he was of an age for war, and my subconscious filled in the rest based on movies and pop culture. Someone named *Kid Rocket* would have been young, the same as any soldier John served alongside. He hadn't pushed back on my guesses out of a desire to avoid confrontation, or to let me work through it on my own. Maybe there were no messages to discover, no hidden or deeper anything, so I could dismiss the dreams.

*Except…*Sera was there, in the courtyard, in the polar ocean, in the porch-dream, and even in the needles of that small pine tree outside John's cabin. Not the Sera from Zeebrugge, not the Sera I'd hallucinated after her death, but another version of her. I asked her in the porch-dream how she could take a man in out of the cold, or the heat, like he was a stray dog. She'd said men could be cats, too. She knew he was good, and he needed to meet her in Oklahoma so she could take him to Louisiana so he could return to Iraq so he could end up in Montana. The dream ended, the chill breeze cutting off her words, sending me down this road.

The noise of the insects reached a breaking point before snapping into utter silence. The scene ahead stunned me immobile. Long past the last house, the road narrowed and the river tumbled along rocks and logs, creating almost a waterfall. Ten posts pierced the ground, heavy metal wire connecting them to guard against running off the road over a steep embankment and into a ravine. The timbers were roughly hewn and flat-topped.

And on each post sat a giant black bird, all ten watching me.

No way to tell how long they'd waited for me, or whether I should call them crows or ravens or something else entirely. Their black eyes, black as their feathers as their beaks as their feet, followed me when I found the strength to move forward again, slowly, the sudden and overwhelming imperative to run not powerful enough to move my feet any quicker.

The nearest bird, gray tinges to the edge of its wings, bigger than the others, had only one eye. This elder corvid winked at me every time it blinked.

An angry explosion in a garbage bin broke the spell. The birds took flight as one.

I spun toward the sound. The forest here was thick, dark, and ancient.

Just past the first rank of trunks, a deer lifted his head, looked right at me, his fully formed antlers dripping with wet moss, before turning and bounding into the woods. For a moment, I swore he ran away on his back two legs.

Someone had carved a half-sized basketball court with a net-free hoop at one end of the jungle. A set of bleachers on the far side, just past where I'd lost sight of the buck, caught my attention. Stepping forward, I saw they weren't bleachers, but a set of stairs, like someone had wanted to build a house and started with the staircase before giving up. The court looked new, unbroken concrete, fresh paint demarcating the free throw line, at which stood a man in khaki slacks and a white button-up shirt playing by himself, lobbing easy arcing shots, recovering his own rebounds. He broke into motion, smooth and fluid as he made soft layups and dribbled between his legs beneath the basket.

He stopped just before taking a shot and approached me, tucking the ball against his hip.

The insect choir returned, quieter than before, a different pitch and tenor to their call.

I found my tongue. "Sorry, got lost in thought for a minute."

"Better to get lost in thought than on the road." His voice was as warm and humid as the forest. He was taller than John, athletic and strong, his face that kind of striking that could almost be *too* good-looking if it weren't tempered by a ready smile and…*impossibly* beautiful eyelashes. "But best not to get lost at all. Are you?"

"Am I what?"

His grin expanded and any previous guess at his age was dashed. "Lost?"

I tried looking over my shoulder, but couldn't break away from him or the stairs, nor remember how far I'd come, or from where.

"We've never seen your face in these parts," he continued, "though I'm somewhat newly returned myself." He looked me up and down. "I'd recognize a face such as yours."

OK, I thought, *too much.*

"That was too much," he said.

"I'm just—" If only the insects would stop. "I'm not lost. I'm staying… with friends?"

The sound of the bugs subsided, though they hovered on the border between the clearing and the forest.

His laughter set my skin to tingling.

My hand landed on my leg, patted the pocket on my shorts and came up empty. I left…somewhere…without my phone. Would a phone even work out here? "I should be getting back." I struggled to remember where that was. "To my friends."

"Brother Crossroads," the man said. "That's what *my* friends call me. Though they are fewer each year, they are more dear." He stood in place, but I swore he came closer. All the energy from the insects and the decay of the old trees pushed at me, like they wanted inside, like they knew the touch insight could work in both directions. "You and I could be friends."

"Well, Brother Crossroads, I'll tell *my* friends, I'll tell them you're back."

"Everyone will know I've returned." He knelt and set the basketball at his feet before retying the laces on one sneaker. "I've been gone a spell, true, but now I'm here and I intend on staying." He stood and offered me the ball. "You can stay, too."

"My shoes," I tried. "Not court legal."

More laughter, this time like ice chips falling on glass. "Just a little game of Horse, Miss…" He raised his eyebrows.

"Mo," I said, not wanting to.

"Not short for something holy like *Moriah*." His teeth flashed as he spoke.

"Haven't heard that one before."

"Divine like *Mohini*, then." His smile faded. "Bonaventure truly is one of the drains in the basin of the world, collecting lost and broken things.

Why here," he asked, narrowing his eyes at me, "of all places in creation to run after being cut adrift?" This time he did step forward, extended his hand toward me, palm down, fingers splayed. The ball dropped silently without bouncing, resting at his feet. My hand lifted to return his greeting, heavy but unstoppable, not wondering why only now he offered it, and what would grabbing an electric fence do to my touch insight—

The crunch of wheels on gravel and a car hurrying to a stop demanded my attention. I gasped for air, unaware of my need to do so. My hand pulled away and the insect drone vanished.

Thank the gods, here was one of their messengers. Sophie, small as a starling behind the wheel of John's truck, but big as life, leaned out of the window and smiled at me.

Brother Crossroads couldn't hide his visceral reaction to her arrival, which made me like her even more and him even less. "What are you doing here?" he asked.

"Hey there, Mo!" She beamed at me from behind gigantic dorky sunglasses, her wild and curly hair fluttering in the breeze that suddenly returned. "C'mon, we're gonna be late for dinner. Everybody's waiting."

"Everybody, wow, all of them." I injected false bravado into my reply. "Gotta go, Crossroads." Anger poured off him, some other emotion close to hunger, and I leapt into the car before he touched me or kidnapped us both and hid our bodies under the staircase by the basketball court.

Wishing I hadn't, I glanced in the mirror as Sophie whipped the truck around. There he was, hands at his side, clenching and unclenching, deprived of their target, his face twisted in petulant rage. The image disappeared as Sophie sped around a bend in the road.

"What," I said, "the *fuck* was *that*?"

She focused on the road ahead and put a hand on my shoulder, rubbing life back into me, cool water running from her touch into my muscles. I almost closed my eyes and cried.

"John didn't think he'd be back this year," she said, "otherwise we would've warned you." She glanced at me. "His name used to be Simon Titerville, we think. He had a reputation in Arizona, where he came from, and started a camp here for religious youth, the kind that make the fundamentalists look reasonable. He turned out to be too much fire and brimstone even for the deep-red out-of-state families that packed their kids off to study under him. Eventually they stopped sending them."

"And now he just, what, hangs out in the forest playing basketball by himself?"

We passed John's cabin and Sophie removed her hand, energy lingering and sweeping away the last of the cobwebs from the encounter in the clearing. She pointed to the cup holder between us. "I got your phone and stuff. Anyway, the camp shut down, some of it burned down—insurance scam, but they fell for it—and that's what's left." She shook her head. "I'd recommend not going back that way."

"You said *out-of-state* families." The last shreds of pressure left me. "Not locals?"

She stopped where the gravel road connected to the paved highway into town. "Montana might surprise you." She glanced both ways and let a speeding truck pass before pulling out. "They got an odd streak about a lot of things. Surprised me the first time I came out."

"You're not from here either?"

"Not many people from our end of the rainbow in these parts, are there?" She laughed. "I'm from Los Angeles. Not the fancy little beach towns, I mean for-real L.A." Sophie waved an arm out the window at the mountains. "Montana's one of the few states that lives up to its license plate name. If they'd been thinking, instead of killing everyone and their buffalo, they'd have made this whole Big Sky place a national park. Better yet, just leave it to those who know how to love the land without hurting it."

"Is that what brought you from L.A.? The land?"

"The land, the people, the possibilities." She shrugged. "I'm still there as much as I'm anywhere. Winters here are too much for my blood, though I *love* the summers. Carter claims it's *middle-of-nowhere-adjacent*, but Bonaventure is really a waystation on the path across our big awkward continent. We're on the way to and from loads of places: San Francisco, Seattle, the Twin Cities, Chicago, Denver, Calgary. Bands come and go all season long, the type that can't afford airfare or those who don't want to miss out on the broad shoulders of this nation." She drummed on the steering wheel. "My kind of music makers. I convince some of them to stop by, offer them my stage and my backup. Word spreads more every year. We get some real surprises."

"Anything as surprising as Brother Crossroads?"

"What I meant before, there's all kinds of religious, right?" We idled at a four-way stop, no traffic in any direction, just the darkening hills and mountains and gathering clouds. "The folks who claim spirituality without burdening themselves with the obligations of community, those who'd use a holy book as a doorstop—they're the ones damaging it for the rest of us. I'm a fan of those that allow people to be people, want to help them grow, love and bless 'em, and Crossroads, well…" She put the truck in gear and moved us forward. "Simon used to be the thumping kind. Now, he's a special kind of wicked, believes in Hell for sinners *and* believers. Maybe thinks he's smarter for having it figured out before the rest of us, like it'll earn him a better berth down there, like he'll get to do the whipping."

"An asshole, then."

"More than that. Something I can't figure out." She looked at me again. "I mean it, Mo. Please don't go back up there."

"He guessed my full name," I said. "No one does that."

Sophie kept her peace for a moment while the tarred strips of road thumped beneath the tires. "Further evidence he's to be avoided." She lifted a finger from the steering wheel toward the approaching storm. "Ever seen it rain so hard you thought it just *had* to be raining everywhere in the world?"

"How'd he know my name, Sophie?" I asked. "No one ever guesses right. And how'd you know where to find me?" The clouds tore open and let the heavens down hard to the accompaniment of lightning followed fast by thunder. "Why are you driving John's truck? I thought he went down to Liza's Hope."

We pulled up to the Diamond Rough, tourists and locals alike scrambling for cover with their hands over their heads. Sophie cut the engine and faced me. "How much do you know about John and the birds, Mo?"

chapter FOURTEEN

My encounter with Crossroads shook me, but walking into the raucous and overly warm lobby filled with laughter and conversation started to rebalance my nerves. The crowd was, once again, electric. Being around so many people intent on food and entertainment energized me, even without brushing shoulders or touching hands. Not wanting to inadvertently set off whatever metaphysical insight would come from contact, I kept my hands in my pockets and followed Sophie through the crowd to our table. John had asked her to find me before setting off to rescue the sandbags from the riverbank. The birds had known that I needed help, and why.

Carter and Gabby sat next to each other, Badger between them, and the Jersey boys fed the jukebox to fill the room until Sophie took the stage. JJ joined us, clearly having struck out with the blonde bartender, and pulled up a chair.

"Rough day?" Gabby asked him.

"About as expected." He passed bottles around the table and fiddled with the empty one in his hand. Maybe he didn't want the townsfolk or the tourists to see him drunk in public. Sure thing he could get drunk later at the Kane family condo. "The chamber of commerce agreed to step up their support to get the shops resupplied, and I managed to get a beer truck bound for Rabbit Springs to come here instead."

Carter laughed. "That couldn't've been cheap."

"I think you're doing OK."

"Thanks, Mo," JJ replied, "but not meaning to be rude, as a newcomer your opinion isn't as important. Those people live here. If I can't get them onboard, the next couple of months are going to be rough."

"Just because I'm not a local doesn't mean…" I had no idea what it meant, not after a day that started on the top of a mountain picking another fight with John, this time over tattoos and memories, a day that nearly ended with me shaking the hand of the town crank. Maybe I really was just passing through, another few months idling somewhere before the next stop on my destination-free journey until winding up back in Boston.

"Did you at least talk about the litter?" Carter asked.

"We have a whole marketing and public education campaign lined up," JJ said, "remind folks they have to take care of Earth, all that stuff."

Sophie set her drink down. "Tourists aren't gonna care, JJ, not enough. Some of them might, but you bring more crowds onto the river, you bring more people into town, it's gotta change what you say you love about this place."

"And if the town doesn't change," he said, "if we don't get a plan in place, some other group, some corporation is going to buy it up, one that's less interested than I am in keeping folks in place and preserving what we can. Do you think someone without a connection to Bonaventure is going to be interested in saving the Diamond Rough, or restoring it? What if they reopen the mines? This isn't just about the river," he continued, gaining steam. "The last few years, I got so immersed in the Wall Street life—"

"And made a ton of stinking money doing it," Gabby said.

"—that I missed the only things that've ever made me happy. Being on the river." He spread his arms wide. "Celebrating with so many wonderful people. This rafting outfit's just the first step. It's Big Sky. There's no limit!"

"Still sounds like you're trying to sell us on the idea," Sophie said. "Or yourself."

"Why are you so determined to question all of this? You only spend a third of the year here." He turned to me. "Or you. Even if you stick around through Labor Day, what does it matter to you?"

I'd seen these tics before in other faces, signs of an impending eruption, one I could defuse by simply ignoring the jab.

"I pay my taxes." I lowered my voice. "When I make enough money, I pay my taxes. I protested the war in Iraq, even without knowing anyone going there. I've stood up for children, for elders. My voice, same as anyone else's, is no more or less than anyone should have. It's not a big voice, despite what you might think, but I have an obligation to speak."

Mickey and Lucky descended on the table bearing pitchers of root beer before JJ could respond.

"New rule, fellas," Carter said. "What'd we decide, Gabby? They're allowed two? Three?"

"Three," she replied. "We're not bloody tyrants."

"You get three Bruce songs per night. That fine with you guys?"

"We like more than just the Boss," Lucky replied. "But that works for us."

"Sophie is here," Mickey added. "The jukebox can rest."

She stood. "I'm not playing for a couple minutes more," she said, "so I'll shove a couple more quarters in there for you guys."

A song I'd last heard on Baba's favorite oldies radio station spun to life. Gabby took Carter by the hand and hauled him out of his chair to the dance floor. Badger followed, happy to help them twist the night away. Human hands on human hips and shoulders, the dog close beside, and damn if the three of them couldn't cut a rug.

The Jersey boys bounced along to Sam Cooke's voice pouring out of the speakers. I remembered the way they sat together during our nighttime run, and despite missing Gabby and Carter's mutual pull felt a premonition. If a man could talk to birds, then maybe there *was* something beyond science to my touch. My encounter with Crossroads unsettled and confused me. We hadn't touched, but his energy crackled, like a piece of light bulb lodged in my head, and I was hungry and didn't know where John was, no one did, but maybe I could undo that encounter.

"Which one of you kids knows how to dance?"

They made a show of climbing over and pushing past each other to get to their feet for the honor of swinging me around. Mickey won out, bowing solemnly before taking my hand and leading me to the dance floor at the foot of the stage.

Happiness. That's all, no visions pouring off him as we spun. Mickey hardly left Lucky's side, and spoke far less than his chatty companion, but what I once took for reserve was actually protective watchfulness.

His hesitation evaporated on the worn parquet.

"Damn, Mickey," I said, "you take lessons?"

"Many years," he confessed, a gentle hand firm in the textbook location on my back. "At first, my parents are OK, until they tell me there is no career in dancing."

He spun and caught me again. "Tell that to Fred Astaire," I said.

"Ah, Mister Astaire, what a gentleman."

He grinned, and I confirmed weeks belated that he directed his smile over my shoulder, back to the table. Picturing them in the raft, in the dark, the Jersey boys sharing thoughts without words, I didn't need to touch Mickey to learn their secret.

I leaned into him and lowered my voice. "Does Lucky know how to dance, too?"

Panic flashed across his face, accompanied by tingling nervous energy transmitted across his hands. He looked again at his friend.

"Mickey, I didn't mean to pry."

His face softened and his touch eased.

"Is this obvious?" he asked. "Our parents, they meet through refugee resettlement. English language classes. We survived much, where we're from.

When we come to America, the music and the movies, they tell us we can be anything. Our parents." He shrugged. "Not as much."

"Is that why you like coming to Montana?"

He beamed. "In Bonaventure," he said, "all things are possible."

I squeezed his shoulder, caught the smile Lucky sent back while we twirled, and hoped that if I could feel Mickey's feelings, then he could feel the warmth and strength I sent back. *Gods*, to be so young, but to literally dance around the truth.

My partner dipped me, spun me again, and didn't miss a beat.

"What does the song say?" I asked. "*Dancing with the chicken slacks?*"

Mickey's eyebrows lifted and he started laughing. "Mo, do you mean… It's the *chick in slacks*. How could a chicken have pants?"

My laughter rose to join his, until the only thing keeping me on my feet was his momentum. *These kids are brave*, I thought, *and I can be brave, too.*

I CAUGHT SOPHIE before she took the stage. The crowd was restless, but it could wait for me to make my request.

"Anything," she said. Clad in a rhinestone vest and cowgirl hat, an entire summer ahead of us, in Bonaventure, all things were possible.

"Teach me how to do what you do."

BORN TO RUN AND BLONDIE sat ready on the trailer. The red-shouldered mountains west of Bonaventure glowed pink and then purple under the first truly warm dawn of the season. The waters of Lake Pando reflected the stately pine trees on its far banks with stunning clarity, like the boathouse perched on the edge of a cliff overlooking a hole in the world, through which someone could fall and emerge completely changed in the mirrored realm below the docks. Piles of clouds with hard edges caught and amplified the sunrise, far brighter than the day had a right to be so early.

The heat of the breakfast burrito in my hand focused my attention. John had left a plate of them for me and Carter, and we'd each eaten one on the drive to the boathouse and started more slowly on our second helpings. I brought one for John, seated on Blondie's edge, and tossed it to him. Snores from inside the raft suggested he wasn't alone.

John devoured the burrito, crumpled the foil into a ball, and lobbed it at the nearer of the two Jersey boys.

"Are we late?" I asked.

"Right on time," he replied. "First tour's not for an hour. Deacon and I rigged up the two rafts for this morning, and now he's checking the bus one last time. Gabby should be by shortly, and JJ likely won't be in until closer to nine. Heard he had a long day, getting grilled by business folks."

Carter and Badger settled in the raft between the kids, sliding his ball cap over his eyes. John stood and walked with me to the office.

"Where were you last night?" I unlocked and propped the door. "The jukebox was on fire, and then Sophie played nothing but dancing music. Mickey and Lucky took turns cutting a rug with me. Did you know they're professionally trained? Even JJ managed to have fun."

"That explains why they're all still asleep."

I opened the laptop that JJ's investment brought to the little office. "Don't tell me you're one of those guys who're like," I dropped my voice, "*Oh, sorry, Mo, I don't dance.*"

"I would've danced if you asked."

I turned away to hide the unbidden smile and flicked on the radio, fine-tuning the dial to catch the college station's signal.

"Anyway," he continued, "it took me longer than it should have to get all the sandbags."

The window looking from the front desk over the water would let me see when the rafts returned. A little set of shades covered the leaded glass. I paused before pulling them up.

"I don't know if you kept us off of Liza's Hope the other night because of a bad feeling you had, or because you knew something the rest of us didn't." I drew the shades up. "Something has always felt a little off about that place, and it was worse in the dark." I tied the drawstring off on a hook and faced John. "I met a guy yesterday who gave me the same weird vibes."

"Brother Crossroads. Are you OK?"

The laptop was still booting up so I made a face at it. "Sophie said he'd been run out of town on a rail, or exiled or something, but I ran into him at a basketball court in the middle of the woods, of all places."

"I'm sorry you had to meet him that way, or at all. He's…I wouldn't go back up there, not alone."

"Not planning on it," I said. "Just glad you and the birds knew I needed some help."

By the time we wrapped up the office chores and returned to the parking lot, the Jersey boys were awake and upright, engaged in conversation with our extraordinary bus driver.

"How come you don't run the river with us, Deacon?" I leaned on the porch railing.

"I am much too old to keep pace with such a young bunch."

"You're way younger than Ollie," I pointed out, "and not that much older than our head guide."

"Aren't you and I the same age?" John asked me.

"The reality is, I don't swim," Deacon said.

"Don't, or can't?" I said. "You're the only one who actually grew up here, right?"

"I was born in Bonaventure," he replied, "but my grandparents raised me in Idaho, along the Snake River, and I never swam."

"Too many snakes?" Lucky asked, eyes wide.

Deacon's smile acknowledged the earnestness of a question that, coming from anyone else, might not have sounded so sincere. "The Snake is a misnamed river," he said. "The white settlers asked the people they found near the water who they were, what they called the river. The language barrier, though, meant the question did not translate, nor did the thinking behind even asking. The people of the river replied like this…" He pressed his palms together in front of his chest and made wavy side-to-side motions. "The whites took this to mean a snake traveling through grass, for they rode horses and feared snakes. Really, the people of the river were craftspeople, and the hands showed the path the plaits of their baskets as they weaved."

"Probably an honest mistake."

We turned as JJ descended from the second story of the boathouse.

"The history of our people has not been marked by much honesty with outsiders," Deacon said, his voice holding no malice, "but what's a little mistake between friends?"

"Did you sleep at the boathouse?" John asked.

"Stayed up late trying to answer questions from townsfolk, replying to investor emails from back east." JJ smiled. "Big day, first day. Wouldn't want to miss a minute of it; wanted to be here to greet our first guests." He leaned around John to address the Jersey boys. "You two ready for the first load of passengers?"

"Wait a second," I said. "Deacon, what did you mean *the thinking behind even asking* what a river is called?"

He paused before answering. "Another story is that the hands represented the salmon that used to fill our rivers. The true meaning behind the gesture is stolen history. When your storytellers are killed, the *idea* of a true meaning is something we can never fully understand. We had, and still have, names for our places, yes, but not in the same way as marking a map, once and forever. The mountain we call Metis Peak," he said, pointing west, "has had many names in many lifetimes. Someone might want to name it, thinking the mountain is unchanging, but it moves, slower than the river, but moves just the same. What matters is that it's a mountain, a prominent one, visible for miles, and holds the headwaters of our river. One day, it may not be called the Big Steep, and Metis Peak may answer to something else. It's good, at times, to be reminded of impermanence."

Before any of us could approach an idea that big, the sound of crunching gravel demanded our attention. This time it was a car none of us knew, and out poured a group of humans we had never met.

"Big day, first day," I whispered.

The script, the spiel, the monologue. The rafters called it different things and, as Deacon alluded to, impermanence meant a lot to them. They rehearsed different versions and varied content and delivery by the day, based on the passengers and their moods. Their tone could be humorous or serious, academic or imaginary. A family with children received something unlike what a boatful of young women got. The rafters had practiced all week alongside their practical river skills, as Carter insisted the ability to gab and jaw was as important as the ability to tie a knot.

Here and now, though, before they set foot in a raft, I had the passengers' attention. Facing this family from Wisconsin (where they had *plenty* of rivers, according to one son, so why was *this* one any better) and a foursome of retirees from Arizona, my teacher's voice took over, verifying names and ages and account details, confirming medical information where necessary, and dispensing the first of three safety briefs.

Something inside me shifted when the passengers shuffled aboard the bus. Deacon closed the door and left me with JJ in the parking lot. I caught John's eyes before he gave the second safety brief. Despite the distance, no matter the glass and metal between us, an element of our repeated incidental contacts let me read his thoughts and send my own.

I want to be on the river, I told him, before he rode out of sight.

CHAPTER FIFTEEN

Log in to the laptop charged overnight. Check for new messages, cancellations, inquiries, or instructions from JJ or the investors. Erase the chalkboard from the day before and mark sunrise, sunset, air and water temperature, official USGS flow rates at the Bighorn and Blue Creek Dams upriver, the Diamond Dam at the east end of Lake Pando, crew assignments, trivia, and noteworthy animal sightings. Set out life preservers for the first trips.

Check the passengers in, give the safety brief, stand back and watch them pile onto the school bus and depart for the Slip. Wait for their return while preparing for the next run, juggle the aforementioned and unforeseen, and itch the entire time to be on the water with them, with him.

Clean up after the last run departs, set up for the next day, and plug in the laptop.

Dinner at the Diamond Rough, quick musical lesson from Sophie before she takes the stage, late night practice alone in my room, set an alarm for an early jog, avoiding all paths up the canyon. John joins me as often as not, Sophie as well, and start it all over again.

JOHN CAUGHT ME STARING at the point where the river dumped into the lake. I tried to cover my envy with a silent shrug. He tilted his head toward the bus. I didn't wait to confirm my interpretation of his gesture, just grabbed a life vest and asked Mickey to cover the desk and phone. I'd take care of the laptop when I got back, *please-OK-thanks-bye* and I ran aboard, passing Deacon and his congratulatory smile.

JJ and Carter put in at the Slip riding Little Durham and John asked if I wanted to narrate. Again, no chance for hesitation. If this were an audition, I didn't want to flub a line. Blondie slipped into the current and I slid the floppy lost-and-found hat off my head, drawstring tethering it around my neck. For all the passengers knew, I did this all the time. How could they know this was the best damn thing to happen to me this summer?

The raft ahead was full of rowdy aunts and boisterous uncles, ours filled with cousins no quieter, an entire extended family of commotion. I tried telling them that the Big Steep River was the dominant waterway in this part of southwest Pando County, which was technically true, tried sharing the story of FDR and his boys damming it up and bequeathing us a lake, but the only one giving me any attention was a little dark-haired girl seated amongst larger, noisier boys. I asked the passengers what animals they hoped to see, as though I could conjure them from thin air, and gods did I try to summon an elk or mule deer or even a duck just for her, the others too busy snapping selfies and chattering excitedly about evening plans to pay either of us any heed.

The little girl smiled when the resident flock of geese took off, beating the water and air with their heavy wings on their way out of the Kitchen. John timed our march downriver to approach the Natty Gann just as the morning tourist train blew its whistle. We passed under to the thundering declaration of iron and steam.

A motley assemblage of birds greeted us as our raft entered the Mill Pond—jays, magpies, even a sighting of the lone blue heron stalking fish in the reedy shallows evoking memories of its dinosaur ancestors. The Great Northern Flyway, I told the girl, was real, composed of millions of birds, maybe more, flapping over us on their way across continents, using the Mill

Pond as sanctuary and waystation on their journey. *It was real*, I repeated, as magical as it sounded, though her cousin took a break from his conversation to insist it had to be fake.

How could someone so young be so cynical?

John caught my attention with a subtle hand gesture lost on the passengers, though the little girl recognized the sudden tension in my shoulders. He pointed ahead and I turned, covering my nerves with recitations about grebes and loons. JJ had one hand on his tiller and the other pointed to a spot between our rafts.

A hawk struggled in the middle of the pond, wings trying to climb above the breaking surface of the water, flailing and failing to gain altitude. I'd never seen a bird gasp for breath before and wondered if anyone had ever watched a raptor drown.

John leaned into the tiller and the raft eased closer. The little girl watched me. I asked the passengers to stay calm and seated, though I could do neither. For all the practice and training we'd done in the last week, our crew had never discussed *recovery of a sinking bird of prey.*

John slid the emergency oar out from its resting spot under the gunwale, cradling the blunt end under his elbow. To the credit of those assembled, they stayed in their seats, hushed and rapt. John dipped the blade in the water as he nudged the raft the last few feet to close the gap. In one simple motion, he lifted the hawk from the water. Balanced on the flat end of the oar, it was too soaked and stunned to do anything other than blink in amazement and open its beak.

The passengers flinched when the bird let loose its call, something between a squawk and a cough, a guttural protest against its near-drowning and the plastic garbage wrapped around its talons, an exclamation of shock at being rescued by a human, recognition of the man who'd done it, and an exhortation that we do something, and do it quick. The call echoed off the trees and rocks and set every other bird to flight. The little girl didn't move a muscle.

The sound of rushing water brought me back to the present moment. No way could John hold the hawk on the oar while we ran the Speedway, nor could it join us in the raft. With the six-pack ring clinging to its feet, dumping it back in the water was a death sentence.

I tore my flannel shirt over my head, wrestling it past the big floppy hat and ponytail, and then balled it up and flung it aft. John caught my shirt and covered the bird, mouth moving silently as he comforted our guest. He held the hawk under his arm and used a pocketknife to slice the garbage from the bird's feet.

Finished, John stretched his arms over the side of the raft and deposited the raptor atop the nearer of the Twins. Freed from plastic and flannel, it preened its feathers. John nodded at me and I had time enough to utter a quick reminder to keep life vests zipped as the current grabbed us. Before we sped away and left the bird behind, it looked at me, then John, and called out once more.

The hawk's cry, piercing and urgent over the sound of water fighting stone, convinced me that Sera was right, Sophie was right, and I was right for hoping it was true—John could talk to birds. My connection to him gave me bird knowledge secondhand, gifted through the shards of a CD burning into my palms, the last act of love from my best friend, and we let the passengers ride without comment the rest of the way to the boathouse.

What else could be possible in a world such as ours?

TURNS OUT, ANYTHING WAS POSSIBLE. Everything was possible.

John got me on the water every few days, responsible for not much beyond keeping the vests on and spinning the river's story. I watched and listened to the Big Steep and its residents with open ears and new eyes, learning how the morning, midday, and afternoon runs each held their differences. In early June we added early evening trips, which opened up an entirely new perspective on the river. Deer at the water's edge in the Kitchen watched us with caution on our first run, but when we saw them later in the day near the Natty Gann, they couldn't have cared less about our intrusion. A month passed before we saw the buck, powerful and suspicious, standing sentinel with early-season antlers under the canopy of aspens.

The family of otters living on the border between river and lake surprised John. He and JJ were the only ones who had seen them before, years ago. A little boy near the absolute lower age limit for what JJ's insurance company would cover on the water was the first to spot them, and I nearly offered him the opportunity to name the creatures. Deacon's story about basket weavers and mountains stayed my suggestion. Instead, I informed the young adventurer of his solemn duty to tell his friends back home, tell them why the otters deserved our respect.

After John's hawk rescue, we noticed a change in the habits of our local birds. Ducks gave way more easily, geese watched us with something like avian understanding, and even the raptors studied us calmly from their dead-tree perches as we passed. Each time I looked to the rafter with the birdspeak power, but he said not one word about it, whether on the water or in the Diamond Rough or at the cabin. The few times I asked him about it on our morning jogs he would increase the pace. The music from Sophie and her guest artists swept us away each night and I promised myself to ask John again the next day. Once, I forgot to throw the question at him and gave up caring. His magic had as little explanation as my own, was there just the same, and that was fine by me.

I used my touch insight sparingly, if at all, avoiding handshakes with customers and rationing hugs with the rafters. Each time my skin touched another person a flash of understanding appeared, the longer the connection the more pronounced the peek, and my dreams became glimpses of other lives. By the middle of June, I gave up contact almost altogether, except among the crew, and only talked about it with Sophie. Through trial and error I figured out how to dampen the omnipresent buzz generated by other living creatures, images and thoughts leaking through even without physical connection, and learned to tune much of it out.

The days grew longer even as they ticked by faster. Part of me wished for a genie's lamp, if only for one wish, the other two be damned. My one wish would have been to slow it all down.

We had the enchantment of Sophie's guitar and piano backed by traveling bands and minstrels. The love between the Jersey boys and the constancy of Carter and Gabby and the cracking of JJ's curated façade that revealed a human beneath provided strength and security in a makeshift family. Even with all that, and supported by Deacon and Ollie in our daily endeavors, we still had plenty of encounters with the most annoying, if not dangerous, animal in all of Montana—the irrational tourist.

A family from Indiana dominated a Monday afternoon ride with preseason football conversations, river be forgotten. We nearly didn't depart with that load, not until the father and his corn-fed sons put on their life jackets and put them on the right way. The glares from the other passengers convinced them to comply.

A California church group reserved three rafts for a massive morning run, and then insisted on monopolizing the time to sing hosannas and hymns, ministering to the unsuspecting humans in the fourth raft. The missionaries asked if we could stop in the Mill Pond for a series of impromptu baptisms, and I reminded them of the contracts they signed, that they would not voluntarily exit the rafts until we returned to the boathouse. One preteen proselytizer challenged my geology lesson, insisting the Big Steep Canyon couldn't *possibly* be older than six thousand years because his grandma *said that God said so*. I told him *my* Nani worshiped *hundreds* of gods, including one with the head of an elephant, and when we hauled ashore, the little missionary insisted to his mother that *he* wanted a god with the head of an elephant. I neither expected nor received a tip that day.

A bachelor party arrived—*this time on purpose*, I told John—and insisted on going down the river with me and Gabby as their guides, promised gratuities and then some, came close to demanding it as some sort of tribute for the groom-to-be. John countered each of their hints, entreaties, bribes, and threats with monosyllabic refusals until, deflated, they piled into a raft with Carter and JJ, who promised them recompense at a bar in Rabbit Springs replete with women. Gabby told me after their vehicles departed our parking lot, cars crammed full of hooting and hollering cavemen, that she knew the bar JJ was taking them to, it was only popular with ranchers and their wives, and our boss had somehow done a good deed.

Even as the solstice approached, replaying those incidents and others, I recognized they weren't really *that* terrible, just people mostly good-natured and looking to connect with something that didn't have an outlet or an off switch, and the smile stayed on my face for all of June.

OF ALL THE UPDATES AND CHANGES to our operation remaining on the project list, moving into a bigger space would have to wait until JJ's promised riches came pouring in. For now, we managed to squeeze him, me, Mickey, and sometimes Ollie (when he wasn't fishing with his buddies), other times Deacon, off-duty rafters, and stray passengers into the cramped office where I'd first met the ancient merchant mariner.

Badger had a permanent bed under the counter. Other than that, the office was in a constant state of flux, a transitory evolution and devolution of life jackets and chalkboards and spare paddles and the expanding lost and found bucket. The last four years of detritus, according to Gabby, had already been eclipsed by what the rafters collected since opening day. This worked out well for me, continuing to dress in other people's cast-offs and the unintentional hand-me-downs, to the point where I could be selective about my wardrobe. The bucket contained a baffling variety of items, and we spent the better part of one morning trying out theories to determine how a brassiere ended up being *donated*—as Carter put it—to the collection.

According to river lore, a similar event occurred during one of John's runs years before, but he refused to confirm or refute any of our hypothetical explanations.

I pressed against the counter to let JJ pass behind me. He was in rare form, his normal harried look replaced with an actual smile. Granting me access to the corporate email account provided a glimpse of the familial, masculine, and patriarchal pressure that hinted at why he ran the river less and less often. Only snippets of conversation came through his ever-present earpiece, and my attention was split between replying to an irate customer's email and showing Mickey how to update the records. The rest of the rafters played a variation of the rock-throwing game the Jersey boys invented in the parking lot, now all the rage, and the noise combined so that eavesdropping on JJ, fun and informative as that might have been, was almost a futile effort.

Almost futile, since his voice rose to compete with every other sound in the vicinity.

"You're not hearing what I'm saying, bro," he said, again. I wasn't sure which bro he was talking to, or how many were on the call. He and I traded places, his turn to squeeze against the counter as I grabbed another of Ollie's ancient logbooks off a shelf.

"We're doing big things, Hutch. I've emailed you guys the documents, all the investor portfolio stuff, but that's just the *numbers*. You have to see this place to believe it."

One last shuffle and I was back at the counter with Mickey to hand him the leather-bound ledger. We were only about halfway done with transcribing the old logbooks. The biggest obstacle was deciphering the cryptic daily notes written in an inscrutable hand on disintegrating yellow paper. We were almost up to 1980, and I was curious to see what the log entry reflected for my birthday.

Thankfully, Mickey's calm and patient nature and his childhood exposure to Cyrillic letters gave him a preternatural ability to read the old boatwright's handwriting.

"It's better than Moab, Boomer. No, different, but better. Yes, I've rafted the Grand Canyon. We were all there, Cap. It's so crowded. This isn't whitewater, but it's different. I don't know, animals, nature, all that stuff." JJ looked at me, threw his arms up, and shook his head. "What can I say to get you guys out here?"

I waved Mickey away from the logbook and reached for the laptop.

"Fly from Westchester so your sorry ass can get some fresh air, Boomer. Your dad never uses the jet. If you guys could just see—"

I spun the computer to face him and pointed at the screen. The Big Steep River Expeditions homepage was a small miracle. Lucky was an amateur web designer and had built it over the course of one coffee-fueled weekend. Ollie accepted the creation but was wholly uninterested in the website or the internet on which it resided.

JJ's face lit up. A photo slideshow, populated at first by scanned images from years past, gradually updated with digital pictures from the last month, was as good an advertisement as any.

"Go to our website, guys. Yes, we have electricity out here, Cap, how do you think I'm talking to you dummies? Are you there yet? How can you look at these pictures and not wanna come?" He gave me a thumbs up. "That's what I'm *saying*, bros! We've got the best guides in the West, there's a whole section about the town and stuff to do, this isn't some fly-by-night thing. You can drop some serious cash out here, but you'll have a blast." He winked at me like a cartoon character. "We're having an investor weekend in August. I'll send you guys the date. We'll open up for a second round, you guys can still get in on the ground floor. It'll be a huge show." He lay his hand on mine and the desperate gratitude radiated off his body. "That's right, the best guides in the West."

JOHN ROCKED IN THE CHAIR on the porch. I hopped on the railing and swung my feet.

"You have a whole picture book of Yellowstone."

"Saves you the trip." He set his feet on a stool.

"Not the same thing." I pointed a foot in his direction. "We're off tomorrow. I'm going to make the drive."

"That's something people do," he said. "It's a place people go."

"Oh, that's right, you think it gets *too crowded*." I smiled and jumped down. "You have seen your own picture book, right? Old Faithful, giant herds of bison, wolves for the first time in a hundred years. Do you want to come with?"

"I have to run to Sherman, help Deacon pick up the new transmission for the bus. Do you want to come with us instead?"

I knocked the stool out from under his feet, setting him back to rocking. "If I don't go now, I never will."

"Let me know what you think when you get back."

I LET THE DOOR SLAM and sought out John. He stood at the stove, stirring what smelled like delicious and hearty soup, but I wasn't about to let my stomach get in the way of the frustration saved up over the previous twelve hours, just for him. He turned his head over his shoulder and read my face. He put the spoon down and, to his credit, did not offer anything like a grin, which somehow made me angrier.

"You weren't joking about the crowds, mountain man," I said, "but you didn't say anything about the absolute *hordes* of humanity, and the lines. Everywhere the lines."

"Did you see any buffalo?" He fully turned to face me and a hint of smile appeared before he forced it back into hiding.

"Oh, *tons* of them." I would have swung at him if he hadn't passed me a glass of wine. Off days for us were off days for Sophie, and after my dawn-to-dusk trek I had no desire to be around any humans, John partially excepted, so the Diamond Rough was not on the evening's agenda. "They come right up to the window when you're stuck in a thirty-minute traffic jam, and they're a lot bigger than my little Camry."

We finished the entire pot of wild rice soup, reduced the fresh loaf of bread to crumbs, and sat sipping our second glasses of wine. I'd chugged the first, which was not advisable but necessary, given my mental state. The night symphony of crickets, bats, and birds helped settle my lingering agitation.

"Is that what JJ wants to do to Bonaventure?"

John shrugged the first part of his reply. "Maybe worse. Maybe not. At least there they have rangers to help corral the crowds, make sure no one tries to ride the animals."

"How come you let me go? You knew it would not be a…pleasant experience."

"You should make your own choices," he replied. "If I gave you my detailed negative review you might not have made the decision on your own."

"How come you never fight me on anything?" I asked. "You hardly fight anyone. It was a noteworthy event when you pushed back against JJ during the practice run, and that was more than a month ago."

"I gave up fighting after I saved the world."

"That argument we had, the confrontation in Zeebrugge, when I basically accused you of being a war criminal after you'd cooked us dinner—"

"You don't give yourself enough credit," he said. "You never actually said *war criminal*."

"That's just it!" I swung forward, the creak of the chair disrupting the crickets and owls. "That night, you never talked about making the world safe for democracy. You admitted you never thought in those terms, so how can you sit there and say you *made the world safe for*—"

"That's not what I said."

The first time John cut me off had been perfunctory. The second time, there was nothing like violence in his words, but there was urgency, like he was once again trying to rescue someone.

If I could have touched him without strangling him, just to get the insight, I would have.

Replaying his words, though, I realized he was right.

I gave up fighting after I saved the world.

Saved the world.

"How come," I said, "in all your storytelling, all our late-night talks and morning jogs and river running, all the time we talk, you've never told me what really happened over there?" The dreams about the courtyard and the snake and the dog and the man with triangle eyes haunted my sleep, every fifth night a more detailed exploration of those five minutes that seemed to take an entire lifetime to tell. "You gave me a rundown on my first night here, but it didn't make sense. Maybe I was too tired. You've hardly touched upon anything that happened between the time you left Louisiana and when you left Iraq for good."

Where did he get the scars? Who were the men inked on his arms? What actually *happened in that courtyard?*

We both shut up, though I ached for an answer.

He stood and I reached out, tapping his leg with my foot, just enough for me to know he was OK. Even that small contact felt like running my feet against carpet and touching a doorknob.

"The rangers," I said, "the ones at Old Faithful, they entertained us while we waited for the geyser to go off. They talked about the trash cans in Yellowstone, how they're bear-proof."

His silence and presence were permission enough for me to continue.

"This one ranger, she told us that crows will work together, one of them opening the trapdoor on the bear-proof can so the other can fly in and get the food. She flies in knowing he'll let her out."

The night was dark enough that we couldn't see each other.

"It's fine if you have a bear-proof heart, John. Just be sure it's not bird-proof."

CHAPTER **SIXTEEN**

Nothing—not JJ's increasing demands on my time and energy, not the heat of midsummer, not even the hare-brained antics of the growing throngs of tourists—knocked me off the upward trajectory of late June. Our free days came less often as word of our magic little river got out, which meant I rotated out of the office and into a raft each week. Nightly concerts courtesy of our transcendent entertainment coordinator kept our spirits high, and a regular rotation of guest artists ensured no two shows were the same.

A punk band from Los Angeles had just wrapped up their first set. Their half-hour break would be enough time to refuel and recharge, musicians and audience alike. The Jersey boys fed a roll of quarters into the jukebox and bestowed baskets of fries upon our table.

"Your guests not joining us for dinner, Sophie?" Carter asked.

"Fries aren't dinner, babe." Gabby offered him a handful.

"They wanted to see the night sky," Sophie said. "The bassist's an old flame of mine and he's a sucker for stargazing. I suggested they head to the edge of town before starting the second set. They promised to kick it into high gear once the families with kids leave."

JJ rolled an empty bottle between his hands. "Let them know if they stick around, we'll run them down the river tomorrow, free of charge."

"That's mighty generous of you," the singer replied. "What's put you in such a mood?"

"A guy can't be friendly with the entertainment?" He leaned forward and grabbed the bottle in one hand. "Am I the only one here who follows the election? Mitt just won Utah. No surprise there, but it means he's officially wrapped up the nomination. I can afford to be magnanimous." He winked at Sophie. "Besides, a few promotional shots of the hottest band from southern California in one of our rafts, maybe Mo writes up a little article for the website, that's gotta drum up some business, get us attention from a younger demographic."

"There's an election this year?" We laughed at Carter's question.

JJ sat back, refusing to let his excitement abate. "Why am I the only one who ever gets political? You guys should pay more attention to the news."

Sophie leaned forward, claiming the space he vacated. "You're the only one among us who gets to use politics as a hobby, JJ. The rest of us live political lives by virtue of who we are."

"What do you mean?" Lucky asked.

Sophie swept a hand around the table, starting with the Jersey boys. "Refugees from east and west, countries bombed by our own. Black woman who wants to be a doctor. Person with a disability. Daughter of immigrants, woman of color, and a teacher. Veteran of another war. Queer *and* a person of color," she said, ending with herself.

JJ paused long enough that I wondered if some of Sophie's words actually made it past his ears. He knew each of our identities, but didn't *know* them, and the calculations in his head were apparent to me even without touching him. None of us looked for an apology, but the fact he took a second to weigh the singer's words counted for something.

A *little* something.

"John's a veteran, huh?" JJ grinned. "We could advertise that for the Fourth of July."

"*That's* what you took away?" Sophie said.

I leaned toward John. "Guess he knows you're a vet now."

"Think it changes anything?" he asked.

"Most of the seven or so billion people on this planet don't hate me, JJ, because they don't think about me. They hold no ill will." Sophie put her hands flat on the table. "Though they're few, there are a couple of people I've wronged, or have a grudge against me, one that's earned because of something I did."

"I was just—"

She cut him off. "I don't count you as one of them, cowboy." I could tell she *needed* JJ to understand her words. "But there are some, and too many, who *do* hate me, and those of us at this table, though they don't know us, on account of who and what we are. *That's* what living a political life means."

These two sparred often, mostly over well-worn ground, references and innuendo and shorthand enough to sustain what Carter described as a *lukewarm* war. Instead of pursuing this new line of conflict, though, Sophie broke away from what could have been an interesting argument, if only for its novelty, and caught my attention. She nodded toward the back of the stage. "We have a few minutes," she said.

"What is it you two do back there?" Lucky asked.

Sophie threw an arm around my waist. "Whatever she's doing, she's getting better each time we do it."

"YOU REALLY MEAN IT?" I settled onto the small wooden stool in the cramped storage room that passed for Sophie's office space and practice studio. "You think I'm getting better?"

"We shouldn't say things we don't mean." She sank into the cushions of a ratty armchair and passed me the loaner guitar. Another one stayed under my bed back at the cabin. "You've been practicing in your free time."

"When I can." Tuning the strings helped warm up my fingers, the instrument no longer strange or heavy in my hands. "Less and less of it recently."

"John still doesn't know?"

"I don't think he does. He sleeps pretty soundly." I picked out the chords of a song she and I had been working on, one that felt…appropriate, if that made a lick of sense outside my own head. My first lesson had been just the two of us discussing songs and memories, and I'd told her about the burned CD Sera left me. Sophie helped me browse a collection of sheet music to find a song to learn in a few weeks, one that would express some of the words and feelings bouncing around my insides. "Still not sure he's what this is all about."

Sophie didn't react, flipping instead through the pages of a photo album. "This one." She handed me the book. I balanced it and the guitar on my lap and examined the picture. The date was scrawled in the upper corner of the page. Someone had snapped the photo at the beginning of last summer, the same day Kirk took me to a Cubs game, just before he started consuming the next year of my life. The image faded already, picking up delicate weeping tones that made it look far older. Sophie wore a long skirt and camisole, John squinted at the camera, JJ, Gabby, the Jersey boys, Carter and Badger, Ollie, a few others I didn't recognize…and there was Deacon, leaning out of the school bus door with a rubber clown nose on his face and a paintbrush in his hand.

"We gotta take another picture like this." I looked up. Sophie's expression made me feel as if she waited for more, that I missed a key element. I glanced back at the photo.

Between last year and this, Deacon had painted BIG STEEP RIVER EXPEDITIONS on the flank of the bus, covering up the name of the previous owner in big block letters. Here though, frozen in time, the bus was new and fresh, or newer and fresher than I knew it in Montana, but older and more tired than the last time I'd seen it in its previous incarnation. The original words blared from the picture and echoed inside my head.

ZEEBRUGGE PARISH SCHOOLS.

"The." No other words manifested on my tongue, dumbstruck and unsure what this revelation meant.

"He went down to Louisiana," she said. The music from the jukebox in the main hall filtered past the wall, through the door, the lyrics indecipherable but urgent. "Last year, early May. He told me about his time there, with Sera and Anita and you, all of it. He had a hunch and said he needed to go." The cushions of the armchair nearly swallowed her up. "When he got there the town was being sold off for spare parts, hardly anyone was left. Ollie's previous bus broke down at the end of the summer before, so John came away with something, if not what or who or why he went down there in the first place."

Words finally found their way into my mind, too many to get out of my mouth, unsure what sequence to fit them in, so instead I tightened my grip on the guitar. Sophie extricated herself from the cushions and found another stool, dragged it over, and sat facing me, our knees nearly brushing, small sparks leaping across the gap. It felt like waving a fork near an outlet.

She took the album back. "You sing these songs because you want them sung, Mohini," she said, "not for any other reason. If you can't find what you want to say in words, sometimes music can help, more often it can't. John's a good man, sure, but you have a history neither can change and a future that'll take two to create."

I jammed the heel of a hand into my eye to rub away the tension and laughed. "Kirk had a point," I admitted, voicing whichever thoughts managed to muscle their way out first. "When he was bored with something, not good at it, he moved on. He was bored with us, with me, because I was boring, on autopilot, maybe the whole time we were together. I was part of the problem."

"Doesn't excuse how he treated you."

"No." My tears didn't arrive, but I plowed ahead. "I want to acknowledge my part in it all, though, even if Kirk never does. There're times I'm not sure I know how to, you know, *be* that way for someone anymore. One whole year, still gut-punched from losing Sera, then having Zeebrugge and our kids taken away, and then I had no idea what the next step in my life was supposed to be."

"Nothing is *supposed* to be anything." She moved my fingers back to the strings, inviting me to strum them again. The basic chords she taught me gave me strength.

"I had goals, Sophie. Plans. I was gonna be *somebody*. My parents were so…put together, capable. Every week I talk to Mama and every week I'm reminded that they had far harder things to face and came away with the life they wanted, became who they wanted to be, who their parents wanted them to be. The thing is, she's never the one reminding me. She just wants me to be happy, but I don't know if I know what that'll take. They've never pressured me about my choices, but I always felt…adrift. Not even like a river, a river has places to go," I said, echoing Carter. "Sometimes I don't even feel like an adult. If only I had a map."

Her laughter was my answer and my anchor. "You don't need a map, just a compass. The minute you figure out everyone else is as scared as you, that's the minute you become an adult." She stood up and brushed the hair from my face, and then leaned forward and kissed me gently on the forehead. "And you *are* somebody, Mo."

"WE'VE MAXED OUT OUR RUNS," JJ declared. "Mo's run the numbers—four trips a day, two rafts per trip, twelve people per raft—and we're constrained by math."

John and Gabby looked at me while Carter massaged Badger's shoulders. Ollie and Deacon worked on the new bus engine, and the Jersey boys washed JJ's Land Rover. Every time he tossed the keys at them, it was for a quick rinse of his car, which stayed relatively spotless while the rest of our trucks and bikes and bodies gathered dirt and dust amid a rapidly heating summer's worth of sweat.

Not that I minded. By the time July rolled around, I embraced the grime for a day or two at a time, tying my hair back in a ponytail each morning and stuffing it under my floppy hat, showering mostly at night. I realized just then that I hadn't shaved my legs in almost a week.

We assembled on the boathouse porch once again and JJ was giving us *another* earful about how hard it was to *actually run* a company.

"There's only so much daylight," John said.

"Still some things money can't buy," Carter added.

"And we're already flippin' exhausted at the end of each dad-gum day," Gabby said. JJ's language restrictions must have permanently warped her dialect, even though there were no passengers present. "Less time off, that's tough, fine. More runs mean more money, and I like money as much as the next girl. Med school won't be cheap, but we gotta be *safe*, JJ."

"And we can't split the crews up any, even if we had more rafts, which we don't," Carter said, finishing another round of discussion unchanged in three days. JJ was right, math was right, everyone was right. We ran at maximum occupancy in all four rafts and still turned people away at the docks, in the parking lot, at the Slip, even at the Diamond Rough. I stopped replying to customer emails complaining about the lack of capacity and had nothing more to add to the discussion. Hadn't, in fact, since the first round of arguments. Tomorrow was an honest-to-goodness day off for everyone, our first full rest period since my trip to Yellowstone, and it fell on the Fourth of July. We'd threatened a mutiny to get JJ to honor the holiday with temporary independence. Sophie would host an Old Crow Medicine Show tribute band tonight. They would stick around to ring in the Fourth tomorrow and, rumor was, this band had the original lead singer's second cousin, or something. We were in danger of missing their opening set. I had no clue who Old Crow Medicine Show was, didn't know their music but, if they were as good as the Los Lonely Lobos from the week before, then the Diamond Rough would be packed to capacity.

"That settles things." JJ clapped his hands together. We perked up, as we'd not reached this point on either of the previous two nights. "We'll bring on some rafters from Gardiner."

"That was an option?" John asked.

"We're actually killing them in new bookings," JJ replied, "and don't look to slow at all. I can pay the guides more than what they get down there, and I can snatch up some surplus rafts for next to nothing. We've got a hell of an online presence, and we've got better-looking guides."

I stopped tapping the clipboard against my leg when he looked at me and Gabby.

"Did you say *better-looking guides*?"

"We've been plastering pictures all over social media," he said. "You, Gabby, the Jersey boys, heck, even Badger attracts a certain clientele. We're playing the cards we have, using the tools at our disposal."

"Capitalism in action," I said.

"Exactly. We run a tamer river, they have more actual wildlife, and they're closer to the national parks, but we're beating them hands down in reservations and online reviews. Five stars all around. I'm not kidding when I say y'all are a large part of why we're doing so well, so far ahead of the competition."

"Didn't use to talk about *competition*," Gabby muttered. "Poaching river guides."

"It'll take time to train them," John said.

"These guys come pre-trained," he replied. "Plus you trained Mo in less than a week, and she was a complete rookie."

"She was a special case," John answered.

Before I could challenge either of them on any of what they said, JJ pressed on. "We just have to get them up to speed on the Big Steep. We have a big investor weekend in early August. Big. I need good numbers in the next few weeks to show them, really pull out all the stops for what we can do in Bonaventure, set us up for next year and beyond. The next few weeks are going to be *busy*." He rubbed his hands. "Running the company takes too much of my time for me to be on the water, at least until after the investor weekend. I'm officially pulling myself out of Carter's raft. Gabby," he said, turning first to her, then me, "you'll ride with him in my place. And Mo, John and I agree you're ready to be a part of his crew for good."

None of the rest of the conversation, not John's begrudging acceptance of the Gardiner plan, Gabby's teasing of her new rafting partner, not even the bus engine coughing to life under Deacon's ministrations registered in my consciousness. We got to the Diamond Rough and the first song blasted from Sophie and her New Raven Homeopathy Revue friends, fiddles and accordions and a penny whistle unstopping my ears before I could take a full breath again.

I'm going on the river…for good.

WE DRAGGED BLONDIE to the water's edge. I managed not to stub my toe on any rocks in the dark. The other rafts ventured toward the center of the lake, propelled by gentle paddle strokes.

"We just sit in the rafts? And we can see the town fireworks from here?"

"You can lie down if you want," John said.

I held the tether line tight and looked up. "The views *are* better out here. Maybe we'll see a shooting star."

"Maybe."

I scrambled into the raft and John leaned forward, shoving it the last few feet before hopping in to join me. We took our time paddling to join the others, the sounds of nature quieting as we left the world behind. I passed John the line and looked for the cooler. He put a foot on the gunwale, waited a moment, and then heaved the line through the air to Mickey. The Jersey boy caught it and tied us off to Born to Run, already hooked to Magnolia. I passed John a cold can, which he cracked open and used to salute the others before settling down on the bottom of our raft, draping his legs over the side and lying back to stare up at the firmament.

I joined him, our heads meeting in the middle and feet pointed outboard. I bundled my flannel shirt beneath my head and hoped my sandals would stay on, though part of me didn't care if they fell in the lake. There were plenty more in the lost and found bin, and sandals floated.

Most of the time.

"Carter dropped an anchor," John said, "so we shouldn't drift too much. And we're all tethered, so if we drift we'll do it together."

"Nice to have company if we get lost," I joked. "That was a beautiful sunset."

"I like that you haven't grown tired of the sunsets yet."

"Does that happen?"

A pair of ospreys winged overhead, maybe on their way home.

"I saw Brother Crossroads the other day. Didn't mean to. I haven't been back up the canyon in his direction since that first time, but he saw me after my run. He looked to be headed toward town."

"He's creepy," John said, "and I don't want to tempt anything by claiming he's likely not dangerous. Nothing that can be proved, at least. There's a reason no one likes having him around. I don't think he has any power, and I've never seen him in town."

A splash that could have come from a fish or a bird broke the tension. "Why'd you get out of the Army? You never told me."

"When you and I met in Zeebrugge, that was my third time in Iraq in four years. When our battalion got back to America, the Army promoted me to staff sergeant."

"Is that high up?"

"It's high enough to consider making it a career. Our battalion was new at the time; the Army made it just before they sent us over. We got… enough of us didn't make it back that they deactivated the battalion, then sent us all to different units." He finished his beer and I could tell he didn't want a second one. The rise and fall of our chests set the raft to trembling. "My new unit, they didn't believe what we'd been through. Can't blame them. If I wasn't there myself I'd have a hard time believing it, too. Still, based on my experiences they figured some of it had to be true. There was a big seminar in North Carolina for the guys the Army wanted to keep, the ones like me trying to decide what to do next. A lot of the others were excited for it, but I thought that a free hotel room and trip out of Georgia would help clear my mind."

"It didn't."

"Not at all. They brought in a bunch of bigwig generals, a guy who earned the Medal of Honor in the Korean War, lots of motivational speakers to get us all pumped. I'll admit, it nearly worked. But then they let this author talk to us. A Vietnam vet. He got up and started talking about the *natural warrior*, the born soldier."

"What's that?"

"Most societies, they don't have a permanent warrior caste. Guys like to fetishize the ones that do, but even those—the Spartans, the samurai—aren't how we picture them. A standing peacetime Army is only a recent invention. Most of the time society calls up citizens to fight on its behalf, they go to war, do what they have to, and then come home. The natural warriors, though, the born soldiers are the ones that might be teachers, or barkeepers, or factory workers."

"Or college students."

"Exactly. They come from other walks of life. Civilians with no concept of war. Once they're exposed to combat, though, not just the danger, but the amplitude—the way smoke smells, they hear the gunfire—not gonna lie, there's a…a *rush* to war that, for some, once they get it, there's nothing else they want to do."

I turned toward him. "You didn't think that was you." Not a question. I could pull the knowledge out of him with a touch, but his guilt radiated off him like the ripples set off by our rafts, touching everything and everyone around him. His sorrow for the men he'd lost there, guilt over losing Sera back here, and anger over the inability to change the past combined to stoke a fire deep inside his soul. "You don't think you're a warrior." I lifted a hand to brush the side of his face, not seeking insight, offering only comfort, something to calm the turmoil. "You're wrong, John."

"How?"

I sat up, turned around, blocking his view of the stars, and pulled my hand back.

"There's more to being a warrior than just killing," I said. "Last week, you defused a fistfight at the Diamond Rough with nothing more than a terrible joke. You could probably face down Brother Crossroads if it came to it, and I've never even heard you raise your voice. The way you are with Mickey and Lucky?" I stroked the side of his face again, catching a tear and carrying it away to fall in Lake Pando. "You're a father to both boys. You're a true friend to Deacon and Carter, Gabby and Sophie think of you as a brother, Ollie acts like a proud dad around you, and you're even kind of a role model to JJ. You might not see it, but he wants to impress you so badly."

"What am I to you?"

My hair hung down, framing his face. "Are you still in love with Sera?" The question circled above us like the ospreys. He said nothing, but nothing was still an answer. I leaned away, back against the gunwale, and he sat up to look at me across the darkness. Our feet tangled together. Neither of us moved them. "I've been lost since she died." My arms wrapped around my chest to prevent the sobs from coming. "I don't know who I am."

"Who do you want to be?" He tapped my foot with his. "I'd like you whoever you decide to be, whoever you have it in your power to become.

And you have an amazing amount of power."

"Thanks to that burned CD?"

"Even before that."

The dome above us erupted, first one, then two, then a hundred shooting stars streaked from one end of the heavens to the other. The meteor shower intensified, wishes beyond counting, enough for everyone in creation. My lips moved with the flares of light. The mountains west of us joined the show. Storm clouds dark and invisible loomed over Mount Metis and Sherman Peak and the other unnamed summits, lightning flashes illuminating the slopes and striving to outshine the meteors. I leaned over the side of the raft, trying to watch it all at once, and the water beneath us glowed. The other humans in other rafts sat up and watched the universe unfold. The energy entered me and I sent it back tenfold, the amplifications reaching the shore to the north and the hills hiding mountains and we saw, ever so dimly, a hint of the aurora borealis, supercharged solar ions celebrating their journey across the cosmos and their arrival at our world and their extinction above us.

CHAPTER **Seventeen**

"You should pick up strange men more often," I'd told Sera.

"More salad, Mo?" John offered me the bowl.

"We ask the man to bring home milk and he makes us dinner three nights in a row. I could get used to that kind of initiative."

Sera winked at John. "Enjoy the five-star treatment while you can, ladies. We'll be dining out at least a couple of times in the next few days."

Anita laughed. "Where, Luigi's? That hardly qualifies as *dining out.*" She spooned grilled asparagus onto her plate. "Pains me to say it," she'd continued, "but you want fancy dining, you might as well cross the state line."

"Or Leesville," I added. "Leesville's OK. Seriously though, where'd an Army guy learn how to cook risotto like this?"

"Maybe I'm just full of surprises," John replied. "I cooked a lot growing up, and knowing how to cook for yourself when you can sure beats relying on Army chow."

The first morning he'd appeared in our kitchen—surprise at our unexpected guest unnecessary, given Sera's penchant for whims—Anita finished the milk and John had volunteered to get more. He returned to our rickety little Louisiana house with milk, meat, beans, and fresh vegetables. If nothing else, he was resourceful and polite, almost gratingly polite.

Anita leaned forward. "What do you guys even eat over there?"

John had shrugged. "Lots of stuff. American stuff. The bigger bases have something like a food court. Burger King and Domino's, that kind of stuff. But you get tired of the options pretty quick. My base isn't that big. In the field sometimes it's MREs."

"Those are those terrible little meals in a bag, right?"

"Not really little," he said. "They're a couple thousand calories each."

I lifted a forkful of asparagus and paused. "So, what is it you guys are doing over there?"

"That's a pretty broad question, Mo. Mostly we go out on patrol, try to find IEDs, or maybe the guys setting the IEDs, but we're also training the Iraqi Army and their National Police."

"Train them to do what?"

He had breathed in and out slowly, maybe detecting the unasked portion of my inquiry. "How to operate on their own. Defend their borders on their own. Be a military, be cops. They have to be able to defend themselves."

"How will you know what a win looks like?" Anita asked. She'd probably sensed the underlying tension in my words and tried to deflect it, knowing I still hadn't warmed up to the soldier.

"We're fighting street to street, day at a time. We're trying to win it here." He'd pointed to his chest, "and here," his head. "That's the idea."

"Hearts and minds? I don't think that worked too well in Vietnam."

"Not theirs, and not even ours. It's yours—America's—hearts and minds. We can't win until the folks back home tell us they think we're done. We're not going to be there forever, you know?"

"Not if some of these politicians have their way. We're still in Germany and Korea, right?" The comparison wasn't exact, but my pulse had quickened just the same.

"Mostly I'm interested in getting my guys back in one piece."

My stomach had trembled as I cast my last stone, wondering if he would surprise us with his answer. "Meaning what, you'll do whatever it takes to get them back, fuck the consequences?"

"Whoa, Mo." Anita put her fork down. "That's not what he said. I'm pretty sure he's not over there shooting up civilians."

"We don't know much of what he's doing over there, just what he tells us."

John nodded. "I guess that's true. But what does Iraq look like to you? How much would you know about anything going on over there if I weren't here to tell you?"

"Just whatever they play on the news," I replied, "or what we read in the papers."

"Or what our family tells us." Anita had glared at me. Her brother was a Marine, also in Iraq, but none of my feelings about that stupid war had ever come out so strongly in front of her before. "Seriously, Mo, chill out. John's our guest. And he cooked us dinner."

"He's Sera's guest." I'd set my own fork down, wondering why Sera remained silent. The tension since his arrival came from a variety of places, but mostly from John's confounding of my expectations. I'd protested the invasion four years before by marching in Forest Park, distributed flyers outside of recruiting stations on the day the president declared *mission accomplished*, and maintained a *screw the man* attitude after Bush stumbled into reelection. Now, face to face with a soldier in our kitchen, my defenses sprang to the fore, ready to wage metaphorical and rhetorical battle against a jingoistic thug once again.

I'd quickly realized that John didn't fit the mold and was, in fact, made from some other material entirely, but my anxieties had remained. Deprived of a lightning rod to focus my angst, it morphed, seeping out now like magma from a fissure.

I'd been testing Sera as much as I'd challenged John, too, baffled how she could claim an immediate connection to the man.

"All the same," I told them both, "I do hope this is a nice break for him from whatever they're really doing over there."

"We're fighting a war." His voice softened. Sera had rested her hand atop his and he closed his eyes. "Every day. I got soldiers over there who haven't seen their kids. Not just haven't seen them in a while or missed a birthday—they missed the births."

"Didn't you all volunteer?" My voice matched his. "Weren't you in college, John? So what the hell are you doing over there? You studied literature. *War makes good men bad and bad men worse.*"

"We did volunteer. Every man and woman there. But we didn't vote on going to war, the country did." John opened his eyes. "Ain't this a democracy? Didn't you send us to war?"

"Wasn't my vote. And you could have refused. Any of you could have."

Sera closed her fingers over his, but he pulled away. "I think it gets pretty dangerous," he'd said, "us picking and choosing which wars we go to, whose orders we follow. You let the military do that and eventually we'll start picking and choosing other things. Wouldn't you rather someone with a brain be there, fighting, instead of someone too dumb to know why?"

"But, even if you're smart enough to know what you're doing, you're still doing it."

Anita had jumped in. "What, you think he should desert?"

"How is it that in a house of raging hippies I'm the only one advocating that he really think about what he's doing?"

"What other laws do you think he should break?" Anita had pressed. "And where's he supposed to go, huh? Fort Polk has twenty thousand soldiers just down the road. Yeah, he'd blend in real well around here."

"What do you want from me?" John had directed his question at everyone. "We're fighting a war over there."

Sera's hand found his again and had stayed when he tried to move it.

I leaned forward, finally seeing a man not yet made bad. "We're fighting a war here, too." My voice broke above a whisper. "Ours is a slow-motion war. Damn it, John, you know what we're dealing with here. You've seen it already; they don't even hide it anymore. Our state has money for oil rigs and tax breaks for lumber mills, but some of our students don't even have desks. The three of us have to buy pencils for them, and there's a fucking *pencil* factory just closed down. This whole nation's being taken apart and sold off while the guys like you are out of the country." I wanted to shove the table aside and wrap him and Sera and Anita in my arms, wanted to hit him and console him and shout and cry. "I've read about what you're going through over there, John. I have no idea what it feels like, but I try to imagine. I do. Here we've got no front either, no rear, no battle lines but what's been drawn by others, and it's all just collateral damage. Katrina nearly killed this town. Same thing that's killing this country, bleeding it every day." I rolled the dice and put my hand atop Sera's, atop his. "We need good people here, John. We need reinforcements."

Making a man cry had not been among my goals for that day. John shivered, eyes unfocused and mouth unmoving. I knew little about PTSD and wouldn't diagnose a man over dinner, but how close to the edge we'd just come wasn't as terrifying as how close he remained, and my hand would not be enough to pull him back from the brink.

Sera had pulled his head to her, resting it against her chest. She looked at me. Accusation or spite or even pity in her eyes I could understand and absorb. In their place had been grace and comprehension and, like a fist to my gut, gratitude.

"It's not like that," John said, and I'd wondered at the memories and ghosts in his life.

My hand had stayed with theirs. "We need good people."

I HOPPED IN PLACE while Sophie tied her laces. The past many weeks had finally undone my distaste for early morning runs, and a large part of the pleasure came from the company.

"John not coming today?" Sophie stretched her calves against the bottom porch step.

"He's going up to Rabbit Springs again, something about getting more life preservers from an old YMCA camp. Gabby says she'll meet us when we pass her place." The doctor-to-be rented a room from a family on the edge of Bonaventure. She'd had a few more summers than I to build up a tolerance to Sophie's insistence on dawn exercise routines, but agreed to join us today to shake off the post-fireworks hangover.

"And you're making dinner tonight?" Sophie asked with an eager grin.

Our local letter carrier was so diligent he'd deposited a package on our porch the day before, holiday be damned. During our weekly phone call, I'd made an offhand comment to Mama about the lack of authentic food in the county and she'd leapt into action. The box contained what some might consider an entire pantry worth of spices but what in my family was the bare minimum acceptable to make a few regular dishes. With a little creativity, I could stretch the supply to the end of rafting season.

"I'll be sure to make at least one dish that isn't too spicy."

"Oh, I like spicy food." Sophie stepped off without warning, forcing me to leap to keep up. We settled on a demanding but sustainable pace after our sneakers landed on the edge of the road, fast enough to get my heart racing, but not yet enough to preclude conversation.

"Never thought," I said, "that a talented and gorgeous rock star would also be in peak physical condition. Doesn't seem fair to the rest of us."

"Funny thing," she replied, arms pumping in rhythm to the music in her head, "I never attended a school with any sports, no P.E., so it's all been independent study. If you grow up as a control freak and a perfectionist, that can be a double-edged sword."

"Really?" My words needed to come early. She was not slowing down, and once Gabby joined us this light workout might turn into a real footrace.

"Magnet school for art nerds in Los Feliz meant no gym classes, no competitive sports of any kind, probably out of mercy. They still wanted us healthy, but left us to our own devices. After high school, Juilliard—"

"Wait, like, freaking *Juilliard*-Juilliard?"

"Surprised?"

"Guess not. Makes sense, you're a phenomenal musician and teacher, it's just…"

"You think I'm wasting my potential, playing in a cowboy bar and tattooing on the side?"

The charge of wasting potential (not the bar and ink stuff) had been leveled against me often enough, mostly by my own guilty conscience, more times than I cared to count, so I resolved not to level it against a friend.

"If what you're doing makes you happy," I said, "who am I to judge?"

We rounded a corner and came upon the outskirts of town. Gabby's apartment was a few hundred yards ahead.

"That's not what I mean," Sophie said. "Yes, making music activates something inside me, but I believe that denying your calling in life is a sure way to upset the balance of the universe. That kind of rebellion invites discord and misery."

"You're saying we have to submit to fate?"

The sideways glances that punctuated her remarks had to carry meaning. Everything with Sophie carried meaning.

"Not fate. Calling. You liked being a teacher, didn't you?"

I tensed before replying, hoping Gabby would join us and we could find a new debate topic…though knowing her, she'd probably take Sophie's side just to push me out of my comfort zone. "Only thing I've ever done that I've been good at, felt like I was contributing to society while doing it."

"The school here is always looking for experienced teachers. They need reinforcements."

"Huh. That's what I told John once, about something else." I skipped over a pothole. "In addition to being a singer and tattoo artist you're a guidance counselor and life coach, too?"

"*Part time* tattooist," she replied. "Gives me something to do when y'all are out on the water. The parlor in town is shorthanded, too, especially with this year's influx of tourists."

"That reminds me," I said. "Lucky said you do covers?" I searched for the right word. "Cover tattoos. You can cover up old ink?"

"One of my specialties," she replied. "I do some new stuff, but mostly help folks reframe earlier life choices."

"That in itself could be a career."

"What'd you have in mind?"

I slowed, then hopped on one leg to pull a sock down to reveal three simple Greek letters on my ankle. We got back up to speed and Sophie was quiet for a moment.

"Lucky makes a lot of sense," she finally said. "Cover bands, cover tattoos. It's all about taking a thing and making it new again, not just making it disappear. You have anything specific you'd want to see instead?"

"I'm open to suggestions. When can you fit me in?"

Sophie laughed. "You may want to hold off. It'll take me a few days to think of the right thing, a few more for you to think about it, plus you don't want to submerge a tattoo for a few weeks."

"I haven't fallen out of the raft in weeks," I pointed out.

"Every Greek letter carries lots of meaning, Mo. Math, science, even history. You don't want to just ditch that kind of burden overnight. One of those letters you have represents the Golden Ratio. Would you be open to getting a fresh design, too?"

"More than just the cover up?"

"It's all about balance," she said. "Covering up letters on your right ankle, you should get something on your…left arm, maybe even the wrist. That's a big commitment, though, getting a tattoo you can see every day." She winked at me. "And if you're interested in covering up that bunny you keep trying to hide, I have a few ideas there, too. Now, when are you gonna get back into teaching? Summer doesn't last forever, especially in Montana."

"You think I should stay." Part of me played with that idea every few days, though the larger part of me was currently unsettled by the exact re-enactment of the dinner table argument that had taken place in my dreams last night, prompted by the nighttime encounter with John in the middle of the lake. That had been the start of the argument that snowballed into the fight with Sera the morning she left town and the world. "I'm stuck being a teacher, if that's the only thing I'm good at."

"I feel safe saying you'd be good at whatever you put your heart to, Mo. But sometimes you have to think about what's best for the ones who love you."

What she left unsaid echoed the questions circling me since, well, since leaving Kirk, maybe before, brought to the surface by last night's light show and my proximity to John. The awe of the aurora and the energy of the shooting stars and the lightning without thunder led us to expose a small part of our hearts to each other. *What* part exactly, I didn't know, but the unaltered memory of our confrontation in Zeebrugge presenting as a dream confused me as much as my desire to explore something new with the quiet man who saved me after my unplanned departure from Chicago.

Fourth of July filled the role of an actual midsummer night as much as any other. The end of the season was now closer than the beginning, time marching if not rapidly, then inevitably. I could only put off post-September plans for so long.

"It may sound weird," I said, letting my thoughts turn into words without editing, "but I've tried praying on this kind of stuff before. For guidance, wisdom, a sign. Not sure to whom I'm praying, but no one's ever responded."

She hopped on a curb and ran along the top for a minute. "That's the funny thing about prayer. You pray for some sort of external intervention, it feels like there's no one there to help. Your prayer goes unanswered, you question your faith and your choices, even your understanding of the uni-verse. You pray for something like strength or patience, though, you might have a chance of getting it, since you're praying to yourself."

"Hey there, ladies." Gabby *had* spent her youth on sports teams, mostly dominating them, and ran for fun year-round. She sprinted around us, and then slowed her pace to match ours as we left the highway for Public Road, skirting a construction zone that would one day bring a proper running path to follow the Big Steep's course through Bonaventure's soon-to-be revitalized downtown.

"We were just talking career plans," I told her. "You two seem to have it all figured out: full-time muse, aspiring gynecologist. I've lost my direction, so maybe I'll just pull up roots and find another town where I can waste a few more—"

"Whoa." Sophie reached an arm out to stop the run. "That's not what I meant."

"Forget about it." I tried covering the lump in my chest with laughter that came out like a coughing fit. "We gonna run or what? I was just working up a sweat."

Gabby recognized what would have been an uncomfortable silence and launched into a detailed description of what drew her to a career of helping pregnant people through the most difficult times in their lives. The fact she wanted to provide women's healthcare in Georgia only confirmed her bravery.

"The women are the brave ones," she said. "Asking for help always takes a bit of courage. Being able to accept it, too."

Gabby didn't look at me when she said that, and Sophie kept her eyes on the path ahead, and I knew they weren't talking about me, but I was thankful for the reminder, as hard as it was to hear.

CHAPTER EIGHTEEN

"Big day."

I didn't take John's bait and managed to keep from cracking a smile.

"Every day's a big day," I said.

We sat on the boat trailer, Blondie and Magnolia strapped aboard, and he watched the road. I made a point to ignore the pair of vans with GARDINER ADVENTURES plastered across their sides, each with a trailer behind and a stack of smaller rafts aboard.

"He must've planned this and had it in the works before he ever mentioned it to us," John continued. "No way he could've swung all of this, not over a holiday."

"Hmm."

The guides JJ poached from the Yellowstone River seemed like a good bunch. Some had more years on the water than any of our crew. One of them had run rafts when Mickey and Lucky were still Mikhail and Luc. None of the guides had a problem listening to a relative youngster like John, not that he would try to lord anything like the title of *head guide* over them.

John swung his feet. "Think the boss already has a paint job lined up for the vans?"

The subject of our bus and its rescue from Louisiana had yet to come up, though I wanted to talk when the time was right.

"Never asked if you knew how to swim."

This brought out a smile and a laugh. "You're just *now* asking that?" I tipped my floppy hat back, lowered my sunglasses, and stared at him. "And isn't the point to *stay* in the raft?"

"Sure," he replied. "It's just peace of mind knowing if you can swim."

"I know how. Captain of the swim team, in fact." I reset my hat and shades and went back to staring at nothing. "I wasn't any better than most of the girls," I continued. "I did the butterfly, which everyone else hated." I slid back into the raft, propped myself against the tiller seat, and picked up the emergency oar. I held it like a guitar, idly strumming against its grain, picturing the chords in my fingertips. "My teammates voted me captain because I swam to beat the water, not them."

JJ's gleaming white Land Rover pulled off the road into the lot.

"Here we go." John hopped off the raft and offered me his hand. I climbed out on my own and handed John the oar.

"Here you go." I walked to the office as JJ introduced the pair of finance bros who spilled from his car as Martin and Tyler. They were the first to accept JJ's invitation and wanted to *scope out* the rafting, *check out* the town, and help our CEO put his grandiose business plans into action…with the hope of a return on their investment. John promised to call them *Boomer* and *Hutch* only until we could fashion real river nicknames for them. He introduced the bros to the Gardiner guides—Todd, Benjamin, and a mostly silent Garth—and excused himself.

"They seem OK," he told me.

I tried to look busy with the laptop, though we both knew by this time of morning most everything had been passed to JJ or Mickey.

"They do, don't they."

"Four new rafts, three new guides," John said, "and a pair of investment bankers at our once-hidden summer camp." He leaned on the counter, still cradling the oar.

"And a partridge in a pear tree."

"Maybe when the bankers all get back from their run we can hold another ceremony."

"We can't name the new rafts and have it mean something." I looked up. "They didn't come from Gardiner with names, so maybe naming rafts isn't something a proper outfit does."

"Who ever said we were a proper outfit?"

Men in the parking lot greeted and tested each other against the backdrop of pine trees and birdsong. "You really think it'll be OK?" I asked.

"They're joining us today, maybe a couple times over the next few weeks," he said. "JJ has that big meeting scheduled for August, after that they'll probably be gone. Those guys might seem familiar, but they're not Kirk. JJ turned out to be better than you expected, right? There's only so much the river can throw at us."

I shut the laptop. "They're not him, of course. I thought JJ was him, at first, but still…"

Another car entered the lot, disgorging customers, and I put those feelings aside.

THE GARDINER GUIDES were, as promised, exceptional. They came without egos, a remarkable achievement given the serious river they ran and the crowds they normally handled. Coming to Bonaventure must have felt like a summer off for them, what with the easier schedule and larger paychecks. They were good men. Todd and Benjamin reminded me of older versions of Carter and John, and Garth could easily be an even quieter Mickey.

JJ's buddies turned out to be decent humans. Martin and Tyler didn't insist on being called by their frat monikers. Their sincere awe at the river and the countryside blunted their natural inclination to puff chests and establish dominance, turning their boisterousness toward each other. When they met Sophie that night at Diamond Rough, they fell right into a kind of puppy love. The best part was she loved them back, the pair becoming the most devoted members of our fan club. They managed not to overdo their affection, earnestly appearing each night at the foot of her stage and leading the audience in applause.

After one week with the expanded crew, our new routine let us haul in money by the busload. Two weeks in and the tourists were happy. Three weeks and Bonaventure finally learned to absorb the crowds, and July was gone before we knew it.

"ANOTHER DAY, ANOTHER RIVER." No one knew what it meant. Carter picked up the phrase from a boatload of Spanish tourists, his utterance now the unofficial demarcation between daytime on the water and nights at the Diamond Rough.

We piled out of trucks and vans and the immaculate Land Rover and onto the sidewalk in front of the bar. Our reserved tables awaited. The nerves in my stomach activated those in my hands and face and every cell of my body. Sophie said that all of her lessons were for this hot August night.

A troupe in the style of a brass-and-thunder big band had wheeled into town, hinting at a night unlike any we had seen so far. A U-Haul full of instrument cases and amplifiers spoke to the power behind Sophie's promise. A few of the guest musicians stopped unloading their equipment long enough to wave at us, perhaps tipped off about who would cheer the loudest.

Teach me to play guitar. Sophie had agreed to my sudden springtime request without hesitation, suggesting that rather than just learning chords and fingerings and scales, she could teach me a whole song, maybe two, and even if I didn't have the knowledge I would have the skill, and one would come with the other, in time.

Or something like that, she said. We shared stolen half hours before she performed, sometimes on our off-days—back when we had them—and I'd practiced late at night, strumming quietly lest my housemate hear too soon.

Sophie came to the boathouse once in June, while John and the others were on the river, to gift me her beat-up old practice guitar. *I replaced the strings,* she said. *Let's hear what they tell you.*

Gabby knew of my clandestine project, her experience with piano and viola enough to help bring me up to speed after a long time of singing to the radio without the benefit of formal musical training. *For a beginner you're pretty flipping good,* she'd admitted, *though might be nice to ask you to play a dang G chord and for you to know what the flack we're talking about.*

Sophie played alongside. *It's like learning a new language,* she'd said, eyes closed. *You can learn the conjugations and proper endings, or you can learn how to find the library, where the food is, ask for help.* Her eyes opened. *It's all about purposes.*

One July afternoon on the steps of the boathouse, Ollie watching from his fishing spot by the lake, Sophie challenged me to pick one of the songs we worked on, one I could pull forth, and sing it aloud in front of people.

Like, actual people?

If you want him to know, she'd said.

You still think this is about him?

Isn't it?

I'd set the guitar down. *This isn't Noah's Ark,* I protested. *Mickey and Lucky are more than friends, their love is deeper than that. And I know why Carter and Badger spend fewer nights at John's cabin than they do at Gabby's apartment.*

I'd stopped myself, not wanting to name something, not sure if it existed or not.

Nothing wrong with a little summer love, Sophie had said.

Even though the guitar was tuned I still twisted the pegs. *That's not what I want, not from him. I want more than the summer.*

And we had more than the summer, more excitement and adventure packed into a handful of months than should fit, and I would try something tonight never before attempted in the life of one Mohini Chopra, I was going to say what I felt to someone who—

A man with his back to us blocked the entrance to the Diamond Rough. Todd from Gardiner tried to get his attention. "Excuse us." The strange man turned, arms folded across his chest, a smug grin plastered on his sharp and handsome face.

"I will not."

Carter perked up. "Oh shoot, is that Brother Crosswalk, or whatever he's calling himself these days? Been a long time since anyone let him come into town. Now, ask him to step aside, for we are thirsty, and music awaits us."

Crossroads scowled. "You have been in a desert, and you shall thirst. I can split the rock and bring forth the water, but I will not, not for you."

John stepped forward, putting himself between the group and Crossroads. "Come on, Simon. We just want to relax, you want to preach. Step aside and we can all go about our business. Try bothering the tourists down at Town Square."

The preacher's face turned from sneering judgment to an outright snarl. "From now until your doom I will speak of new things," he said, "of things hidden and unknown. Of old your ears have been stopped and I will unstop them."

The Gardiner guides, unfamiliar with Crossroads, shifted on their feet. Maybe not every town had a disgraced creep handling snakes in public.

"You hurry to your destruction," the man continued. "To revel in sinful music from the mouth of miscegenation." He leveled a finger at each of us in turn. "Cursed with ignorance. Blasphemer. Sinful fornication, gluttony, afflicted with avarice." He looked at me without casting a curse. His smile was far more terrifying. His crooked digit pointed at John, inches from his face. "And a coward, a man who pretends to be brave, fighting and killing in defense of scum such as this. You all play at things that anger our brothers, and our work will be revealed by fire."

JJ and his fraternity brothers moved from the back of the group forward. My arm came up, not to stop, but to caution them.

"For the sake of our plan, from the one unknown, I delay my wrath." A grating rasp infected the space between Simon's words. The more he talked, the more the hum grew into a sickening buzz filling my ears alongside his bombast. Dizziness swamped me and I put a hand on Gabby's shoulder, hoping to receive strength from our firecracker.

"Is that a threat?" John's body was relaxed, but his tone reminded me of the Mill Pond.

"John, leave it." I forced the words out and kept my bile down. "We can just go around the—"

I didn't know that people still used the word *harlot*. The syllables barely passed the sidewalk prophet's lips before John stepped forward, closing the gap between the two men. No doubt, he could call upon his soldier training to knock Crossroads across the street, and the rest of the boys would join in, but something about the man's stance, his carriage, the raw belligerence with which he confronted us felt at once familiar and deeply disturbing.

My hand moved from Gabby's shoulder to John's back, urging nothing and taking nothing, just a reminder of my presence. John took half a step back and a full breath. The grating buzz subsided.

"I knew your kind," John said, "over there. Your friend Samuel tried to hurt us. He met his end in an Iraqi courtyard amid a tornado, and you're not even a shade of what he was."

I remembered John describing his final combat tour and wondered if there was a connection between Crossroads and Samuel.

A fleeting look of anger and panic washed across the preacher's face. He shrank, regaining what little of his senses remained. He watched the assembled crowd grow larger, our own group swelling with tourists and locals, and covered his revulsion and fear with a final curse.

"Fire and water." He stepped aside, permitting the masses to enter. "This world will end in fire and water."

JJ ERUPTED INSIDE THE DOOR, incredulous at the confrontation, threatening some sort of follow up, and disappointed that John didn't do something to Simon. He said he would try to convince the town elders to permanently rid themselves of the nuisance in the interest of cementing Bonaventure's reputation as a family-friendly destination.

"You should've done something," JJ said again.

"By the end Gabby and Mo were ready to take care of him," John replied. "Have you been drinking already?"

"Celebrating. Martin drove. Seriously, though, wish we could've seen you use some of your soldier skills to turn him upside down."

John moved through the crowd, large and raucous before the music had even started. "There's people at our tables, JJ."

"Not just people, John—investors!"

The noise and similarity of names made the introductions almost impossible to hear, but I learned that JJ's dad was Jared, Senior. Mickey and Lucky peeled off to place mass orders for the table at the bar, and Gabby and Garth joined them to help ferry drinks and food. Jared, Senior commanded and demanded even more attention than his son, launching right into his pitch, practicing once more before the town meeting on Monday.

The band set up while our food arrived. I couldn't eat a bite. The investors peppered the crew with questions about the river and trails and mountains around us, animated by their envy of those of us who were still young and living for adventure, not a bottom line.

I took this opportunity to slip away.

I changed my outfit in Sophie's little spare room and snuck back out. There were no theater curtains to hide behind, so I watched from the shadows as Sophie took the microphone in hand, resplendent in a sequined top and black skirt, and described the evening's entertainment as *big band karaoke*. She offered the patrons of the Diamond Rough on this, the most crowded night of the year, the chance to come on stage and sing along, not to an electronic knock-off track of their favorite tune, but in front of a live band that could perform any song a tourist requested.

The idea was an immediate hit with out-of-towners and locals alike, even a few of the investors lining up to pencil their selections in Sophie's magic book. The band was amazing, powerful, the songs swelling to fill the room, and the crowd was enthusiastic and devoted.

"And coming to the stage next," Sophie announced after a half dozen singers had performed their hearts out, "our very own roving river rafter, Mohini."

In the nerves and anticipation, I had forgotten to put shoes on. The stage was surprisingly cool and the wood smooth. The stool cushion beneath me was soft but firm. Sophie angled the microphone to catch my words and the strings of my guitar. I smiled, tight-lipped and nervous, afraid that, if I spoke one word before singing, I would never have the power to do either ever again.

Sophie took her place at the keyboard. Real musicians assembled behind me with saxophone, trombone, and an entire standup bass, and I gave thanks for the overhead light shining directly in my eyes.

The hem of the dress Allison gave me in Chicago all those lifetimes ago hid my bare feet perched upon the middle rung of the stool. I leaned over my guitar toward the microphone and touched my fingertips to the strings.

The band held their instruments, the audience their breath, and Sophie joined me on the second line. My hair spilled over my face, rustling against the microphone. I pulled one hand away from my guitar and brushed the strand away, tucked it behind my ear, and picked up the lyrics.

Putting aside thoughts of anything other than my fingers and the strings, the words as I knew them and had sung them, high on hilltops and on the road and Lake Pando under a meteor shower, I forgot, if only for a minute, the heavy bitterness of the year before Montana and the loneliness before that.

My soul poured out and I felt as brave as Mickey, as Gabby, as brave as…as brave as me. I sung for my audience of one, whatever he might think, and that would be it. I had avoided watching or listening to other versions of the song when I practiced with Sophie, lest it not be my own when the time came, and the time had come. The weight and expectations of every woman who'd sang it before me and everyone who would sing it after, women who sang other words to other men and other women, lifted, leaving only acceptance, and I meant every word spilled, vowing to never not mean my words again.

The song ended. The crowd sat in silence, and I wondered how badly I'd flubbed the performance before their shouted approval crashed into me like waves after an earthquake. They demanded more, but I was already off the stage. I left my guitar in Sophie's office and wrapped one hand around the other, squeezing tightly until the shaking stopped. I couldn't hold an instrument right now, maybe ever, let alone a bottle of beer, though my throat begged for relief. I wanted to find John and wanted him to find me. I watched the next singer take the stage and gave thanks for the distraction. They sang the eclipse into existence, elevating it beyond cliché into high art, the band swelling to match the moment, and the crowd joined forces, not a soul singing off-key or ironically. Even those who couldn't find their voices sat in mute admiration. My thoughts wandered into a cavern, plumbed the depths of the Earth, and soared to the clouds.

When the song ended the world returned to a life more ordinary. I emerged from the back hallway, wanting to find a seat next to John, but ended up standing next to Gabby.

"What the hell, Mo?" Even though she'd been privy to my lessons, she was more than impressed, maybe fearful of the energy building in the bar.

"Sophie's a pretty good teacher," I said. "And you, too. Thank you."

I ignored the looks, whether from the Gardiner guides or the frat bros or the investors or the assembled crowd, lest anyone get anything like an idea, right or wrong, and thanked the gods when another singer took the stage, sang a sedate folk song, and we all let out our collective breath. The newcomers congratulated me on a job well done, but the Bonaventure guides knew there was more to it. Even JJ recognized something had shifted, jumping up and offering me his seat.

I found myself facing John across the table.

"Hey." As far as second-chance first lines, my attempt was pretty dumb.

He at least offered peace in his reply. "Hey."

The next song started, the opening chords shivering my memories. "Oh, man." I shook the tension out of my shoulders with a theatrical shudder and a laugh. "I hate this song."

"Why?" Mickey asked. "It is a lovely song."

"Listen to the lyrics," Lucky said. "It's about an affair. The woman, she leaves in secret, there is shame, though perhaps there shouldn't be. Very complicated."

"An ex declared this *our song* without asking me," I said. My chances to pull John away and talk to him in the heat of the moment evaporated. Part of me wanted to delay, to collect my wits, and the other part of me couldn't wait.

"Ain't a woman singing tonight." Gabby nodded toward the stage.

Summoning what courage remained to me, wanting to cheat and know his thoughts now, to get my insight before it disappeared, before the light of the morning could wash away the heady rush that lodged in my chest, I reached out and took John's hand and felt—

Nothing.

The flesh of his hand was warm, but trying to see anything more was like trying to push against the ocean. I squeezed harder, tried to find a flicker of—

The singer behind me doubled his effort, straying from *over-the-top* into *too much*. I turned to look at the man on stage singing and caught the rising excitement among the investors and JJ's frat brothers. Martin held aloft a cell phone, ready to capture the moment.

That had been *our* song, *his* declaration, a love song from someone incapable of feeling that emotion, and how had he found me here on the edge of the world?

Kirk launched into the chorus, extravagant and ridiculous and a million stupid things, and smiled at me from behind the microphone.

CHAPTER **nineteen**

Fat, lumpy black clouds brooded over the mountains, stalled from a barometric inversion, unleashing a month's worth of rain in just hours. That water would find its way to our course tomorrow, but today we had to run with the investors.

"River feels strange," Deacon told John.

Those of us ashore didn't feel any better. The residual effects of last night's performance, the unwelcome appearance of a man I'd hoped never to see again, and the lack of resolution for any of it combined with the morning heat to aggravate nerves already frayed by preparation for what JJ declared *the biggest day of the year*.

I avoided any path that took me within ten feet of Kirk, deflecting his efforts to *make up*. Last night he'd come off the stage and wrapped me in a hug before I could evade his arms. He'd tried to make a joke about wanting to present me my portion of the mortgage—*the rent*—in person, after helpfully deducting the cost of the typewriter I liberated, then started in on what he thought counted as a confession and declaration, and what a fool he'd been.

I did the math. He and JJ were about the same age, must have connected in college over binge drinking and harassing freshmen, and one of the pictures of our crew made its way to his laptop. Hell, it could have been that conference call JJ had, imploring his fraternity brothers to visit Bonaventure.

Fuck. I was the one who'd suggested showing off our website.

Knowing the kinds of movies Kirk watched, I could guess at what he thought would transpire, either over the next few days or, gods, maybe just tonight. I had seen more films than he had and, more importantly, read more books.

"The river's unbalanced," John said.

"Too much water in the wrong spots," Deacon replied. "The forest is crackling dry while the mountains drown."

"We're lucky we haven't had a serious fire yet." He pointed at the cars and SUVs packing the gravel lot.

"Any fire is a serious fire," Deacon added, "depending on time and place."

JJ wanted as many rafts as could fit on the trailers, the Zeebrugge bus and both Gardiner vans and even John's truck pressed into service. The CEO jiggered the schedule to free up everyone, shuffled seating assignments to put two or three investors in each raft so they could speak directly with the paying customers, gain firsthand appreciation for their enjoyment, measure the potential return on their investment, or something like that. I left off paying attention when JJ launched into business school jargon. John interrupted the boss's spiel about quarterly profits to insist I not be moved out of Blondie and into Little Durham. JJ would crew his raft with his father, who was an old raft-hand in his youth, and Kirk, who'd never set foot in a raft before.

To his credit, JJ accepted John's decision without even a pro forma fight, despite my ex's demands.

We squeezed everyone in along the Slip, river guides and paying passengers and Wall Street tycoons, Deacon trying to direct traffic, Gabby posted on a tree stump barking instructions about raft assignments, the Jersey boys handing out life preservers like we were on the *Titanic*. I looked for John. We hadn't talked last night after, well, after I sang my heart out at him, not after Kirk's unexpected and melodramatic arrival knocked the wind from my sails. What *had* been my plan if I'd managed to find time alone with—

"Hey," he said, appearing at my side.

"John." I hadn't smiled since Sophie and the band finished off the night, bringing the roof down around our heads belting out joyous tunes. I'd finally recovered enough strength to offer him a smile now. "This is a shipload of people."

"And you thought Yellowstone was crowded."

Badger pressed close to Carter, quivering and protective. The passengers finished zipping up their life vests under the watchful eyes of Mickey and Lucky. The investors would have direct access to hear from a mix of families, couples, and retirees. We had an entire summer of stories dumped at our feet, but would learn only a few, if any of them. The touch insight was still muted, muddled. Given the proximity to so many bodies, I was grateful for the silence.

"We're still going out, right?" I asked. "On the water. In the raft. Oh, gods."

"You, me, a family from Oregon, one of JJ's investors, and the investor's two sons." He tilted his head toward a pair of kids, two specimens of that indeterminate age range where children, especially boys, were hardheaded and hard of hearing. One of them used his oversized hiking boots to try and stomp on the smaller one's feet, failing, and growing frustrated at his failure.

"This oughta be a breeze," I said.

We stumbled through the Kitchen and under the Natty Gann as a semi-cohesive cluster of rafts. John instructed Gabby and the Jersey boys to run their rafts ahead while he kept the rest of us back, which would shorten their ride but clear out the potential traffic jam in the Mill Pond. At this time of day, nature wasn't enough to distract the guests; if Gabby managed to take a few of the Gardiner guides along, then we all might clear the Twins without bunching up.

"Stop." The younger child elongated the word into a multisyllabic plea. The older boy, he of the boots, did not stop. Their investor father was otherwise engaged with the matriarch of the Oregon family, her own hus-band fiddling with a camera hung around his neck, and offered only a few half-hearted corrections.

"Your life vest needs to stay zipped."

The older boy ignored my command. "This river is lame." He turned back to his brother, harassment interrupted resulting in harassment doubled. "No one's ever even fallen out of a dumb *raft* before."

"I said *stop*," came the younger's plaintive cry again. "Please."

The older brother ceased using his boots as weapons and instead leaned over the side to shovel water from the Mill Pond into his brother's face. The collateral spray landed on their dad, enough to finally break the conversation with the woman who had grown weary of his attempts at flirting. The man turned and hissed something at his children.

"Sir," I said, "your son needs to keep his vest zipped up."

"We're halfway through the river, miss," he replied. "And my son is right. How could someone fall out of a raft going this slowly?"

The older son stood, vest flapping in the wind, hands on hips, the younger boy clutching his own vest and perhaps considering retaliation—

The older boy flew backward before his brother could act, tumbling over the gunwale into the water.

Everyone in the raft froze.

There, splayed across the surface of the Mill Pond, the vest floated, no kid in sight.

The father stood, maybe he shouted. John commanded him back to his seat, looked for the closest raft to render aid. Blondie was the last raft in line, though, so there were no crews behind to help. The kid should have popped back to the surface by now, good swimmer or bad.

Those boots.

The raft below us shuddered, the river moving us past the expanding circles that marked where he sank. I came off my seat, planted one foot on the side of the raft, and heaved my life preserver as far downriver as my arms allowed. I caught John's eye for a second, looking not for permission but his acceptance, then lunged forward, hands clasped, arms extended, and split the river's surface.

A FOUNTAIN OF WATER accompanied my return to the surface world. Hands reached over the side of the raft, grabbing the sputtering child in my arms. I clung to the ropes stretched across the gunwale, passing him up first. The passengers slid spare life vests over his head and then mine as they hauled me aboard. The boy cried for his mother, miles away.

If he could cry, he could breathe. John found me and I held fast to his side, my own chest heaving for air, my eyes fixed on the Mill Pond as we passed the Twins.

JJ CANCELED THE REST OF THE TRIPS for the day, promising to pay the guides the same and eat the refunds himself. He ordered the stand-down in the name of a safety review, though the crew recognized a glimmer of humanity in the gesture. No night at the Diamond Rough, though the porch and yard at John's cabin felt as full and frenetic as the movie theater-turned-dive bar when we held an impromptu celebration of life-snatched-from-death. Sophie played DJ to the party and mother to us all.

The storm broke early upon Bonaventure, sending everyone inside. Mickey and Lucky, who refused to leave my side, observed that we would have been back on the river in the worst of it, another auspicious consequence of my actions. The Gardiner guides offered their praise and affirmed I could ride the Yellowstone or any crazier river in the Rockies.

John didn't let me out of his sight, my two teenage bodyguards not-withstanding. Kirk tried to corner me, declared his awe at my bravery, his stupidity in how he'd treated me, vowed to make up for lost time and any pain he inflicted. He was ready to talk.

"Even when we talked," I said, breaking my silence and draping a plaid wool blanket across my shoulder, "we never really *said* anything."

He made an excuse, muttered a platitude about giving me time and space to recover my senses, and threw John a challenging look as he brushed past, leaving with the first wave of investors and frat bros, bound for the bar in Rabbit Springs. Others left after offering their own assessments of my deed. They scattered back to their homes and cabins and RVs. Carter and Gabby were among the last to leave, wondering if Kirk was right about my need to be alone.

I made my way back to the porch to watch the deluge up close. Sophie turned the music down, just enough for me to hear it above the rain, and found John on her way out.

"Maybe she does need some time to herself," he told her.

"Mo might need time and space," Sophie replied, tapping her hand against his chest before grabbing her jacket. "But she doesn't need to be alone."

He joined me on the porch and offered a mug of hot cocoa.

"The last time we watched the rain together…" He trailed off, letting history fill the gap.

"I was yelling at you." I didn't look at him. "Is that what memories are? Just, every time it rains, we'll think of that day?"

We hadn't known then, but it was almost the last time John saw Sera.

"It wasn't yelling, more like…" He searched for the word. "Lecturing."

I pulled the blanket tighter around me. "That doesn't sound any better."

"How are you?"

"I'm cold, John. Down to my bones. JJ says we're pulling the plug again tomorrow. The storm came too quickly, dumped too much water." I drank from the mug and passed it to him. "You here to tell me what I did was stupid?"

He sipped and passed the cocoa back. "Most people in there called it *brave*."

"Didn't you say once there's not much difference between brave and stupid?"

"Gus said that."

I reached out and brushed his arm, just where the name *Atwood* was inked. "Pretty much everyone called it brave, but they wanted to call it stupid, especially jumping in after a brat like that."

"Bring 'em back alive, Mo," he recited. "Even the brats."

I stepped away from the post and let the blanket fall off my shoulders, holding it between my elbows and body. I set the empty mug on the railing. "Did you see what happened?" I asked. "No one else did, or at least none of them said anything."

He'd seen it. The kid was full-fledged harassing his little brother, who would've been justified in lashing out, but at the instant the older boy fell out of the raft, the two were nowhere near touching. He hadn't been pushed—he was pulled.

"When I was down there." The words caught in my throat. "I wasn't alone. The kid was there, of course." I looked past John into the rain, tried and failed to hide my tears. "The current caught him, but it was pulling him straight *down*, not downriver. Gods, it was fast...and *strong*. I had no idea the Mill Pond was that deep."

He gave me time and space.

"Remember I was on the swim team?"

"Captain," he said.

"How long do you think I was down there?"

He rubbed the stubble on his chin. "Based on how far Blondie made it down the river, it was about fifteen, maybe twenty seconds."

"I can hold my breath for three minutes," I said. "Ever since I was a kid, I took pride in being able to hold my breath that long. Down there? I almost had to come back up for air, and it wasn't just because of stress. I remembered...no, I was back there, the first time ever standing on the blocks. Just a kid, younger than this one, maybe six or seven, and no one in my family really swam. We knew how, of course, but to race against others? I begged my parents to let me. And down there, I was suddenly back in Boston, the morning of my first-ever swim meet. Baba made me breakfast and told me I might never be the fastest swimmer, someone could always outswim me, but I could be the toughest. *No one can take that from you, Mohini.*" For some reason, sniffing back a tear let the rest flow. "Driving me to the meet, Mama said it was good to be tough, that's the world we live in, and it's tougher for some than for others. I could beat my fists against the water all I wanted, though, and it would not obey. *The mountain is tough,* she said, *but water grinds it down.* I would have to be both, she told me, to survive." I laughed. "Seven years old and they're giving me these pep talks. So, at the meet, I kicked like hell, stole a half-second off the block from that little blonde dolphin. She won, of course, won lots of medals that year. She always beat me *in* the water, but never *to* the water."

I stepped to face John and looked up into his eyes. "I kicked, I kicked like *hell* down there, kicked out of my shoes, out of my socks, and still he drew away from me. I was too slow. It wasn't just that the current was too strong, there was something else down there."

"What did you do?"

"I couldn't get back to the surface, take another chest-full of air, and get back down in time. I kept trying to beat the water, and I was filled with anger. That wasn't working," I said, "so I asked the universe for help. I gave a small prayer and grabbed his wrist."

I took John's hand in mine and a flood went in both directions, staggering us both without breaking our connection.

It's back.

"I felt something else down there…*holding* his other wrist, tugging him away from me. Touching the kid allowed me to feel him, every bit of him was scared, but I could feel what held him as well. It felt like Brother

Crossroads on the other end. It was like jumping on a transmission line." I stepped closer. "I asked the universe for help, and Sera was the one who answered me. She broke the grip Crossroads had on him and we brought him up, together."

I let John's hand go and thumped him on the chest.

"She's been dead for *years*, John." My voice rose. "But she was down there. It wasn't a dream, or a hallucination, or an aneurysm. How is that *possible*? Did you know? What can't I see?"

He couldn't keep his eyes from flickering beyond me, across the yard, landing on the small, stunted tree. I felt sick and let the blanket fall entirely off my body as I walked into the storm. The downpour intensified, pummeling the ground and demanding I turn back.

I fell to my knees at the base of the baby redwood, stroked the needles battered by heavy pounding drops, and recoiled as if lightning struck the tree. Undeterred, I buried my head in the tender limbs of the sapling and wept.

John followed me and threw the blanket over my shoulders. When he touched me, Sera reached out to him, using my body as a conduit, and offered both of us absolution. We fell back from the redwood, the lingering resonance of my best friend and his true love pushing us away before we were lost to the chasm of eternity, to the canyon where her energy resided, knowledge not meant for mortals like us.

"It's her!" Thunder swallowed up my words. "How?"

I pulled my hand back, not sure if I wanted to hit him, knew that he wanted me to, his own tears mixing with mine and the rain. Instead, I pitched forward, pressed my forehead to his chest. John wrapped me with the sodden blanket and we stumbled back to the porch. He pulled the wet wool away from my shoulders and held me in his arms. The storm bellowed above us.

"How?"

"You may be the only one who'd believe me," he said.

"This is more than just the birdspeak, isn't it?"

"I can't lose someone else to the magic, even if you have a piece of your own."

"But you saved her." I pulled away, just enough to hold his cheek in my hand. "Some part of her is in that tree." Time froze in the river. Time slowed now, inching forward to a future that threatened to consume our present. Each drop of rain hit the roof, rivulets of water gathering and gushing off the metal over our heads to splatter against mud and rock and wood, the slow absorption of moisture into soil and root and back into the world as the respiration of a tree that contained what was left of Sera.

Each beat of John's heart rang against mine.

"You want to kiss me," I said, silly with fear and love and finally untethered from anything like my past or unexplained insights, all because I beat death and rediscovered my best friend in the river and a tree. "Now that I'm a hero, I mean."

"I wanted to before," he admitted. "And you were a hero before, too."

Was this where we were headed, ever since a late-night email and a shattered CD and an adopted school bus? Maybe before that? Had we been set upon a path, herded back when we strayed from destiny? What had it cost, what was taken from us to get here? Why did the universe keep me stumbling for so long? I chose to sing him a song, elected to acknowledge my feelings not just to myself, but out loud, in public, to him. Those feelings were real and strong and would not be delayed any longer.

"I'm not her," I said.

He didn't flinch. "Neither am I."

"Is this moving on, then? Gods, I've tried. We both lost her, I might have seen her last, but you held her last, and I should have been with her when she was taken. Maybe I should have been taken instead. Even what's left of her in that tree is like an echo. Are we abandoning Sera in a sapling?"

John didn't answer, even as the wheels of his mind worked, his thoughts pouring into me through my hand against his face.

"Is this a surrender?" I insisted. "Or is it two people making a choice?"

He leaned down and kissed me on the forehead, leaving his lips pressed to my skin.

I lifted my hands up and brought his mouth to mine.

CHAPTER TWENTY

I traced my fingers over the names again, not rushing, not seeking, just sounding out the letters and fitting together the syllables in my head, wondering at the histories of these men before their paths had crossed John's, whether their families knew about the corporeal monuments to their sons, brothers, and lovers.

After last night's performance at the Diamond Rough, no insights had come. Getting trapped in Kirk's hug showed me nothing in his mind or heart. Being surrounded by dozens of rafters and passengers and investors this morning provided no more knowledge than anyone else could get. When I grabbed the boy underwater, the power came surging back for a moment. After burying my face in the needles of Sera's tree—a complete story I'd get from John when he offered—I discovered the ability to open and close the floodgates at will, allowing thoughts and memories and dreams to come and go.

"When you were a kid," I said, my voice muffled under the quilts and his other arm, "how much did you think about rain?" He shifted behind me, repositioning to perhaps hear me better, or speak more clearly, or because his arm was falling asleep. "When it rained like this," I continued, "I thought it was raining this hard the world over. How could it not?"

The deluge intensified again after we left the porch behind, stumbling into walls and furniture and nearly tipping over the desk that held the typewriter I'd wanted to steal, only to end up buying, on the way to my room. Despite the rush to get indoors, John had been slow and patient since, asking gentle permission at each step, until we'd fumbled through each other's buttons and zippers, tossed aside clothing and finally, *finally* got into bed and under the covers. The quilts came off and were snatched back from the floor. The cold of the river had settled deep inside me, wrapped around my bones, and even the heat of our exertions and the warmth of John's body was barely enough to stave off the shivers, though I shook for other reasons, too.

"That's what sadness is like," I said. His arms tightened. "You think everyone else should be sad, too, so you don't understand when they're not. When Sera died, I had no clue how the whole world didn't just die along with her."

"It very nearly did." His voice covered up his thoughts again. I could force my way to insight, open up his feelings for display with the lightest of touch, but knew John would speak on his own time. No more intrusions, only offerings. In addition to turning it on and off, I could send my thoughts out as easily as receive them from others.

I changed the subject. "I never picked up a guitar before this summer."

"Could've fooled me. Sophie's a great teacher."

"I wanted to try something *bold*. I knew about Carter and Gabby, Mickey and Lucky, and wanted something like what they have."

He ran his fingers through my hair. "Theirs aren't summer flings."

"I know." My breath caught. "I didn't want that, either, I don't want that, not with you, but it still felt like I was…"

"Like you were going behind Sera's back?"

Here it came. "That last day, before she went up to the Delta, to find some town named Tully," I said, closing my eyes, "we got into an argument. We argued a fair bit most days, mostly one-sided, but this was a *fight*. I had no idea what she was thinking, why she wanted to go off in search of a town from some story she heard from some guy she had just met, but she was committed. I turned it into something bigger, about her promise to wait for you." I opened my eyes. "She asked me to go with her, to continue the conversation, and I refused." I tried to move deeper into John's embrace. "She offered me a hug before she left, the way she always did, and I refused that, too. You wanna talk about feeling guilty?"

"I'm the one who told her the stories that got her curious about Tully." His mouth pressed against the back of my head. "There's enough guilt to go around."

"You came to Louisiana," I said, "after our town shut down, after Anita and I got scattered to the winds. That's where Deacon's bus comes from. Sophie showed me the picture."

"I thought you might still be there," he replied. "Last year, just before we got the crew back together, I got a…" He searched for another word. "Something told me I had to go. Zeebrugge's not an easy place to get to, and Bonaventure isn't an easy place to start from. I arrived too late. The town was already being sold off, piece by piece, and no one knew where you or Anita had gone."

We breathed together, the only sounds our heartbeats and rain thundering down above our heads. I gave thanks for the roof and hoped the world was still there in the morning.

"You're OK with this moving as fast as it did?"

"We have to believe in loving fast," he said. "As fast as the world's being destroyed, we have to learn to love even faster."

The CD, the one she burned for me, for us, carried that message from before the grave, a message that found me when I needed it the most, the shards imparting or unlocking whatever this power was.

I turned to see his face. "Is this you opening that bear-proof heart of yours?"

He kissed my forehead again. "Remember what the ranger said—though the bears can't get in, ravens can, if they work together."

"Does that make us birds?"

He answered me with another kiss, this time on my lips, and I kissed him back. When we visited each other again, when we explored our bodies and the ways we could move together, the ways we traded energy, we still fumbled, but I *giggled* and he laughed. Reading a man's entire psyche while making love to him might have been unfair except he made love to me the same way, open and receptive and inquisitive and responsive. He was strong and tender, and I gave every piece of my heart, the small parts I'd kept in a safe in a mistaken belief I had to, and his smile could have beat back the thunderclouds.

"AND HERE I THOUGHT you talking to birds was the most special thing about you." I rested my back against the headboard, John in my arms, my legs around his waist. "What happened in the river? What you and I have, what we can do, that might be a certain kind of magic, something powerful and good, even if we don't fully understand it, but Brother Crossroads was under the Mill Pond. He's been on Liza's Hope, too. He's obsessed with us."

"I'd like to tell you what…" His chest rose and fell. "I started to tell you the first night you came to Montana, but I think you were so tired none of it made sense. I've avoided bringing it up since because it still doesn't make sense what happened over there."

"In Iraq."

He told me about three ghost stories that he had shared with Sera on the edge of Keep's Creek, tales gathered from other soldiers and traded during a competition to see who could tell the scariest tale. John told me about a little black dog with the hair of a woman…about a soul-collecting demon on the outskirts of Tully, Mississippi …and about a malevolent force of nature called taliment that stalked an ancient Iraqi city. He left out details, fearful of conjuring the spirits in the stories as he had before, but I could see all of it, just as it had appeared in my dream on my first night in

Montana. Triangle eyes, a tornado, and the end of the world.

Sera had gone in search of the town of Tully, intent on seeing for herself the truth behind these stories. That was the day she and I had fought for the last time, the day I rejected her. In her search, she'd caught the attention of the demon named Moonlit Samuel. No longer content collecting souls one at a time, eager to move up in the hierarchy of evil, Samuel had stolen the rest of the stories from Sera and traveled to the hottest combat zone in the world: Iraq. There, he'd set taliment free from its confinement deep beneath the city of al Noor—the same city that John and his soldiers patrolled.

The man who could talk to birds had seen signs of the coming super-natural struggle: a body so badly broken that every bone, even the three in the inner ear, was snapped cleanly in two; a crematorium in the middle of a freak sandstorm that consumed men like cigarettes; and an exquisite corpse, a profane giant body etched in blood with thousands of names, warning of impending doom. Through it all, a guardian jackal stood vigil over the men of his platoon.

Samuel had killed Sera in a car accident as an act of evil, as a taunt to the man who'd pieced together the truth of the impending unholy war, but the demon hadn't predicted that Sera would find a way to delay the trans-migration of her soul or the transfer of her energy or whatever came after death, delay it long enough to appear before John in Iraq. Not a figment or a hallucination or the result of a busted blood vessel in his brain, she was there, offering herself as a shield to the women and children of the city, a guide and protector to John and his men.

She walked the soldiers through firefights and ambushes, saved as many of them as she could from snipers and bombs, and, when the time came, found them in the courtyard I'd seen in my dreams. Moonlit Samuel wanted to test his mettle against taliment, and he'd trapped John and his men in the middle of an apocalyptic battle, a snake with triangle eyes fighting against a tornado of fire. Whichever entity had prevailed would have gone on to destroy the world.

Sera had offered up herself, pinning the demon in place long enough for John to kill its serpent body with one shot, transferring Samuel's evil energy into the storm above and ending both threats. He'd saved the world and lost his last, ephemeral connection to the woman who loved him more than life itself.

After John left the Army, he'd found the courage to visit Sera's family in California, a belated paying of respects that did nothing to diminish the guilt he felt at sending her down the path of death and temporary displaced resurrection, and for his role in her final sacrifice. Her parents, burdened with the loss of their only child, had been too kind, kinder than he felt he deserved. They gave him some of her belongings, including the journal she kept in Louisiana, which he still hadn't read.

Before leaving California, he'd uprooted a tiny redwood from a state park near her childhood home, an ill-conceived and desperate attempt to transplant one final keepsake. He managed to keep the tree alive long enough to replant it outside this cabin and, for years, it grew, every day collecting echoes of her from out of the ether. It was the last little piece of her that existed, he said.

We wondered if this rainstorm would be too much for the sapling.

If you leave, he thought, knowing that I could hear, *now would be the worst time. I can live the rest of my life without Sera, knowing almost all of her is gone from this plane of reality, and that she gave her life to defend life. I've grown used to her absence, though it still hurts. Whatever pieces of her linger in the tree and the river are enough.*

I can live without you, Mohini, probably, but if it's my truth that drives you away, then I would be undone.

"Losing Sera shattered me, John. I literally went blind for an entire day. When my sight came back, everything was death. Do you know how hard it is to look at second graders and worry about when, about how they're gonna die? Didn't matter if it was eighty years into the future, everyone I knew would be dead one day. Doc Bellamy forced me to take time off, but going home was worse than staying in Zeebrugge. My parents still live in the house we grew up in, but suddenly it felt like the inside of an M.C. Escher drawing. The stairs made no sense. I couldn't remember where the cereal was, even though Mama always kept the cereal on the second shelf, and my bedroom was too hot and too cold no matter what I did.

"I looked for Sera everywhere, places I'd never seen her, all over Boston. Any woman with short hair, any man with a full-throated laugh, children, old people, and birds. *Birds*, John; everything reminded me of her. I cut my trip short and went back to Louisiana. Anita came back early from Oakland without talking to me about it, but we returned on the same day, as if we'd been called. We couldn't bring ourselves to touch her room, so we just sat outside the door, like Sera would open it and give me the hug I'd denied, tell us it was all a misunderstanding.

"Someone at school must have mentioned it to one of the local preachers, because he came to our door and offered what he might've thought was wisdom, about seeing Sera resurrected if only I believed, and he had a pamphlet that explained everything. Anita had to pull me off the guy. It's not like I'd never lost a loved one, but this was harder in every way.

"Until one morning it wasn't." I held onto John. "I woke up, went to school, taught the kids without seeing skeletons in their places, and got through the day. Then another, and another. Not long after ending up in Chicago, I stopped thinking about her every day—too busy. There was a buzz whenever I was with Kirk. We moved so fast my brain had time for nothing else. That whole year came crashing down on my head in one night, and I've been working through it ever since landing in Montana." I moved my hands to his chest. "Looking at you, talking with you, damn it, *touching* you is like looking at her, touching her. A piece of her lives in you, too, same as me, same as the redwood. Gods, does it hurt, but nothing can ever compare to the day I lost her. When *we* lost her." I kissed the back of his head. "I believe you. Sera told me about the coyote, the one you saw in Oklahoma, the morning she invited you to Louisiana. You called it a spirit animal; she said it was your guardian angel. It had to be both. I've witnessed your birdspeak in action, when you saved that hawk and when the crows sought you out to help me escape Crossroads. And the first night here, before I knew anything about this touch insight, before I knew the details, I dreamt of your fight in that courtyard, exactly as you just described it. I've had that dream many times since, each time with more detail, details that make sense now. She helped you save the world. I'm still not sure how you two fought off a demon and a force of nature."

"I'm sorry you saw all that."

I laughed and loosened my grip, though my limbs still wrapped around him. "It helps to know I'm not crazy. I've seen insights from Ollie, from Carter, Mickey, Sophie, hell, even Badger, and it helps to know it's all real. I'm just sorry you helped save the world and can't tell anyone about it."

"You're going to stay?"

"Of course, John. Turns out we've been building a life here. We might all be refugees in our own way, or maybe just a collection of stray cats and screw-ups, but this is where I want to be. I'd love to properly meet the redwood in the morning, spend a little more time in her branches." I ran my hand down his chest to his stomach. "But for now…"

"Yeah?"

"I haven't eaten since breakfast."

"You didn't eat anything at the party?"

I laughed and disentangled myself from him, shoved him away and clutched a sheet to cover myself. "I had just saved a *life*," I exclaimed, "and survived a confrontation with something we still haven't figured out, but *gods*, John, let's think—in the last twenty-four hours I sang my feelings for you onstage in front of a million people, my disaster of an ex-boyfriend arrived without warning, we nearly watched a kid drown, and I almost drowned myself because of a disgraced former preacher. I then discovered, in the midst of an epic downpour and some passionate fooling around, that the man I'm falling for battled demons and saved the world with the spirit of my dead best friend."

"'Fooling around'?"

I grabbed a pillow and swung it at him. "*That's* what you took away? Bottom line, I'm freaking starving, and I know for a fact there's cold chicken in the fridge and beer in a cooler on the porch, if it hasn't floated away."

"It's like, two in the morning." He looked for his shorts.

I grabbed a pair of socks from a drawer to replace the ones lost to the current of the Big Steep. "We're probably not sleeping much tonight, and JJ gave us tomorrow off." I slipped a tank top over my head and wrapped John's flannel shirt over it. "C'mon, you heat up the chicken, I'll grab the drinks."

We had the cabin to ourselves, but walked out of my room as if we had a secret. He headed to the kitchen to begin the process of making us a midnight feast and I opened the door onto the porch.

The sound I let loose brought John to me in an instant.

The heavens threw the rain down heavier, angrier than should be possible, like a hurricane stuck in our canyon. Lightning flashed as brightly as the sun, illuminating the tops of pines and our cars in the driveway and the small brave tree.

A pair of socks neatly folded lay on the porch.

My socks.

The ones I'd lost to the raging river.

chapter **TWENTY-ONE**

I f May in Montana was still winter and June a kind of gift spring, July was full summer in a month and August its own special kind of hell. No metaphors of ovens or furnaces could convey the grueling heat to anyone not suffering under its oppressive dome.

The river dried up, exposing banks of mud that baked into hardpan barriers. Trees crinkled whenever the wind blew and no breeze brought relief, merely pushed the heated air around until there was no escape. Lake Pando shriveled and the boat ramps sagged. By the second week of the brutal month, we ran the rafts ashore and dragged them to the boathouse ourselves.

Birds clung to branches, listless and frightened, passing John messages only he could hear and asking him questions he couldn't answer. The deer disappeared and the otters left. The river ran sluggish, the snowmelt long gone, the deluge enough to swell the current for a week without sustaining the flow. Our fourth trip was nearly impossible each day, even with the additional craft and crew. The Gardiner guides departed, giving us one of their vans before they left. Martin and Tyler decamped as well, the former group back to their own river to wait for true winter (when they would lead snowmobiling excursions into Yellowstone's backcountry), the latter to their high-rises to tell exaggerated tales of tangential heroism and secondhand adventure.

I would not care if they said they ran the Big Steep or claimed they saved the kid from the Mill Pond. They could reap the benefits of a wide-eyed Manhattan barmaid gawking at a story only half-told. None of them knew the truth, would ever know it, a truth saved only for me and John.

And, I suspected, Brother Crossroads.

I saw him everywhere, meaning I saw him nowhere. Any time I tried to direct the attention of whoever was with me, Crossroads vanished. He appeared in places he had no business being: on the hilltop above John's cabin; in the boughs of trees along the highway; or hanging from his fingertips beneath the Natty Gann Bridge. There was no way to explain his fascination with me, but he returned my socks as a provocation, a taunt, the way John described Sera's murder at Moonlit Samuel's hands as a challenge against the soldier. There had to be something unholy about the former preacher. I'd felt as much the first time we met, when he voiced my name without hesitation and nearly touched me, again on the night he blocked us from the Diamond Rough. He radiated a harsh buzzing energy that confounded my thoughts, and when he was close, the droning threatened to drown out any sense or sensation, overpowering the growing skill I'd gained in controlling my insights.

We still went to watch Sophie, though her music wasn't enough to keep me from staring at the door, waiting for Crossroads to barge in. My safety briefs grew shorter before our few trips and I left the narration to John, who offered soft stories of hope and redemption, none of them hinting at the dangers below the water. Despite the ebb of the river's flow, every time we passed over the Mill Pond an ancient, unsettling, and incomprehensible aura emanated from its depths, dangerous in a way that none of us could grasp, eclipsing Liza's Hope at night for the pure unease permeating our surroundings.

Kirk stayed. His presence interfered with my insights like a competing radio tower tuned inversely to my own, two signals canceling each other out, leaving a dead silence in place of the static emanating from Crossroads.

Kirk even muted the thoughts in my own head whenever he was near, which was often.

Nothing, he said, would keep him from getting me back.

He couldn't know about the negative pregnancy test, the one I'd thrown away the morning of our abandoned anniversary party, and I would never tell him, but he dropped hints that made me wonder if he had stumbled upon my secret, or if Crossroads had transmitted knowledge, encouraged his attentions, just to bedevil me.

I retreated from Kirk at the same time I poured myself into John. We held each other each night as we opened everything we could and held nothing back. This was our own kind of challenge, to admit every fault and vice and transgression, to cut ourselves asunder and dare the other to turn away or accept us, flaws and all. Trying to live up to the memory of the greatest love either of us would know didn't intimidate me only because Sera wouldn't have seen it that way.

When I sat and read the needles, I realized that her spirit lived in the tree, transformed into something elemental. Touching the branches connected me to more than just my friend, or even the tree itself. It felt like peering through a keyhole into a ballroom filled with living energies, mirrors on walls and ceilings, eavesdropping on the force of nature itself. Hold on too long and I would tap into a vast network of power, more than one mortal woman could bear even with a sliver of magic, so I left the tree alone and turned again to John.

Friendship was the most powerful kind of love for humans. The heart fell for who the heart wanted, often without reciprocation. Family was not a choice for those born into it. Friendship spanning time, and space, and death had to be measurable on a cosmic scale. Sera wasn't a wall. No way could she have known her trip to Tully would be the last she took on this plane of existence, but still she ensured there would be pieces of her left for us after she departed. She was a bridge, bigger and stronger than even the

Natty Gann. She strengthened John's birdspeak through an unread journal and gave me touch insight from a talismanic compact disc, because Sera's power was gift magic. She knew the dangers we would face, whether in a warzone or on the river, and provided tools to survive.

Brother Crossroads was dangerous, strong enough to leave tokens on our doorstep and travel the land at will, though something kept him from violating the sanctity of the cabin. I told John it was the redwood standing sentinel over us, another gift from Sera, and inside our walls we guarded our hearts from the world and showed them to each other.

"THERE'S NOT ENOUGH WATER." John waited for JJ to respond. Something else ate at the boss's attention, so the guide returned to picking the label off his beer bottle. We'd assembled at our usual table, shrunk after the departure of the Gardiner guides and JJ's fraternity brothers. Gabby was set to leave in two days, a family emergency prompting an early return to Georgia. Sophie and Deacon planned a going-away party at the boathouse not just for the future doctor, but also for Carter and Badger, who would join her back east a week later, just before the start of classes. Gabby revealed to me and John that this was their last summer on the Big Steep. If the three of them ever returned to Montana it would be as *freakin' cargo*, and she thanked us for everything.

Mickey and Lucky declared their plans to stick around until Labor Day, if we could even run rafts that late.

Kirk's presence made the nearly deserted bar far too crowded. Striving to find some way into my worldview and failing, he moved past misguided romantic notions to firm insistent commands and teetered on demanding something I could not give. I erected no armor against his advances or energies. My apathetic disregard seemed to energize his misplaced motivation.

JJ finally responded to John's comment. "After Gabby and Carter leave, we'll be down to three rafts and six guides."

"Six?" John asked.

"Kirk can ride with me, it's not that hard."

"Well, there's barely enough river for that," John said. "The snowmelt's gone, and other than the investor weekend monsoon it's been almost a month with no rain."

JJ watched Sophie singing on stage, sorrow on his face. "Maybe we can get more water."

"You can't just buy a river, Jared."

He turned to face John, his own bottle long since stripped of its label.

"That's the first time you've called me *Jared* in years."

"Sorry about that."

"By now I prefer *JJ*." He turned away. "Dad's pulling his investment, encouraging others to do the same."

"They can do that?"

He shrugged. "It's their money. A lot of the land deals fell through. Negotiating the mineral rights alone would've kept us in court for years. The crowds were too much for the town to handle…" He trailed off. "Dad called this my *vanity project*. Said he was done giving me advances on my allowance, even though it was mostly my money. Thing is, he wrote the contracts in a way that he and his buddies won't take a loss on any of it."

Five-star reviews and pictures of beautiful river guides couldn't counter weather reports and a forest fire west of us, small but growing and dissuading would-be tourists.

We felt the electricity and danger of the political campaigns stalking the country, nastiness and vitriol shivering the lines of union and camaraderie even in our small corner of the world. For all of JJ's pronouncements of *principled conservatism* in support of his chosen candidate, Kirk was far more belligerently declarative, wielding his affiliation and John's *soft head and softer heart* as further evidence of his unsuitability for me. Kirk wanted Mitt to lose so *the world can see how terrible this current guy really is* (and hinted at political machinations far beyond the world of amateurs like us), *clearing the way for a true conservative to save America.*

"Dad said I ruined the river, ruined Bonaventure," JJ said. "The one *his* dad helped put on the map, the one *he* used to test *his* manliness. Said I went big without going all the way."

"Maybe your vision wasn't big enough for him," John said, "but you at least tried keeping the spirit of the place intact."

Kirk left and came back with two bottles, setting one in front of me. He sat across from me, Mickey and Lucky unmoving from my sides, and started talking at me. The Jersey boys couldn't fend off his recollections of the trip we took to Miami so they raised their voices to sing along with Sophie.

"Do you still have that crappy little car?" His voice strained to counter theirs. "That thing won't do you any good after it snows out here, once you come to your senses and decide to leave. You should come with me now. Four-wheel drive, the heated seats you always liked. We could swing down through Aspen on the way home. You always wanted to see Aspen."

I watched Sophie and finally spoke to him.

"Who says I'm leaving?"

He looked in John's direction before answering. "Who says you'll stay? The river is almost done for, the whole place is gonna freeze before you know it, and there aren't going to be a lot of parties to plan once the last of the tourists leave."

I looked at him, for maybe the first time in days. "You remember that I was a teacher before I worked at your firm, right?" I pushed the bottle away from me. "I taught for almost a *decade* before Chicago. It's important to me that you know I had a life before we met."

He slid the bottle back my way. "Remember what those first few months were like?" he asked. "First class plane tickets. Box seats. Five-star restaurants." He leaned forward. "You told me once those were happy times."

"I'd lost my best friend, the town I loved was just shut down, and I had nowhere to go."

"And yet you ended up in Chicago," he said. "At Stephen and Allison's house, in their backyard at the same time I was there. That had to be something like fate. You could have ended up anywhere after Louisiana, you were free from—"

"I was untethered. Not the same thing."

"We could be *happy* again. I have a promotion lined up at work; I could even get you your old job back. It'll be better." He shouldered his way over the table. "I've learned a lot in the past few months. Maybe this place made you feel like you can just start over, but—"

"Kirk."

The sound of his name silenced everything except Sophie, and even she sang with newfound caution in her voice.

"My story doesn't begin when you dumped me, and it didn't start in Chicago. Gods, it didn't even start when I came to Montana. My story started centuries ago and it's going to continue long after you finally understand that I'm not going anywhere with you." I stood. "And I never wanted to see Aspen. You did."

DESPERATION WAS THE BEST CATALYST for man and beast.

We stumbled from dry to drought and, perhaps inevitably, lightning struck twice, igniting another fire northwest of the Big Steep River. By the time we could smell smoke it merged with the earlier, older fire.

Gabby embraced me, letting her feelings hit me full force, and departed for Atlanta.

JJ absorbed as much of the financial loss as he could, though the town elders were keen on stringing him up on some sort of charges, promises unfulfilled or hopes oversold, and who could have predicted the first year Bonaventure sat in the nation's spotlight it would also char and choke?

Most of the land aflame was deemed *wilderness*, nearly unpopulated by humanity and left to burn, declared *not worth fighting* until the flames threatened something with a dollar sign affixed. I understood the science behind that thinking, but marking the fire's daily progress cut at our mammalian brains.

Desperation was its own kind of enticement to a cornered animal.

One day, bus and rafts idle due to lack of interest, Kirk spoke with someone dressed as a forest ranger. I did not see money change hands, but an agreement passed between the two men. Later, Kirk acknowledged *something* had happened and hinted that, if I loved the river, he would find a way to bring the river back.

AFTER MY FIRST WEEK OF LESSONS with Sophie, back in the springtime of possibility, once my fingertips ached but before I'd learned a single chord, she'd suggested we put my practice on hold and examine my motivations.

A few drinks deep, heart heavy with the conflict and disappointment still swirling in my wake since Chicago, I slammed the shot glass down and pushed it toward Sophie. She hadn't obliged my request, so I poured myself another question.

"Why," I'd asked, "in all the movies and books and in freaking *life*, why's it always the *woman's* life that has to implode before she can grow? Before my story can even *start?*"

She rested a hand on mine before I brought the drink to my mouth, and her crackling voltage transmitted through our skin. "Your story's been going on this whole time, Mo."

I released the glass and sat back, pulling away and picking at the guitar, tried to strum something out of it. "But what the hell am I even *doing* here?" My outspread arm took in the entire world.

"John's life imploded once," she'd replied. "You were witness to part of that collapse, saw the calm before his battles."

"I knew him for like, two weeks a million years ago." I'd reached again for the glass but just held it, warming the liquid inside.

"And now your life is bumped off the rails," she continued. "Or, better analogy, you're adrift. Maybe he can help hold the water back, or at least keep the boat from flooding long enough for you to get your bearings."

I'd given up on the strings for the moment and looked down at my fingertips, tried to concentrate harder than I was capable of, given my state. "How do you know about his life imploding?"

"He told me." She'd propped her feet on the edge of my chair. "He told me about Sera, about his time overseas. He talked about you, too. After your email, before you got here, he called me and we talked for hours. He and I go way back, but until your email, he'd never scratched the surface of his life before Bonaventure. Once you said you were on your way, he just kind of spilled it all out."

"And what did you tell him?"

"I told him he needed to be as brave with you as you were in seeking help," she'd replied. "There was a reason you asked and a reason he said yes."

"What do you think of John?"

Her eyes had drifted past me to the closed door. "He's closer to me than a brother." She focused her gaze on me. "He's a quiet man."

"Is there truth to the saying about the fury of a quiet man?"

"*Patient* man," Sophie corrected. "Are you asking about a temper?"

"*Quiet* and *patient* cover a lot of ground, can mean a lot of things."

"Whatever he's carrying from his time there, the things he saw, it's not bottled up, but sorted, kept in a drawer. He's…conscientious. Deliberate. John's tied to the present, everything's always happening *now*, but there's strength behind that dam."

I tested the waters. "Did you guys ever—"

"A brother, Mo," she'd reminded me. "Closer than a brother."

"Does it make sense to say I feel safe at the same time I know I'm treading on dangerous ground?"

She grinned. "Maybe that has something to do with you asking for guitar lessons."

"Could be just a guilty pleasure." I returned half of her smile. "Learning the guitar."

"I don't believe in guilty pleasures," she said.

We'd pretended to work on chords, talked about songs and their lyrics while teetering closer to both of us being drunk, when I slapped my hand across the body of the guitar.

"He's not the lake," I said, "he's the river."

CHAPTER TWENTY-TWO

"Can you swim?"

The sun set the trees on the far side of the lake to shimmering. Kirk repeated his question. "Can. You. Swim, Mohini?"

The lake receded so fast we could almost watch it shrink. Deacon cleaned the windows of the bus again, even though it had been idle for days. Carter whittled in the shade of the trees near the Durham, Badger curled at his feet, the two of them waiting for their ride to Georgia.

"I've got a surprise for you," Kirk said. "I lined up some customers. JJ and John ran off to Rabbit Springs on some errand, and they asked if we'd take a raft out."

The otters used to live where the river dumped into the lake. I hoped they had the sense to make for safer waters and the luck to make it there, if such a place existed.

"That doesn't sound like John. Or even JJ."

"Fine, *I* asked *him*, OK?"

"Where are Mickey and Lucky? They're more experienced than either of us."

"There's four passengers." Kirk plowed ahead. "They should be here any minute. We can make it a triple date, and we'll split the tips. I'll take you to dinner in Big Sky. Can you swim?"

"You think the money is what's keeping me from saying yes?"

"Don't tell me you don't need it."

"I've never sat as the senior rafter." I used up my last few arguments. "And you're barely qualified to ride as cargo."

"You said yourself that the river was low, might be the easiest run we do all season."

"Yes, Kirk, I can swim. I was—"

"Good. Here they are."

A dusty SUV pulled into the parking lot. Two men and two women piled out. A beautiful blonde with a giant smile on her face came straight for me, and Allison wrapped me in her arms before I could say her name.

"I CAN'T BELIEVE you're thinking of getting back with Kirk." She turned in her seat to smile at me, ignoring the river. Allison and Stephen had left Emma with his parents for their first vacation since she was born, and of all the places in the world, they came to this sick and dismal river.

Kirk. He'd probably implored Stephen to come to Montana and play a part in his plot to get me back. Part of me was glad to see Allison, the only person I could have turned to in my moment of desperation last year. We hadn't spoken in months, not since I texted her to ask if she could bring some wine for the misbegotten anniversary party, the one where Kirk dumped me, and now here she was, perhaps unwittingly helping his cause, perhaps unwillingly. She tried to catch me up on their trip from Chicago, but I couldn't concentrate on her words.

The Kitchen was boring, neither the hot spring nor the blast of water from Blue Creek enough to change the river's indifferent temperature. The Natty Gann Bridge loomed large but silent, no train to pass over for fear that a spark thrown from the engine could ignite a third fire in Pando County, right on the doorstep of Bonaventure. Even the Mill Pond, devoid of nearly all animal life, the reeds cracked and muddy brown, held no power, on the surface or below.

"Is it as bad as it feels?" Carter sat next to me in the stern, Badger pressed between us. Kirk could sit up front all he wanted; there was nothing for him to keep an eye on.

"Worse."

Allison's friend Vicki was attached to one of the men Allison had suggested I meet at her backyard party. If I'd taken her up on that offer instead of busying myself with the redwood mulch, maybe my year with Kirk would have been twelve months with…*Brett?* There'd been a couple of guys named Brett at the party. Perhaps the intervening year would have been better, maybe worse, but it would have been *different*, a series of events that would not have catapulted me toward Bonaventure and John.

Vicki leaned in my direction. "It's so cool you get to run the river with your boyfriend. He's really good at his job."

"He is," I replied, "but he's not here right now."

"Oh," Vicki said, glancing to the bow and then back at me. "Kirk said the two of you—"

"You shouldn't trust him. I wouldn't trust him to watch a bee in a jar."

"Would you even *consider* getting back with him?" Allison asked. "It's not like he was abusive, and he didn't cheat on you. He's getting promoted, and even talked about moving out to the suburbs to be closer to us."

"That's the best he can do? I don't have bruises and he's rich, so he gets a second chance? You know what he put me through, what he did to me." I didn't want to fight with her, but I wasn't sure why she'd take his side over mine, not after all the undergrad breakups I'd walked her through, not after our backpacking disaster across Europe. We hadn't spoken for months before I asked her for help last year, so what was different about these months without speaking?

"He's a decent guy and he's changed. He can provide a good life, a comfortable life." She swept her arms across the landscape. "This? This isn't you, Mo. It might be fun, but it isn't sustainable. You really see yourself here in ten years? Five? Next year?"

"Why not?"

She hadn't met John.

"What happened to you, Mo? You used to have serious plans."

"So did you," I replied. Apathy hadn't blunted her inquiries, so maybe matching her pique would convince her of my sincerity. "In college, you talked about being an advocate, working on causes, making a difference. Heck, you were the one who inspired me to apply to Teach for America. What happened?"

She looked away from me, staring hard at pine trees with yellowed needles on the far bank. "You think you're in a position to lecture me?" she asked. "We all make choices, Mo. I've made mine."

"You can still make a difference, Allison. You have a daughter. What's more important than making sure Emma has a better world than we did?"

The edges of her eyes softened, but she kept her gaze on the hills north of us, away from me. "This John guy have anything to do with your newfound confidence?"

"Not newfound." I reached out and touched her on the shoulder. Kirk's radioactivity prevented any transmission or reception of a message, but I wanted to offer Allison my peace. "Just rediscovered."

Did I owe Kirk something for sending me on a path that reunited me with John? Gratitude? Acknowledgment? People in time travel movies liked to talk about the butterfly effect, about the dangers of stepping on something in the past to alter their present, but how many creatures great and small did we stomp on in the present without worrying about our future?

Did Allison have a point, though? Sure, maybe going back with Kirk wasn't sustainable, either, but did I have anything beyond a summer life here? For all our deep conversations, John and I had yet to make anything like a plan, so focused on surviving the *now*.

The raft slipped between the Twins, moving down the Speedway at barely a walking pace before landing in Teflon Flats. I turned my head away from Liza's Hope, watching the shallows exposed on our side of the river, steering as far away from the burned-out husk of a cabin as possible without running us aground on the opposite bank. I had no desire to portage over the sandbar, and little idea if we even could.

All the feelings of uneasiness around the Hope came from the overwhelming sense of nothingness that the point of land radiated. Even those without my touch insight could feel the strange and eerie energy contained in the charred timbers and crumbled rocks.

Kirk continued talking politics with Brett and Stephen, hoping the television star got serious for the next cycle.

"Please don't antagonize them," I asked.

"I wasn't gonna say nothing, Mo," Carter replied.

Vicki waved to someone on shore. "He's cute," she said. "Is he some sort of mountain man? You should dress like that, Brett."

The gaping silence inside my head imposed by Kirk's presence in the raft was replaced with a harsh buzz. My eyes watered as Badger leapt to her feet, nose pointed toward Liza's Hope, her fur electrified.

Brother Crossroads stood atop the ruined foundations of the cabin, hands on hips, an oversized wicked grin directed at me. Once he knew that I saw him, he hopped off the stones and disappeared into the trees.

"Who was that?" Brett asked.

An angry rumble came from the thickets behind the cabin.

"Oh, wow! Look, Al," Stephen said. "You said you wanted to see a black bear."

The ranger at Yellowstone, while talking to tourists about geysers and ravens and trashcans, had also detailed the differences between black bears and grizzlies. She'd said that black bears could sport a coat of fur in shades from deepest ebony or dark brown to cinnamon and blond, so the quickest way to tell them apart from their larger, more potentially dangerous cousins was not by their color, but by their size and shape.

While this animal had fur to match a moonless, starless night, it was no black bear. The creature was no ordinary grizzly, either. After it cleared the forest's edge, shoving aside pines and quaking aspens as if they were blades of grass, it stood on its hind legs amidst the ruins. Had the one-story cabin survived the cataclysm that had consumed it decades before, this creature could have knocked a hole through its roof.

The claws of its forepaws sheathed and flexed as the beast breathed, watching us.

"Is it safe," Vicki asked, voice falling, "to be this close to—"

The monster roared and set a flock of ravens in a dead oak tree to flight, their own shrieks and alarms drowned out by a second bellowing challenge from the mouth of the beast.

The raft shuddered over rocks beneath our feet.

The sandbar.

The bear-thing dropped to all fours and approached, knocking aside stones and timbers, bearing down on our raft.

On us.

On me.

Badger returned the bear-thing's growl, like a rowboat facing down a tsunami.

Rowboat.

I grabbed two of the emergency oars and handed them to Brett and Stephen. Entranced by the creature coming our way, it took them a second to shake themselves awake.

"What the hell do you want me to do with *this*?" Stephen cried. "No way I can fight that thing off."

"Paddle," I ordered. "Hard." I caught Kirk's attention. "C'mon, we gotta get the raft off the sandbar."

I leapt out of the raft, digging my heels into the loose gravel and mud, wedging my shoulder against the gunwale. My muscles ached like I'd already run a marathon, my head throbbed from the buzzing, and I wanted to retch.

"Badger, no. No girl, *please.*" Carter wrapped his arms around Badger's shoulders, her fur ruffled ten times larger than normal in a vain attempt to intimidate the abnormal creation headed toward the water. She strained against his embrace, hell-bent on defending her human.

Kirk regained enough sense to join me in muscling the raft off the sandbar. With five people and a dog aboard the task wasn't easy, but I had no illusions about our ability to outrun the bear-thing on land, or Carter's ability to restrain his girl much longer, or the tourists' ability to get back in the raft if we broke free before—

The creature splashed into the water, a constant groan coming from deep within its belly. Brother Crossroads sent it or conjured it out of meat and madness. The bear-thing was too big to be natural, its limbs moving in painful articulation.

The raft lifted free, what little water still flowing through the Big Steep enough to move us along the course. Kirk threw himself into the bow headfirst, one foot kicking the air behind him, and the raft picked up speed.

Badger lunged over the gunwale, intent on protecting her charges. Carter fumbled for her back legs.

Allison reached for me. I grabbed her hand and she hauled me aboard, her fear breaking through the buzz and washing over me like nausea, my own terror stifled and false bravado sent back along our touch. I wrapped Badger in my free arm, urged her with simple thoughts to *stay with us*, and we all tumbled to the bottom of the raft. I pushed her toward Carter and grabbed the third stubby oar.

The bear-thing sucked in a chest full of air and thundered at us, furious at our attempt to flee, thrashing farther into the water.

"Paddle!" My order was nearly covered up by the echoing rage from our pursuer.

The bear-thing picked up speed, stomping through the shallows faster than we could travel. If we could make it the few hundred yards to Lake Pando, then we would—

Fuck. I had no idea what we would do, or even *could* do if we reached the lake, but gods I did not want to face this thing in the narrows of the river.

Just stop paddling.

I couldn't tell who said that, or what was real or imagined anymore, but the urge to stop paddling grew. Maybe it would be for the best. *Just give in, just stop paddling.* The thought became a command. *This is too hard.* My arms slowed, too heavy to move, my hands too weak to hold the tiny wooden oar. *Everything is too hard.* How stupid to think we could outrun our fates.

Just stop paddling. All my problems would solve themselves.

Stop paddling. Who was I to want more?

Stop paddling. To think I deserved anything?

Stop.

A dragonfly, wings shiny and brilliant under the midday sun, landed on my knees, drops of water on six small feet enough to tingle through the mental haze and silence the urgent command to quit.

Help us, I asked. The insect zipped away too fast to follow.

A raven, one of those startled into flight, circled back over the bear-thing, diving at the giant shaggy head. The monster barely registered the attack until another raven, and another joined the assault, swooping and shouting and snapping at our pursuer until it slowed. The creature heaved its body out of the water, swiping at the birds, turning its rage from us to them, and it caught a raven, then a second, but more took up the attack, crows and jays reinforcing, and even the ducks and geese joined in.

No one else in the raft witnessed the battle, everyone paddling with oars or hands to propel us to the boathouse.

Breath returned to my chest. *Thank you.*

The bear-thing flailed in the water, taking out our defenders in ones and twos, but struggling against superior numbers and coordination. A trio of geese flew just above the water straight at its head. The hawk John rescued gave a battle cry as it slashed at the beast's face with its talons. The monster snarled, sank lower in the water, the current catching it, every effort expended in slaying birds less energy devoted to staying afloat.

The river dug out a little cavern near its connection to the lake, where the otters once lived, and the birds must have known this. They redoubled their efforts, targeting the bear-thing until finally the beast sank below the surface, bobbed up to release a desperate angry howl, and then disappeared from view.

CHAPTER TWENTY-THREE

"The season is over." JJ's proclamation was early in comparison to his hopes for the year, late relative to the reality on the water, but surprised none of us. We assembled the last of the crew. Mickey and Lucky shared a tree stump, Carter and Badger were on their way to Georgia, and Kirk hung off JJ's shoulders like his shadow.

Ollie sold most of the rafts to outfits down Gardiner-way, keeping Blondie for posterity, and spent most of his time sprucing up the Durham, hauled clear of its forest canopy and brighter than new. Deacon worked alongside him, the two men laboring long into the hot nights in silence, attuning themselves to the needs of the boat and ignoring nearly everything else.

There was no simple word in English for being immune to smell, and I wished something other than smoke and fire filled our noses. The conflagration encroached closer every minute, mandatory evacuation orders at most forty-eight hours away, likely fewer, according to John.

"Thanks for a good run, everybody," JJ continued. "May, June, even July were some of the best months on the river I've ever had. Hell of a way to…Reminded me of coming out here as a kid, my grandfather and Ollie trading stories about…"

If he had a speech prepared, the emotion welling up in his eyes negated the need to share the words with us. Part of his sorrow could rightly be attributed to failing at this, his first independent business venture, but not everything came down to dollars and cents, even for a guy with JJ's heritage.

Kirk leaned forward. "Hold it together, man."

The soon-to-be-former CEO coughed into his hand and plowed back on course. "All right, listen up. Everyone should have their last paycheck, and I gave everyone an end-of-season bonus. It's what you would've earned through Labor Day, plus a little extra." Kirk rolled his eyes and I felt John suppress the sudden urge to help them roll deeper into his skull. "Mickey, Lucky—you guys have a ride to Bozeman?" They nodded. "Deacon told me he's going back to Idaho to be with family, wait out the winter there." He smirked. "Not that there'll be much to come back to next year."

"And Ollie?" John asked.

"I bought everything out from under him," JJ replied. "It's what he asked for. I have the boathouse, the land, what's left of the equipment. Everything but the Durham, which Deacon's taking to Idaho." He looked past us to the mountains in the west. "Again, not sure how much will be left in a few days, but I'm going to include the insurance payout in what I'm offering Ollie. Maybe he can rebuild in a few years."

We turned to follow his gaze, though we'd all been watching the same thing for a week.

A sullen, burling, charred glimpse into the oncoming apocalypse. Stacks of seething dark clouds made of combusted pine and grass and mountain life, heaped and growing fast as a mushroom, churning and whirling under the weather system it created. Even at midday, the hillsides gave off a cherry glow, promising destruction and an end to all things.

I pressed against John.

No. Not all things.

Kirk jutted his chin at me. "Are you ready to leave, Mohini?" He'd crossed from desperate to hopeless to delusional. The brush with peril at Liza's Hope surely colored his thinking, if it didn't break his cocky spirit. Without closing the physical distance, he still loomed over me at the boathouse, in the lot, at the Diamond Rough. Like Brother Crossroads, he couldn't violate the cabin's perimeter, but still sapped my energy and blanked my thoughts just the same.

"You've had your summer of fun." He bulled ahead. "Now it's time to come back to the real world. You know, an actual grown-up job. Mortgage, parties, daily showers."

My unbroken stare, more than any protest or insult or even correction, upset him enough to step forward and throw his arms wide.

"I was wrong, OK? Is that what you want me to admit? I never should've said we needed to take a break. I shouldn't have dated anyone in the meantime. I should've let you talk more. If you want to be a substitute teacher that's great. I'll make it happen. I'm not the same guy anymore, OK? I've changed; I'll change more for you. You can't hate me forever."

Words from Sera drifted into my memory.

Hate can be heavy, or hate can be light, she said, *the one thing it can't be is indifferent.*

I stood, grazed John's arm with my fingertips, and left the huddle to join Ollie and Deacon while they refinished the bench seats on the Durham boat. Kirk turned his rage toward John. "You'll see. She just needs a little more time. I'm gonna show you all that I can save the river, even if JJ can't."

Mickey sat up straight, like the tree stump electrocuted him. "What does he mean, *save the river?*"

JOHN SHUT THE CAMPER on the back of his truck, now stuffed full of what we'd determined was worth saving. My Camry was similarly stuffed. The typewriter sat next to my duffel, the green dress once again wrapped around a redwood chip inside the bag with clothes I'd pulled from the lost and found bucket, and the box of spices from home occupied the trunk alongside the picture book of Yellowstone. I wore the BSR shirt with the unofficial motto on the back—*Bring 'em Back Alive*—and cargo shorts. I'd tucked Sera's unread journal into one of the pockets. A bandana around my neck covered my mouth when the air became too smoky.

The cabin itself, a Mackenzie family dwelling passed down to its last male heir, was nowhere near empty. John spent time each week walking the grounds, clearing brush and cutting back trees, following the forest service's best advice for maximizing a structure's chance of surviving a fire, but even the experts hadn't reckoned on an inferno like the one blazing a handful of miles away.

Turns out, they named fires. Not like hurricanes, from a ready-made list of human names, but after their point of origin or a local geographic feature. This one had spawned, to the best estimation of those who worked at such things, at the junction of two numbered county roads in southeastern Idaho, not quite enough for a memorable name on its own.

The Crossroads Fire drove us from our home, the preacher not so much breaching our perimeter as just consuming it, along with everything else in the valley, maybe the world.

"We have enough room in the truck to fit the Jersey boys?" I asked. "My little car is full."

John nodded. "They travel light," he said. "We'll swing by the boathouse and pick them up. You can follow us to the airport from there. We'll stay at the evacuation center in Bozeman for a few days and see what's left when we get back."

I looked at the cabin, so many memories made in just a few months. We'd split our nights between his room and mine, more than once the porch, and I would miss the kitchen where I met Badger and her human, and the hearth, the living room rug stained with a small patch of tea, and the bedroom where I learned to dream and love again.

The fate of the young redwood tree, though, broke my heart. It would not survive another transplant, not now that it was almost fully established in this land so far from its ancestors. Its larger cousins could withstand fire, might have even withstood this one, but the sapling would be ignited almost instantly once the flames arrived. I brushed my hands through its branches, perhaps for the last time, and felt the tingle of the needles on my palm and wrist and arm. Whatever John did to maintain its magic worked. The tree wasn't an embodiment of Sera, more like a lens, a lighthouse, an antenna, a bottle containing her last message. Her spirit had once refused to leave this reality long enough to save John and his men in Iraq, and then burrowed into this tree's roots. John protected it so it could protect us, for as long as it could, and soon its job would be complete.

I cut no keepsakes or mementos from its branches, gave a silent apology for being unable to save it, and received absolution back. The tree didn't blame us, just as Sera wouldn't blame us.

The roar of an automotive engine racing up the highway and barreling into the driveway stole our attention. A white Land Rover, once immaculate, now covered with dark flecks of falling ash, slid to a stop. JJ leaned out the window, face of desperation beneath a white hat.

"They're taking the raft out!"

"What?" John and I asked at the same time.

"The kids—Mickey and Lucky. C'mon, I'll explain on the way."

Someone had approached Kirk asking for one last guided tour before the world burned down. The man presented a sum more than sufficient to stiffen any hesitation on Kirk's part while also promising that such a run, such a story, would demonstrate the young man's bravery and determination: the last ride of the Big Steep River. Who could say *no* to that kind of resolve? Being new and untested, Kirk enlisted the assistance of the Jersey boys, who saw not fame, but a way to help Ollie save something of the river for the future.

"But there's no water," I pointed out from the back seat.

JJ gunned the engine and shook his head. "Kirk bribed a forest service engineer, the guy who oversees the Bighorn Dam, the biggest one west of us. It controls the flow of the Big Steep, and most of the year the flow is fine." He crossed the double-yellow line to pass another car. "We usually see a drop-off this time of year, but nothing like this. They've been holding back most of the water to fight the fires."

"And someone thought they could make a quick buck by, what, releasing water our way so some mysterious fancy guy can have one last glory ride?" I asked.

JJ smiled at me in the mirror. "Fucking rich people, right?" Another heavy foot on the accelerator and we surged ahead. "The fire planes can fill up at Pando just as easily as they can upriver, the water ends up there anyway, but he had no right to unleash that flood."

The problem with the plan was that the Bighorn Dam had been slated for upgrade for years, the embankment far beyond its intended service life. The state deferred maintenance until appropriate legislation could be signed and funds set aside. When the engineer opened the floodgates for Kirk, the water crumbled the bulwark like a sandcastle before the coming tide.

Now, a bolus of reservoir water hurtled east.

We passed the Slip. I saw the Gardiner van and an empty trailer.

"So just when the kids are hitting the Mill Pond," John said, "they're gonna get stuck in the reeds or slammed by a wall of water."

"Or both," JJ said.

"The Mill Pond is too far from the road to get them," I said, "so how do we—"

John turned in his seat. "There's a secondary put-in, just below the Natty Gann. We can run the river, catch the boys, and get them out before they get caught in the Speedway."

"Bring 'em back alive," JJ said.

"Are you planning to swim?" I asked. "Hate to remind you guys, but they took Blondie. They took the last raft."

John smiled. "I know."

JJ cut across the highway, violating just about every traffic law to slide off the road to a stop. I recognized the trellis of the railroad bridge, saw Deacon's yellow school bus and the boat trailer—

—with an actual boat, not a raft, already backing down to the river's edge.

"The Durham?" My heart thundered against my ribs.

John leapt from the Land Rover, tossing two sets of keys at JJ. He caught them easily.

"Get to the boathouse." The sharp edge of a soldier's voice gave his words a commanding bite. "Take Ollie and Kirk, then head back to the cabin."

"Wait, Kirk?" I asked. "But he went out with the boys and the rich guy."

JJ shook his head. "The mystery benefactor insisted it just be him and the boys. That's when Kirk called me and spilled everything."

We muscled the Durham to the water's edge, easing the mechanical addition at its stern into the river first. Deacon held the safety line as we boarded. He and JJ would retrieve any humans left at the boathouse, return to John's cabin for his truck and my car, and evacuate everything east. By that time, we hoped to have the boys and (if the rich man survived John's beating) our last patron at the docks and we could all get the hell out of town before the fire found us.

A new sensation joined the choking smell of smoke. The air pushed before the inferno was heated and crisp, and we heard it, a menacing sound all its own. The fire neither roared nor bellowed, not this close, but emitted a low and steady thrum, like ten thousand wasps bellied in on each other, hissing like vipers grown to the size of roads, a raw and grating shriek.

I didn't need to touch the fire for the insight to push behind my eyes into my mind, smothering all thoughts and memories, nothing but pain and devastation. I gripped the edge of the Durham and breathed, felt echoes from the worn timbers, and tried to draw strength from whatever life was left inside the wood.

Somewhere in the midst of this towering disaster, winters of snow and summers of rain no longer held back by the Bighorn Dam raced toward our little family.

John put his hand on my shoulder.

I GAVE CONFLICTED THANKS for the outboard motor lashed to the stern. Perched in the bow, I knew we'd be on the boys in minutes. I felt a slight pang of regret at the modern convenience strapped to the tail of this hulking anachronism.

No. The Durhams of old had been hardy, daring watercraft, and *yes*, rescue boats, and this was its intended purpose.

John kept us to the middle of the channel, shying away from the shallows on both sides. I leaned forward and hunkered down, though by now I knew the Mill Pond in a way no one else did. Maybe the fire had driven off whatever lived below.

I pointed. "There!"

Blondie, the last of our rafts, the final survivor of a dying race, was stuck among the reeds. Mickey stood in muddy water to his waist, trying to shove the raft off the bottom, while Lucky dug the paddle into the water with solid but ineffective strokes.

The boys turned their heads at the whine of the outboard engine cutting through the groan of the Crossroads Fire. We slowed, inching our way forward, aware of the danger in getting *two* craft beached.

"Come on!" John waved them closer. "Leave it."

"Where's the cargo?" I reached for Lucky and hauled him into the Durham.

Mickey waded through muck. I shuddered at the memory of my underwater experience, the sense of pure dread and abandonment lurking below the pond's surface. My hand opened and closed Dand Lucky joined me in leaning forward, reaching for his partner.

"I don't know." Mickey heaved his upper body over the side of the

Durham. We grabbed him, trying to pull him from the suction hold of the river bottom. John eased the boat back, popping the kid free and landing him on the deck. Lucky threw his arms around Mickey's shoulders and they sat up holding each other.

"When we reached the Mill Pond, the man said he wanted to see if the rumors were true. Then he jumped over the side." Lucky shivered. "That's when we got caught in an eddy and ended up in the reeds. I tried not to get stuck, John, I tried."

"I know. It's OK, Luc." John motored us back to the center of the river and lined us up with the Twins. We would run the Speedway at more than full speed, zip past Liza's Hope and return to—

Mickey looked upriver. His eyes widened and his mouth hung open as he squeezed Lucky tighter.

BONAVENTURE SOUNDS EVERY SIREN, signaling fire, flood, disaster. Evacuation orders issued and largely obeyed, the town is almost empty of life. Every time the world ends, though, some refuse to leave, either through disbelief in their own mortality or, more often, because of an accurate assessment of their place in the world.

A rancher loads the last of his horses onto a trailer and orders the driver to head for safer pastures, fulfilling his duty to the animals but exhausted from running his entire life.

A man in a shack deep in the woods believes himself invincible, and in death becomes so.

A couple married nearly eighty years tends their land, raises generations of children and grandchildren and great-grandchildren, and feels so connected to the fertile earth beneath them and the orchard around them they see any departure as surrender.

The river cutting through town is the focus of proposed investments to add pavement and benches, to turn it from mere geographic feature to a destination in its own right for imagined future tourists. It now swells to unreasonable proportions, shattering bridges and viaducts, shoving aside cars and trucks as it blows through Public Road and the heart of Bonaventure's small downtown, vibrant only weeks before, now abandoned.

The river passes by the bar named Diamond Rough and would destroy it, but for a trick of architecture and drainage, a combination of factors diverting the water into empty fields and parking lots around the old iconic movie palace. Inside, on the stage, in darkness sings a woman alone with her guitar, words untranslatable and powerful.

Blizzard after blizzard dumps snow and sleet onto mountaintops, and those beds of ice melt and feed the Bighorn Reservoir, in turn held back by the dam of the same name now let loose, entire centuries of winter coming like a runaway train. The flood catches the van and trailer at the little sliver of land, tearing away at the banks as it douses the hot springs, smothers the flow from Blue Creek, and wipes out the Kitchen.

The river batters the stone and iron of the bridge that stabs across its belly. The Natty Gann holds, not defiant, but indifferent. The water splits and whirls around the trestles, rejoining and renewing its assault.

And here, where birds bathe and deer drink and, on moonless nights, bobcats stalk and leap, a little pond choked with reeds cups a small boat in its hands, an offering to the river. Four little people cling to the sides and each other as they are lifted and hurled down the course they once reveled in, fancying themselves rafters and guides, and never has the river treated them such.

It is not the river, though, that rages against them. It isn't the lake or snow or nature, but something far older and more malicious. The waters scream as they break again, this time on stony points and cracked timbers where once a cabin stood. Two of the little humans are tossed ashore, the other two holding to what is left of their wooden toy until it tumbles into the lake, the one the men made so long ago, and they are pulled ashore by the hands of friends, who ask after the others who are lost.

Taken.

CHAPTER TWENTY-FOUR

Between redwoods and the deep gray sea, we take the name *Lost Coast* a little too seriously, finally stopping a dairy farmer on an ATV to ask for directions. His black and white cows wander behind him on impossibly green fields as Anita tries to describe our destination, and I frown at the map spread over my legs. Pooling our resources and accepting a gift from Doc Bellamy, we fly from Baton Rouge to Redding and rent a car to the edge of the world on a quest to return Sera's ashes to her home.

Even with so few roads in this part of creation, I still somehow get us turned around.

The farmer looks unconcerned about his cows as he listens to Anita's narrative of where exactly we went wrong and where she thinks we are going. The light disappears early this late in the year, and with the hills and ever-present trees it fades even faster.

I look up from the map.

"We're looking for the Cuarón house."

The man on the ATV sits up straight, as if I've uttered the secret password.

"Damn shame." He gives us detailed instructions to a homestead not far from his. Had we continued down the road we would have reached the turnoff, but might have missed it in the dark.

We pull up to a house of some kind, though the lead ball in the pit of my gut prevents me from committing to memory any details past the

Christmas lights strung through the branches of pine trees in the front yard, illuminating a picnic table painted white. The next day before the funeral and after, during the wake, I sit at that picnic table for hours, unable to go inside the house except to sleep and not eat, unable to tell Sera's mom about my role in the loss of her only child.

Terésa tells me and Anita and a dozen others how her daughter changes her name to *Quarron* in high school, not as a challenge or in defiance, but because she likes the way it looks on the page. Perhaps the entire population of this wooded valley attends the wake, including the dairy farmer, and they trade stories of a fearless and impetuous raven-haired girl who makes friends with cows and beavers and forestry students. Anita offers recollections from Louisiana on our behalf, how Sera loves and protects her students—*loved and protected*, she corrects herself—and how she watched a certain spaghetti Western every month, despite having seen it hundreds of times before leaving home.

I keep my silence throughout the entire weekend, sure that if I speak I will admit my guilt. It would spill out not in expiation, but like a stain, smearing everyone with my culpability until none of us are worthy of Sera's love.

Terésa sits at that picnic table next to me the second night, after we watch Sera's favorite movie, that glorious, dumb, and ugly spaghetti Western that plays every week on the local Zeebrugge channel. Most of the visitors return to farmhouses and cabins and dwellings farther up the valley, nearly to the roots of the redwoods, and Terésa says nothing. I want her to talk and will collapse if she does. She has wisdom, though, and I will need it one day.

After an hour of sitting in the embracing darkness together, the sounds of owls and bobcats surrounding us, she puts her hand on my arm and opens her mouth. She mourns, more than I might ever know, and still she seeks to comfort me, but I can't receive insight just from her touch, not yet, because, although Sera has burned the CD for me in anticipation of my need for the magic, right now it is lost beneath my car seat, it won't shatter for a few more years, not until—

The sensations of rocks beneath me pulled me out of the hazy ether of memories. Round river stones worn smooth by time, sharp jagged splinters kicked up by a flood, and heavy wet sand pressed against my chest and stomach. The clammy smack of soaked clothing against my skin blurred my senses. The crash landing might have pierced my flesh.

The words Terésa gave me on that picnic table howled in my ears even though I couldn't make them out. I pushed my hands against the earth to lift my head, gravel and grass beneath my palms. Pebbles clung to my tattered shirt before dropping off, nothing on my body broken or bleeding.

Gods, I hurt to high heaven, though.

Turning over sapped most of my remaining energy so I waited, collecting wits and breath as I looked around me. The charred timbers and broken stones prompted immediate recognition.

Liza's Hope.

At least it wasn't nighttime yet.

A glance at the sky suggested sunset no longer existed, not inside an incandescent gloom like this. The billowing clouds of the Crossroads Fire lent everything a dark hue, and the smoke-filtered light from the fire colored the land and water a menacing scarlet all around me.

Us.

The word rang in my head like an alarm. I tried to stand and fell back to the ground twice before gaining my feet.

"John!" I coughed and choked at the inhalation of superheated air. I tore the soaked bandana from around my neck and held it over my mouth and nose. Sucking in moistened oxygen, I pulled the blue rag from my mouth. "Mickey? Lucky?"

John lay crumpled in a patch of wizened grass, twisted on his side. I collapsed next to him, checking for a pulse, careful not to move him. His heart beat weakly. The sudden rush of blood to my head brought tears that flooded my eyes. I blinked them away and gently probed his neck with trembling fingers. I had no idea if I could find a fracture, but wanted to give myself something like permission to move him.

Backed against what might have been one corner of the cabin, I pulled John along with me, his head resting in my lap. A strip of my shirt torn off and pressed to his head stopped the blood from a long but shallow gash, and I wondered what would be worse for his lungs, the charged air full of embers and sparks or trying to breathe through a soaked cloth. I had clothing enough to rip apart if it meant a chance to save him, but wished for first aid skills more comprehensive than what I'd learned as a Girl Scout.

John stirred beneath me and tried opening his eyes.

"Mo?"

"I'm here, I'm here." I stroked his cheeks and held him. The touch connected me to his pain. I tried to share the onus, maybe lighten it for him, but just like love, agony shared was agony amplified. His anguish blocked any other insights. "Don't move. I don't know how badly you're hurt."

"Kids?" He relaxed against my legs.

I looked around the Hope. No sign of the Durham, not even a smashed frame or keel, and no trace of the Jersey boys. Perhaps they'd stayed aboard and been washed down to the lake. I tried extending my insight outward and felt nothing but grass and worms around us.

A rescue only half-accomplished.

"They're safe," I offered. "We got them."

"Good." He took a few shallow breaths. "Try to…swim?"

The roiling brown river, bigger and angrier than ever, swollen because of the broken dam, choked with logs and rocks and flume—even alone it would have been a risk to brave. Trying to keep John afloat and alive through that would be more than difficult…but was it any more dangerous than waiting for the fire to find us?

A piercing icy breeze blew smoke away from the point of land. *Is this how fires operate?* Some bizarre trick of physics allowed a pocket of breathable air to find its way to us before snuffing out all life, like the eye of a vengeful hurricane.

The entire idea of naming disasters struck me as uselessly dumb.

"Don't want to worry about hypothermia," I teased. We both shivered as our clothes dried. He felt good enough to sit higher, his head resting under my chin, his back against my chest. I rubbed his sternum, trying to keep him awake, fighting against the concussion that had surely beaten his head in. He could be injured in ways made worse by how I treated him, how I held him, but what the fuck else was there to do?

The world was ending, and we'd end it together.

Our bodies finally dry, he asked that I keep him awake.

I told him stories we'd already shared, reminded him of each funny customer or oddball situation of the summer, at least before it all turned deadly, and opined on events political, current, and nonsensical. Baba told me bedtime fables of the predator shark, the last congress of bears, the godhead and the ocean, and I gave those tales to John.

"Remember the Fourth of July?" I asked. "The town had a fireworks show, but the Milky Way, and the meteor shower, and the storms above us put it all to shame. How dumb we are thinking we can compete with nature."

"Can't."

"You gotta talk more, John," I urged. "You're famously terse, but I can't carry this whole conversation by myself."

"Doing great." A smile curled his lips.

Though we no longer sat inside a kiln, the fire continued its unstoppable advance. Dull orange flames trickled along the hilltops west of us. I'd have given up the silly little car that carried me so many thousands of miles and everything in it if we could keep the cabin, but those kinds of trades only worked in fairy tales, and rarely then.

Was the whole world burning by now? Would that be worse, or better, or make no difference at all?

No way could the crew mount another rescue mission for our broken rescue mission. By now, the Slip would be washed away, the Natty Gann torn down, and even the depths of the Mill Pond might not be enough to stave off destruction. A large enough chunk of wood could serve as a raft, and maybe we *could* float down the river.

John stirred again and I traced the names on his arms, saying them aloud, speaking them from memory into this moment, shivering at the ghostly images that paraded before us, men dead too young, each one stopping to thank John for whatever role he'd played in prolonging their lives as long as he had, absolving him of his inability to step between them and their ends.

A spirit I recognized as Gus—Julius Atwood—nodded at me, gratitude that his best friend in a combat zone would not be alone at the end. He knelt and pressed his forehead to John's before dissolving into nothingness.

Would someone write our names on their bodies? Sophie still owed me the cover-up tattoos, but maybe she'd ink her own body on our behalf instead. The raised bumps of the scar from a sniper's bullet on John's other arm felt rough under my fingers.

"How are you feeling?" I asked like an idiot.

"Don't wanna…go on that ride…again," he joked. "You?"

"A little hungry."

"Tired."

"Nah, I could stay awake all night."

He shook his head. "I'm…tired."

I raked my knuckles along his breastbone, perhaps more harshly than necessary, but he jerked awake. "Not yet, soldier." His left arm hung out and I rubbed his wrist, my other hand tripping along his ribs. "You think

Sophie only taught me one song?"

"No guitar."

"Real keen observation. I don't need a guitar to play, I've got you, my love." Recalling the fingerings, I plumbed for the words, singing to him about a fast car and a job in the city. "Sing along if you know it."

He hummed, mostly in tune and in time, as I sang the words.

I made up chords on his body and brought forth every song in me. I gifted him lullabies in a language I couldn't speak, scoured my memory from childhood through college and every radio station I'd ever stumbled across or the dumb mixed tapes from pining guys or sorority sisters, every road trip sing-along I ever participated in, willingly or not. I made up words when I didn't know the lyrics, returning finally to the ten songs Sera had recorded for me in her final act of love. I felt his trauma through my touch, raw and immediate now that he hovered so close to the end.

Every trip John took down the Big Steep River, every journey from the Slip to the boathouse was an effort in washing away another layer of the trauma visited upon this man after three trips to a war zone and the loss of so many people close to him. Each time he returned to Lake Pando he'd shed a few more molecules of sorrow, could breathe a little more easily, but he was still loaded with so much pain, how many more trips would it have taken to ease his burden completely?

We couldn't step in the same river twice, wouldn't want to, not if we were both trying to heal. How many more trips would I need for my own burdens?

Just as I vowed to stay awake and with him all through the night, his muscles slacked. *No*, I would not lose him, not another love taken from me. I dug my knuckles into his sternum again, sang stronger and louder, lifting my voice against the invading darkness, challenging it to keep its distance; we weren't done yet.

Through the shimmering air and mist, I saw a set of stairs…the same staircase I had seen next to a derelict basketball court in the mountains above John's cabin.

My voice caught on the line about the stray cat, choking on big stupid sobs.

"They forgot…" John said, "what they lacked."

I laughed and coughed and sniffed. "Close enough."

His hand squeezed mine, no longer a pretend guitar, and his other arm covered mine, hugging my hug. When he shifted his weight, his body pressed against an object in my pocket, pushing Sera's journal into my thigh.

"You think…those kids…the fast car…they made it…out?"

Before I could answer, the hot wind surged, throwing sand in our faces. I shielded John.

"Mo." A soft voice from my dreams, one I hadn't heard aloud in forever. "Mohini, it's OK. I'm here."

Seated on the lowest step of the staircase, wearing the long blue dress she'd bought at a Louisiana yard sale, the one that billowed around her in the Iraqi courtyard as she intervened in supernatural combat, short dark hair framing an impossibly beautiful smile, tattoos of love and loss etched on skin close enough to touch—

"No."

"Mo, believe me. I fought my way through the void to come back. It wasn't easy."

John shuddered.

I glared at the avatar on the stairs. "If you were going to pretend to be her, you should have done more than copy her looks. She never greeted me without a hug."

The air shimmered. The cool air disappeared as a wave of heat barreled over us. When I could lift my head again my jaw clenched hard enough to pop. Brother Crossroads sat primly on a log, backlit by flames and etched in iron.

"Where'd you come up with the money to pay off Kirk?" I worked my jaw free. "Did you make that like you made the bear-thing?"

"Cast out the sin and sinner alike," he said, ignoring my questions. "Baby with the bathwater, for both are spoiled." He crossed his legs and rested his hands on his knee. "I have sinned, yes, though I can beat a plowshare into a sword to smite the contemptible just the same as angels can."

John shook beneath my grip, whether from the lingering chill or sweltering heat or the sudden arrival of this asshole, I did not know, but I held him tighter, reminding him he wasn't alone.

"Did your version of a god spare you to come ashore and harass us before the fire consumes us all?" I forced myself to laugh. "Looks like he didn't plan for your escape." I wondered if someone this cruel could be harmed by something so petty as a conflagration. Part of me took pleasure in needling him, though anyone with as much belief in a self-anointed wicked mission would respond to needling by—

His smile grew. "You begin to understand." His voice sounded strangled and bitter. "And needles will be returned with scythes."

Can he read minds, too?

"In a way," Crossroads replied to my unasked question. "You may be right that I'm on a mission, but I serve a new master, and revelation is at hand." He stood. "As it was written, so shall we rewrite it, as above as below, far below, far above."

The din of the forest fire was joined by the horrible buzzing, scattering my thoughts under a deafening crackle, drowning out the river and the preacher's taunts and my own mind. A great hot sirocco kicked dry leaves and debris at us. Even though I believed John's stories of demons and chaos battling in a warzone, and that belief was strengthened by what I'd seen inside him, I'd never considered the possibility that the war could come home, that all wars came home, that this, too, was a kind of combat, and we were but collateral damage.

"John told me about Moonlit Samuel." I choked down the revulsion and confusion, focusing on the details of his stories, the emotions beneath my hands pressing against his body. "Samuel had been tethered to a place, broke free and went rogue. The demon paid the price."

Crossroads hissed. "I know of Samuel's rebellion, feckless though it was." The evil spirit stood and paced. "He cast aside the commands he'd been given. For that we weakened him, allowing him to be defeated by a force as weak as mortal love. We then recalled him by the rules of our order, forfeiting his physical form to suffer just punishment at our master's taloned hands."

"Samuel killed my best friend." I gritted my teeth. "Are you here to kill us?" He shrugged. "You started the fire, you destroyed the dam, and you bribed Kirk."

"What's the expression? *Guilty as charged.* Except I don't believe in guilty pleasures. And Kirk took no manipulation to act as he did."

"Why?"

He leveled a finger at John and a wave of nausea swept over me. I twisted to move him from the demon's gaze, to guard him with my body, to suffer the blow on his behalf.

"Even though Moonlit Samuel violated his oaths he was still one of us. We devise plans to punish those who defeat our own, and John's role in Samuel's destruction marked him."

"But why here?" The air made my head swim and swell. "Why not just kill him in Iraq? That would have been quicker, easier."

Crossroads squatted down, face to face with us. "Oh, simple child of man and woman. Time and space mean nothing to eternity and the universe. We only wished to punish him when it would hurt him the most. Our patience has been rewarded." He stood, his bones moving in a dislocated jumble. "You say this man *told* you what he witnessed. You have *seen* this as though you were there, though you were not there."

He knows about the insight.

If he didn't before, he knew as soon as I thought of it.

He pitched forward, bones cracking and articulating like a macabre toy, something from a child's nightmare. For a brief second he looked like the deer from the basketball court, standing on two legs, his antlers dripping with blood. Then, like a candle beneath a flame, his flesh began to melt. His skin sloughed off to reveal mottled gray pus beneath, blackened bones breaking through as his matter swirled, and finally he settled into a freakish creature made of ash and stone, large, beguiling eyes and teeth like knives, body of a hulking red cryptid.

I squeezed my eyelids shut, but still saw this monster before us.

"Everything born of dream or nightmare comes from depths of collective understanding," he growled, voice worse than the fire. "If evil has a human name it has existed in human form."

"You couldn't maximize John's pain after Samuel took Sera, after she passed on." I forced the words out, hoping my deductions had power. The longer I talked the longer we stayed alive. "You had to wait until he could love again, and was *in* love, and then you could strike, using Kirk as your cudgel." I opened my eyes and saw Crossroads, once again in the likeness of a man, seated on a log. "And you want me because of my insights, because I can see the thoughts of others and you think that's somehow useful to you."

"Clever girl."

"But why? You can read minds; surely you don't need a human to help."

He wagged his finger at me. "And I just said you were clever. We can read minds. Many of my kind have that power. We have difficulty reading the human heart, however. So full of confusion and contradiction." He leaned forward. "More importantly, we need your gift for more practical purposes."

"You want me to go around laying hands on people so you can take advantage of what's in their hearts?" I laughed. "Doesn't seem a very effective way to serve evil."

Crossroads sat back. "Think, child. Surely by now you know you are attuned to others, that you need not contact someone physically to read their heart. Well, just as you are a receiver for the energy of others, so too can you be a transmitter. Any antenna can be tuned in both directions. And, if you can send messages, you can send commands."

The fury and rage in my heart grew, threatening to undo me, when John's chest rose and fell against mine. A dragonfly, somehow alive amidst the apocalypse, landed on my knee.

The earth rumbled, a quaking convulsion I'd only felt twice before—once just before the sheriff of Tully, Mississippi, phoned to tell me and Anita that our friend had died in his small town, how truly sorry he was.

The other time I felt it…

"You want to hurt him." I pushed the previous thought down before fully grasping it, buried it deep into my heart, pouring anger into my voice to mask my thoughts. "Hook me up to a battery and use my body like a radio tower so you can conquer the world. You think killing him, using me, achieves your goal?" My laughter caused Crossroads to shake, his edges to glimmer. "You know nothing of misery."

Terésa…her hand on mine, seated across from me at that picnic table, the night she released her only child's ashes into the Pacific Ocean…

The ones we've lost, she said, *need us less than the ones who are left.*

Gods, my heart said, *this* has *to work.*

Every wound and insult hurled my way since birth came into my mind, anger and sorrow and grievance occupying my thoughts, a catalog of human suffering dominating my mind.

And I shoved everything for John into my bear-proof heart, open only to another raven.

"What do you know of pain?" Crossroads snarled.

"What do *you*? You admitted it, you're a demon, you're invincible."

He sneered. "No, not invincible. These meaty forms we inhabit are weak. When we lose them we are recalled to suffer punishment, as Moonlit Samuel was."

"Then what could you ever know about true loss?" I asked again. "It would hurt John far more to live and lose me." I tried not to choke on the words. "Let me leave, let us both get off Liza's Hope alive and I'll…I'll go back to Kirk."

John stirred beneath me. He slipped deeper into the cold embrace of the concussion, but could still protest. I tried to offer comfort through my touch without revealing my thoughts.

"Why do this?" Crossroads narrowed his eyes. "You've grown fond of this man."

"Sera only died because of him, and now I'm caught in a supernatural power struggle that's all his fault. I'm just trying to save myself." I tilted my head toward the fires. "Make up your mind, unless you want your *meaty form* to get cooked, too."

The demon twisted in his seat and waved a hand. Blondie, the raft the Jersey boys had used for their misadventure, floated gently out of dry reeds and down the river until it landed on the shore of Liza's Hope.

"Put him in."

The world rumbled again, stronger, though the demon didn't notice. I focused only on obeying his commands.

I struggled to get John to his feet. When the demon moved to help, I poured hatred into my face and he backed away. I tried to set John gently in the raft, but it was closer to a collapse. I flung his legs over the gunwale and turned to Crossroads. "Let us go."

I wanted to offer one last chance of escape, even if he was evil and deluded.

"You shall stay with me," he said. "To prolong his pain, and yours.

Don't worry, you'll be safe with me until I can reunite you with Kirk. We don't want to lose a transmitter as powerful as you, for we have great plans for this world."

A chill penetrated my body, staggering me under the pain of wrenching cold, anguish older than pyramids, than cave paintings, than bone flutes. My muscles rebelled against my mind and moved me from the raft, closer to the demon and oblivion.

Thankfully, my knees buckled.

Before Crossroads could claim me, I sunk my fingers down between the rocks, shoving them into gravel and sand. I grabbed handfuls of earth and pushed my bleeding knuckles deeper, trying to bury my arms in the mud. Every living thing was connected, worms, and beetles, and grass, and fish, and the soil itself. A small, lone tree heard and amplified my call, relaying my plea to the redwoods on the edge of a continent, to the kelp forests of the ocean, to the birds of the sky. I asked them all for help, sent my desperate message into the world, offering nothing in return for our survival, but still I asked.

Life answered back that there was no need to bargain.

As fast as the world is being destroyed, we have to learn to love even faster.

The shudder in the earth grew, reaching a breaking point that snapped the hold over my body, allowing me to breathe again.

Here goes everything.

Touching Brother Crossroads, even on the ankle, sent every pain we as a species had ever suffered into my body. My hand felt colder than space. The insight into his mind threatened to consume me, hate and venom gushing out of every molecule of his being through my hand, into my mind, which screamed for release.

If an antenna can be tuned in both directions, he was about to receive.

Keeping one hand in the dirt and summoning a power I would never understand, I staked Crossroads to the ground, opening my heart and sharing with him every piece of love ever sent my way.

I am a newborn child, racked with fever. Mama fights to save my life.

Baba teaches me humor and curiosity, showers me with indulgences, shows me bravery.

Sisters of blood and of choice, fierce and standing between me and wanton bigotry.

Friends, boyfriends, girlfriends, strangers. Love lies strewn along my path.

Allison, opening her home to me without hesitation.

Doc Bellamy, who believes in my strength and purpose even after I lose them.

Anita, who shoulders loss beside me when our world splits in half.

Sera, as devoted in death as she is in life, setting me signposts along the way.

And John.

I tightened my grip on Crossroads. He looked down at me, face flickering between human and true form, slow realization animating his hideous features.

I released him, stood, then flung myself into the raft, covered John's body with my own, and shut my eyes.

Sound and fury unleashed from another dam thundered down the valley, hammering Liza's Hope and washing away the last vestiges of a cabin once inhabited by people, now cursed by loss, and the flood picked the raft aloft and threw it to the east. Crossroads tried to move and couldn't. He howled and cursed as a new lake covered him.

I heard music in the maelstrom, a clear commanding note ringing out over everything. The waves carried us from land, back to the river's course and down to Pando. The flames engulfing Liza's Hope now doused by a secondary surge, the lone figure of Brother Crossroads consumed beneath it, ending in fire and water, and I fell back on John's body, bleeding my heart through my hands in hopes he could still hear my cry.

EPILOGUE

Not even middle of September and snow fell again in soft patterns, giant flakes that lingered a heartbeat on the gloves wrapped around the mug, steaming liquid a small defense against a kind of cold that held no hurt.

John would have loved that line. The fact he'd loaned me these exact gloves in May made the poetry that much stronger.

The typewriter once thought liberated, belatedly purchased, the last touchstone from my life before, sat on the desk in the cabin behind me, in the same spot where I'd placed it so many months ago. Turned out, the typewriter still worked, and the cabin still stood, so maybe I *would* hammer that line onto paper and see what came next.

The first snowfall the week before set me to marveling, but this storm promised to be even larger. I wished John were with me on the porch to share in it. Surely the snow would cover up Yellowstone again, blanketing the bison and bedding the world down for another winter. Though earlier than much of the country, I appreciated its arrival.

Maybe I would brave the park again, now that the crowds were gone.

I had yet to crack the leathered cover of Sera's journal. The pages had survived immersion in water and exposure to superheated air, but the longer it remained unread, the more I felt like it should remain that way, if only as a reminder of the lives we'd left behind.

The flames of August had almost reached Lake Pando, cutting off the crew's attempted retrieval of our cars from the cabin. Inside this near-disaster was fortune, as Deacon and JJ and Ollie were there when Mickey and Lucky floated ashore in the remains of the Durham. The Jersey boys demanded they be sent back out to find their erstwhile rescuers, only succumbing to

Deacon's declaration that they stood no chance, and John and I might stand a small one, if favor and grace were on our side.

When our bodies came tumbling down the river on the crest of the surge released by the failure of the Blue Creek Dam—triggered by the earlier collapse of the Bighorn Dam—everyone jumped in the water to pull us ashore. Turns out Deacon *could* swim, and he had to force my arms from around John, my repeated entreaties to make sure he was OK, that I hadn't meant what I said, that what mattered was in my heart and not my head, bargaining with everyone there and Sera to please bring him back or take me with.

I sipped from the mug. Snow accumulated on my car, on John's truck, on the branches of the tree he'd transplanted for the same reason I brought the typewriter from my former life, all of them surviving the fire and flood by dumb luck and physics and maybe something more. The redwood was now taller than the truck, and I did not question this growth spurt.

I set the mug down and approached the tree, offering my daily prayer of gratitude, and collected snow from the branches nearest me, forming a ball between my gloves. The needles beneath my fingertips were quiet, Sera finally at rest.

When I extended my arm, the jacket pulled away from the glove and I saw fresh ink, courtesy of Sophie. A beaded pattern wrapped my left wrist like a watchband, but in place of a clock face sat a compass, the needle pointed back toward my heart.

Since the fire had spared the boathouse, JJ offered to sell the whole outfit back to Ollie for a dollar, or fund his retirement to a sunnier destination, but the old boater refused both offers. *No future anywhere I go, except for where I have a past,* he had said. We found out he didn't live above the office, but in a cozy bungalow on the outskirts of town, a sanctuary that also survived the fire and flood, and he'd invited us to dinner.

Sophie joined us at Ollie's, gently ordering him to sit while she cooked for us, and I wanted to tell her about hearing her voice on the river, how the music she helped me learn had kept John alive long enough to make it off the point of land haunted by undead memories. She asked if a memory could really die so long as someone was left to live it, and we ate and drank and by midnight slept in a pile of wool blankets and sleeping bags in Ollie's living room, a litter of stray puppies he'd collected and shepherded along the way, refugees and screw-ups at home with each other. We phoned Gabby and Carter the next morning, filling them in on the wonders of our survival, and laughed at the sound of Badger in the background. No one had ever heard her bark before.

Kirk fled, of course, nearly immediately after confessing to JJ his bribery and acceptance of a last minute and highly suspicious deal for one last customer in misguided desperation for my attention. He pocketed the money, unsurprisingly, but JJ hinted over a second serving of lasagna and deep into a bottle of red wine that any sum would not be enough to allow Kirk to hide forever. JJ stuck around a few days before he drove Mickey and Lucky to Bozeman to make their rescheduled flight to Newark. When they'd invited him to visit, he promised he would.

I took up permanent residence in the cabin since that's what John wanted. In fact, it's what I wanted as well. This was no longer a landing place or a temporary refuge.

It was home.

The door behind me swung open.

"Hey," I said without looking. "Glad you're feeling up to watching another storm with me. Promise I won't yell at you this time."

I turned and lobbed my snowball. John raised a hand and the projectile scattered back into a million pieces. He swept off a small spot on the top of the stairs and sat down. I joined him, pressed against his side, and watched the trees. My insight was dormant, but I knew enough about him now that maybe I didn't need the extra help.

His own mug steamed against the falling flakes, joining the wisps from mine.

"A little different than a rainstorm," he said. "But you might get tired of it by October."

"How could I get tired of this?"

Nothing indicated, nothing pointed to, but my words encompassed the whole of the world, and almost everyone in it.

THE END.

ACKNOWLEDGMENTS

The second book was harder to write because I knew what went in to getting the first one on the shelf. Luckily, I had an amazing team of support that guided my work down the rivers of generation, drafting, editing, and publishing. Any errors of fact or geography are my own.

My father-in-law David Schwentker took me and my wife on a trip to Wyoming and Montana, which was the inciting incident for my desire to continue Mo and John's story that started in *Have Snakes, Need Birds*. Christopher Lyke of the inestimable *Line of Advance* literary journal published an early version of Mo's Chicago departure and let me know I was on the right track with Kirk's attitude. Russell Helyer and Wes Borre provided specific and helpful feedback. Thank you to Sara Naomi Lewkowicz for the line about a bee in a jar. Peter Molin pointed me in the right direction to get the story in front of a publisher, and Brett Allen provided additional critical and supportive eyes.

I adapted a portion of Edward Bouviere Pusey's translation of Saint Augustine's *Confessions* to inform Mo's speech about her reaction to Sera's death, so thank you to those two dead guys. Karl Marlantes wrote the foreword to an edition of Ernst Junger's *Storm of Steel* from which I took the idea of a "natural warrior." A book on writing by Elizabeth George helped determine when the novel actually started, and this resource was recommended by Cameron Redfern (who I met through Matt Gallagher and Patrick Deer's online writing workshop; such a small world). Phil Klay's essay "False Witnesses" from April 2022's issue of *The Point Magazine* provided background for much of John's experiences as a veteran trying to rejoin the world.

The CD Sera made for Mo contains music from The Cranberries, Peter Murphy, Indigo Girls (covering Dire Straits), Idlewild, Magnetic Fields, Ingrid Michaelson, Carbon Leaf, Royal Teeth (covering The Knife), Cyndi Lauper, and Barenaked Ladies.

Karla Rojas designed the logo for BSR Expeditions, and Amalie Flynn, Andria Williams, and the crew at *Wrath-Bearing Tree* helped make the shirt a reality. (Contact me through social media to get one for yourself or a friend!) Thank you to everyone who read and blurbed the book; maybe their words and names on the cover convinced you to pick this book up.

I owe ongoing and immense gratitude to Tracy Crow, Samantha Brown, and Michelle Bradford at MilSpeak Books, and to Jerri Bell for her assistance in navigating the waters of submission. Any typos or errors that remain belong to me and to Titivillus. The team has been supportive of me and this story every step of the way, and I'm glad to be in the company of such fine writers and artists.

Almost everyone mentioned above has some creative work of their own— novels, poetry, essays, artwork. Please give them and their work a chance; you may find something else you like.

Finally, thank you to Beth, for going to Yellowstone and the Grand Tetons with me, and for every minute before and since. Charlie is in for the ride of his life down a river of adventure, and there's no one else I'd rather be in a raft with than the two of you.

photo credit Beth Klempan

TRAVIS KLEMPAN is the author of the novel, *Have Snakes, Need Birds*, which received the Gold Medal for Wartime Fiction from Independent Publisher Magazine and was a finalist for the Montaigne Medal. His fiction and poetry have appeared in *Line of Advance*, *O Dark Thirty*, *Proximity*, *Flyway Journal*, and *Bombay Gin*, among other outlets. Travis is a graduate of the U.S. Naval Academy, the Jack Kerouac School of Disembodied Poetics, and the University of Colorado Law School. He lives near Red Rocks with his wife, son, and animals.

Thank you for supporting the creative works of veterans and military family members by purchasing this book. If you enjoyed your reading experience, we're certain you'll enjoy these other great reads.

AMERICAN DELPHI
by M.c. Armstrong

During America's summer of plague and protest, fifteen-year-old Zora Box worries her pesky younger brother is a psychopath for sneaking out at night to hang with their suspicious new neighbor, Buck London, who's old enough to be their father. Their father, a combat veteran, is dead—suicide. Or so everyone thinks, until Buck sets Zora and her brother Zach straight, revealing their father as the genius inventor of a truth-telling, future-altering device called American Delphi.

SALMON IN THE SEINE
by Norris Comer

One moment eighteen-year-old Norris Comer is throwing his high school graduation cap in the air and setting off for Alaska to earn money, and the next he's comforting a wounded commercial fisherman who's desperate for the mercy of a rescue helicopter. From landlubber to deckhand, Comer's harrowing adventures at sea and during a solo search in the Denali backcountry for wolves provide a transformative bridge from adolescence to adulthood.

CRY OF THE HEART

by Rlynn Johnson

After law school, a group of women calling themselves the Alphas embark on diverse legal careers—Pauline joins the Army as a Judge Advocate. For twenty years, the Alphas gather for annual weekend retreats where the shenanigans and truth-telling will test and transform the bonds of sisterhood.

COLLATERAL DAMAGE

2nd edition

by Kevin C. Jones

These stories live in the real-world psychedelics of warfare, poverty, love, hate, and just trying to get by. Jones's evocative language, the high stakes, and heartfelt characters create worlds of wonder and grace. The explosions, real and psychological, have a burning effect on the reader. Nothing here is easy, but so much is gained.

—ANTHONY SWOFFORD, author of *Jarhead: A Marine's Chronicle of the Gulf War and Other Battles*

SUB WIFE

by Samantha Otto Brown

A Navy wife's account of life within the super-secret sector of the submarine community, and of the support among spouses who often wait and worry through long stretches of silence from loved ones who are deeply submerged.

BEYOND THEIR LIMITS OF LONGING

edited by

Jennifer Orth-Veillon, PhD

In America, WWI became overshadowed by WWII and Vietnam, further diluting the voices of poets, novelists, essayists, and scholars who unknowingly set a precedent for the sixty-two successive, and notable, war writers who appear in this collection to explore the complexity both of war's physical and mental horrors and of its historical significance in today's world in crises.

THE FINE ART OF CAMOUFLAGE

by LAUREN KAY JOHNSON

A young woman's coming-of-age in the military against a backdrop of war, viewed through her lens as an information operations officer who wrestles with the nature of truth in the stories we hear from the media and official sources, and in the stories we tell about ourselves and our families.

THE SMOKE OF YOU

by AMBER JENSEN

A young couple's love and marriage are tested during and after a military deployment with the National Guard to Iraq that results in a battle with chronic pain and the slow-burning challenges of married life. A story of selfless love and self-discovery, of hardship and hope, *The Smoke of You* will resonate with anyone who has ever suffered, and still bravely loved.

FALLING OFF HORSES

by KAREN DONLEY-HAYES

A mutual love for horses unites two young women as teenagers who forge an undying friendship that will steady them after countless falls from horses, a roller coaster of love losses and triumphs, the emotional pitfalls of equestrian breeding and competing—and finally, through the heartbreaking diagnosis of a fatal illness.

KURTZ

by JOHN LAWSON III

Nick Willard may be three years her junior but he has pined for Annie Kurtz since they were both prep school students. However, after 9/11, Annie joins the Marines, eventually making a split-second decision her superiors never wanted her to make, and wrestles with whether she should have followed orders or her conscience. Nick—now a successful journalist—and Annie explore the tensions between love and friendship, even those between morality and law, as they come of age amid the psychological traumas that result when war makers sweep reality under a rug of ridiculous details.

THE WAITING WORLD

by ANDRIA WILLIAMS

In 1929, two Irish housemaids, Nessa and Aoife, bonded through their journey to America, stumble upon and pocket a strange find on the shoreline of the home belonging to larger-than-life business magnate Titus McAvoy. When their path crosses a young white-passing British World War I veteran, John, who suspects the enormous worth of their find, the three friends forge a different life together—one free from the dark underbelly of how the rich treat the poor, and free from the pervasive rot of nationalist and racist behaviour, not to mention the injustices and dangers that too often befall women. But... nobody walks away from Titus McAvoy.

CELDAN HERESIES

by MEGAN CARNES

A medieval fantasy world of heretics, led by young and brave Gaelle, rebel against a dark, militarized church after discovering a religion based in light. From Annie Dillard, Pulitzer-Prize winning author of *Pilgrim at Tinker Creek: An American Childhood,* "A work of startling imagination... a world both strange and deadly that feels at once feudal and extremely current, Carnes acquaints us with heretics, horse smugglers, poisoners, and church thieves—criminals... they are also wonderful company. Grab this book now. You won't put it down."

SHOALIE'S CROW

by Karen Donley-Hayes

A horrific fatal accident during an equestrian jumping event leads to the reincarnation of a newborn foal who discovers the only being who speaks her non-horseman-like language is, of all things, a crow. Together, Shoalie and her crow-friend struggle to unravel a mystery that's leading toward another horrific fatal accident. (Published under our imprint Family of Light Books)